. . . continued . . .

Buttercream Bump Off

"A charmingly entertaining story paired with a luscious assortment of cupcake recipes that, when combined, made for a deliciously thrilling mystery." —*Fresh Fiction*

"Another tasty entry, complete with cupcake recipes, into what is sure to grow into a perennial favorite series."
—*The Mystery Reader*

Sprinkle with Murder

"A tender cozy full of warm and likable characters and a refreshingly sympathetic murder victim. Readers will look forward to more of McKinlay's tasty concoctions."
—*Publishers Weekly* (starred review)

"Jenn McKinlay delivers all the ingredients for a winning read. Frost me another!"
—Cleo Coyle, *New York Times* bestselling author of the Coffeehouse Mysteries

"A delicious new series featuring a spirited heroine, luscious cupcakes, and a clever murder. Jenn McKinlay has baked a sweet read."
—Krista Davis, *New York Times* bestselling author of the Domestic Diva Mysteries

Praise for the Library Lover's Mysteries
Book, Line, and Sinker

"[A] delightfully charming series." —*Dru's Book Musings*

Due or Die

"[A] terrific addition to an intelligent, fun, and lively series."
—Miranda James, *New York Times* bestselling author of the Cat in the Stacks Mysteries

"What a great read! . . . A winning formula."

—*Library Journal*

Books Can Be Deceiving

"A sparkling setting, lovely characters, books, knitting, and chowder! What more could any reader ask?"

—Lorna Barrett, *New York Times* bestselling author of the Booktown Mysteries

"Is sure to charm cozy readers everywhere."

—Ellery Adams, *New York Times* bestselling author of the Books by the Bay Mysteries

"Fast-paced and fun . . . An endearing protagonist, delightful characters, a lovely New England setting, and a fascinating murder."

—Kate Carlisle, *New York Times* bestselling author of the Bibliophile Mysteries

Praise for the Hat Shop Mysteries
Cloche and Dagger

"A delicious romp through my favorite part of London with a delightful new heroine."

—Deborah Crombie, *New York Times* bestselling author of the Kincade/James novels

"Brimming with McKinlay's trademark wit and snappy one-liners, Anglophiles will love this thoroughly entertaining new murder mystery series. A hat trick of love, laughter, and suspense, and another feather in [Jenn McKinlay's] cap."

—Hannah Dennison, author of the Vicky Hill Exclusive! Mysteries

"Fancy hats and British aristocrats make this my sort of delicious cozy read."

—Rhys Bowen, *New York Times* bestselling author of the Royal Spyness Mysteries

Dark Chocolate Demise

Jenn McKinlay

BERKLEY PRIME CRIME, NEW YORK

THE BERKLEY PUBLISHING GROUP
Published by the Penguin Group
Penguin Group (USA) LLC
375 Hudson Street, New York, New York 10014

USA • Canada • UK • Ireland • Australia • New Zealand • India • South Africa • China

penguin.com

A Penguin Random House Company

DARK CHOCOLATE DEMISE

A Berkley Prime Crime Book / published by arrangement with the author

Berkley Prime Crime Books are published by The Berkley Publishing Group.
BERKLEY® PRIME CRIME and the PRIME CRIME logo are registered trademarks of
Penguin Group (USA) LLC.

For information, address: The Berkley Publishing Group,
a division of Penguin Group (USA) LLC,
375 Hudson Street, New York, New York 10014.

ISBN: 978-0-425-25893-4

PUBLISHING HISTORY
Berkley Prime Crime mass-market edition / April 2015

PRINTED IN THE UNITED STATES OF AMERICA

10 9 8 7 6 5 4 3 2 1

Cover illustration by Jeff Fitz-Maurice.
Cover design by Lesley Worrell.
Interior text design by Laura K. Corless.

For two of my favorite dudes, Austin McKinlay and Phoenix McKinlay. It's a beautiful thing when an aunt gets nephews as wonderful as you. It is a joy to have you in my life. I am so proud of the amazing people you are becoming. Love you always!

One

"He looks really good in there," Angie DeLaura said. "Peaceful even."

"You can't say that about everyone," Melanie Cooper agreed.

"It's all about the casket," Tate Harper said. "You want to choose a lining that complements your skin tone in the postmortem."

Mel and Angie turned and gave him concerned looks.

"How could you possibly know that?" Mel asked.

"The funeral director at the mortuary told me," he said. He threw an arm around Angie. "Since we're engaged and all, maybe we should pick out a double-wide so we can spend eternity snuggling."

Angie beamed at him and giggled. Then she kissed him. It did not maintain its PG-13 rating for more than a moment, and Mel felt her upchuck reflex kick in as she turned away.

She was happy for her best friends in their coupledom, really she was, but sometimes, like now, it was just gag worthy.

"Really you two, how about a little decorum, given the gravity of the situation?" she asked. She knew she sounded a bit snippy but honestly, some days they were just too much.

"Of course, you're right," Tate said. "Sorry."

He and Angie untangled themselves from each other. He smoothed the front of his shirt and straightened his jacket while Angie fluffed her hair and shook out her skirt. Duly subdued, the three of them stood beside the casket that held their friend and employee Marty Zelaznik.

Marty looked particularly spiffy in his white dress shirt and his favorite bold blue tie. His suit was black, and Angie had tucked a blue pocket square into his breast pocket so that just the edge of it was visible. His features were relaxed and his bald head was as shiny as if it had been waxed to a high gloss.

"Hey." Oscar Ruiz, a teen known as Oz, who worked alongside Marty in the bakery Fairy Tale Cupcakes that Mel, Angie, and Tate owned, joined the trio by the casket. "So, we're going with an open lid, huh?"

"We think it's for the best," Mel said.

"His tie is crooked," Angie said. "We should fix that."

"Yeah, and his makeup is a little on the heavy side," Tate said. "He has angry eyebrows."

"Anyone have a handkerchief?" Mel asked. "A little spit will take care of that."

At this, Marty's eyes popped open and he sat up in his coffin and glared. "What am I, five? You are not spit shining me!"

"Ah!" Angie yelped and leaped back with her hand clutching her chest. "Gees, Marty, you scared me to death!"

"Nice one." Tate laughed as he and Oz high-fived and knuckle-bumped Marty.

"What? Did you think I was really dead?" Marty asked, sounding outraged.

"No!" Angie snapped. "I thought you were napping. You had a little drool in the corner of your mouth."

"I was, but that doesn't mean you get to swab my decks," Marty said as he shifted around and rubbed the dried spittle off his chin. "You know, I have to say it's pretty comfy in here. I may have to look into putting a deposit on one of these for the future."

"*Way* in the future," Mel said.

Marty glanced at the four of them. "So when do we leave for the zombie walk? I want to catch a few more Z's. Oh, and by the way, the undead look you've all got going, yeah, I don't want to wake up to that ever again."

Mel glanced at her friends. Tate and Angie were doing the undead bride and groom. In requisite tux and white wedding gown, they had topped off their look with gray makeup and faux partially rotted flesh. Tate had a fake knife lodged in his skull, while Angie had an axe sticking out of her back. They had already taken bogus wedding photos that Angie was seriously considering making their official wedding portrait.

Being single and thinking this was going to become a permanent state, Mel had decided to go as an undead chef complete with her toque, double-breasted white coat, and checkered pants. She wore her pleated hat back on her head to enhance the amazing latex scar Oz had adhered to her forehead. It was pretty badass.

Oz had decided to wear his chef whites as well, but had

changed it up by making the side of his face appear to be rotting off. Every time Mel saw his fake putrid skin flap in the breeze, she had to resist the urge to peel it off.

As the body in the casket, Marty had chosen to be less undead than the rest of them. He was pasty pale and sunken eyed but that was about it. Mel suspected that because he was closer to his actual expiration date than the rest of them, dressing up as a dead man had less appeal for him. Overall, she had to admit, they were fabulously gruesome.

"Sorry, Marty, but no napping," Mel said. She grabbed him by the elbow and hauled him out of the casket, which was sitting on a trailer on the back of the cupcake van. "We've got to load up the van and get over to the Civic Center Park and set up our station before the undead descend upon us."

"Ooh, that sounded nice and grisly." Angie shuddered.

"It did, didn't it?" Mel said. She let go of Marty, ignoring the look of longing he gave the coffin. "Let's move, people."

She hurried to the back of the bakery, where she'd left her rolling cart loaded with boxes of cupcakes. She pushed it alongside the service window of the van and began to hand them off to Oz, who was inside.

"What flavors did you create for zombie cupcakes?" Tate asked.

"No new flavors," Mel said. She flipped open the lid of one of the boxes to show off the cupcakes. "Just new names. In place of the usual suspects we have the Marshmallow Mummy—"

"Hey, you made the frosting look like bandages on a mummy's head," Oz said from the window. "Cool."

"And it has a marshmallow filling," Mel said. "We also

have Vanilla Eyeballs, Strawberry Brains, and Dark Chocolate Demise just to round out the flavors."

"The eyeball one is staring at me," Marty said. "I don't think I could eat that."

"How about the brains?" Tate said. "How did you pipe the frosting in the shape of a pink brain?"

"Fine pastry tip," Angie said. "It was fun."

"Are those little candy coffins on the chocolate ones?" Oz asked. "I dig those. Get it?"

"Aw, man, that stunk worse than rotting flesh," Marty said. He closed the lid on the box, took it from Mel, and handed it through the window. The others stared at him and he asked, "What? I'm just getting into the spirit of things."

"Fine, but please keep the rotten flesh remarks to a minimum when selling the cupcakes," Mel said.

"This from the woman who ruined a perfectly good cupcake by putting a bloodshot eyeball on it," he said. He shook his head as if he couldn't fathom what she'd been thinking.

Mel lowered her head to keep from laughing. She didn't want to offend Marty, as he took his vanilla cupcakes very seriously.

"Melanie!" a voice called from the bakery. Mel glanced up to see her mother, Joyce Cooper, stride out the door. Joyce took three steps and stopped, putting her hand to her throat. "Oh, my!"

"We look amazing, right?" Mel asked. She spread her arms wide to include her entire crew.

"*What* are you?" Joyce asked.

"The baking dead," Oz said from the van.

"Niiiice." Tate nodded.

"Yeah, I'll give you that one," Marty agreed and exchanged a complicated handshake with Oz.

Mel approached her mother, who flinched only a little when she drew near. "Thanks for watching the bakery so we could work the zombie walk, Mom."

"No problem," Joyce said, "But, honey, really I just have to say that white foundation you have on, well, it's really not terribly flattering, and now that you're single, you really might want to consider a little blush and maybe a less prominent eye shadow."

"I'm supposed to look like a zombie," Mel said. "I'm pretty sure they don't wear blush or eye shadow."

"Lipstick?"

"No," Mel said.

Joyce heaved a beleaguered sigh, turned and walked back into the bakery.

"Really?" Mel said to Angie. "She's worried about my pasty foundation, but she blithely ignores the fact that I have a gaping wound on my head."

"She's just looking out for you," Angie said. "Maybe you'll meet a nice undead lawyer at the zombie walk and she'll stop worrying."

"There's only one lawyer I'm interested in," Mel said. "And as far as I know he is alive and kicking."

Angie gave her a half hug as if trying to bolster her spirits. The love of Mel's life was Joe DeLaura, the middle of Angie's seven older brothers. A few months ago, Joe had rejected Mel's proposal of marriage even though he had already proposed to her and she'd said yes. As Mel explained to her mother, it was complicated.

The truth was that Mel had gotten cold feet at the "until death us do part" portion of the whole marriage package, but she had worked through it. Unfortunately, when she had gotten over her case of the wiggins and proposed to Joe, he'd just taken on the trial of a notorious mobster, who was known for wriggling off justice's barbed hook by murdering anyone who tried to lock him up.

Joe had walked away from Mel to keep her from being a target. To Mel it still felt like rejection. She didn't handle that sort of thing well and in the past three months had gained fifteen pounds from comfort eating. For that alone, she hoped Joe brought his mobster to justice.

"Come on, ladies, it's 'time to nut up or shut up,'" Tate said as he dropped an arm around Mel's and Angie's shoulders and began to herd them to the van.

"*Zombieland*," Mel and Angie said, identifying the movie together.

The swapping of movie quotes was one of the foundations of their friendship. Mel and Tate had met first in middle school, but then Angie had come along and the three friends had spent weekends in Tate's parents' home theater, watching old movies and eating junk food. Ever since, they had played a game of stumping one another with movie quotes.

These days just the memory of those happier times made Mel glum. Why did it seem like everything was so difficult now?

"Chin up, Undead Chef," Tate said. "We're going to go sell cupcakes to the shambling masses and make an arm and a leg in profit."

"*Ba dum dum*," Angie made the sound of a drummer's rim shot.

Mel rolled her eyes. "I guess that's better than making a killing."

"That's the spirit," Angie said with a laugh.

"Aw, come on. It's a zombie walk finished off with an outdoor big screen showing of *Night of the Living Dead*," Tate said. "How could we have anything but a good time?"

Two

Because the cupcake van was packed to bursting with food, there was no way to wedge Angie's poufy meringue of a dress into the back. She and Mel opted to walk the half block to the Civic Center, the park in Old Town Scottsdale where the zombie walk would end and the party would begin.

As Mel and Angie strolled through the bakery's neighborhood, Mel hoped they didn't scare any small children in their ghoulish getups. She did not want to be responsible for anyone's nightmares.

As they passed the tattoo parlor on the corner, Mick the owner poked his head out of the doorway. Standing six feet four and covered in ink right to the top of his shaved head, which sported a rising phoenix, he was fearsome to behold.

"Well, look what crawled up from the netherworld," he said. "And here I thought today was going to be ordinary."

Mel glanced at the metal implants on Mick's forehead that made him look like he was about to sprout horns. Did the man even know the meaning of the word *ordinary*?

"It's my new look," Angie said as she twirled, giving him an eyeful of her axe in the back. "What do you think?"

"Totally hot. If you weren't spoken for, I'd ask you to the opera tonight."

"You mean you're going to miss the zombie walk?" Mel asked. She would have thought it was right up Mick's alley, literally.

"Sorry," Mick said with a shrug. "*La Bohème* is tonight. You know how I feel about my man Puccini."

Mel nodded. Mick was an onion with a lot of layers. Despite his outwardly scary appearance, he was a season ticket holder to the Arizona Opera, and she knew from his weekly visits to the bakery that he had a weakness for coconut cupcakes.

"Oh, ew!" Mel turned around to see a young woman in a charcoal gray skirt and suit jacket over a black blouse and black tights, staring at her and Angie in revulsion. Frances Kelly, CPA, was new to the neighborhood as she had just rented office space above Mick's tattoo parlor. Frances twirled her finger at them. "That is so wrong and on so many levels."

"Frances, I'm hurt," Angie said. "I can't believe you don't like my outfit."

"Flirting with damnation is not my idea of a good time," Frances said with a sniff. Frances had a very rigid religious code that as far as Mel had been able to determine meant no fun of any kind ever.

Mel rolled her eyes at Mick, who grinned in return.

"Come on, Frankie, lighten up," he teased the young woman. "A zombie walk is good, clean fun. No harm, no foul."

"It's Frances, Mr. Donnelly; you would do well to remember that," she snapped and jerked on the lapels of her jacket while hoisting her messenger bag up onto her shoulder. "And for your information, playing with Satan is always harmful. I'll pray for you all."

With that she strode past them to the stairs on the side of the building, which led to her office above. When they heard the door shut behind her, Angie turned to Mick with a perplexed expression.

"Explain to me how that"—she paused to point up—"ended up renting space from you."

Mick shrugged. "Price and location. Besides, I think she likes me."

"Oh, yeah, I saw a glimmer of that mixed in with her scathing contempt," Mel said. "Not."

Mick laughed. "Well, she's not indifferent to me, so we have a starting place."

Mel and Angie waved good-bye as Mick ducked back into his shop.

"Is it just me or is he completely deluded?" Angie asked.

"It's not you," Mel said. "For reasons unknown to me, men do not seem to suffer the same self-esteem issues as women do. I mean, have you ever noticed that old, fat bald guys tend to go for young, skinny, pretty girls? What's up with that?"

"I don't know. Maybe they see themselves as they were when they were young," Angie said.

"See? Deluded," Mel said. "Not unlike our inked-up friend there thinking he stands a chance with the poster girl of prim and proper."

"Agreed," Angie said. "Let me just say if Tate ever throws

me over because I've gained a few pounds or let my hair go gray while he did the same, why I'd . . ."

"What?" Mel prompted her.

"Lose the weight, dye my hair, find the youngest, hottest man in town, and make Tate regret his stupidity until he draws his last breath."

"Wow," Mel said. "You're kind of scaring me right now."

Angie gave her a sidelong glance as they crossed the street. "You are not the one who needs to be scared."

"Noted."

As they entered the park, Mel could see other vendors setting up their booths for the zombie walk. She was relieved that most of them had dressed up as well, making her feel much less conspicuous than she had under Frances's censorious gaze.

It was a perfect March day in Arizona with a warm sun and a cool breeze, making it the sort of day that demanded it be spent outside.

"Oh, check them out." Angie nudged Mel with her elbow and pointed to a gruesome twosome.

Mel felt her jaw drop. The woman was dressed like a dominatrix, and she led her zombie man around by a chain around his neck.

"I thought this was a family event," she said.

Angie shrugged. They watched as the man moaned and shambled past them while the woman strutted on stiletto boots that went all the way up to mid-thigh. She smacked a riding crop against her thigh as if just itching to use it.

"That's fifty shades of seriously wrong," Mel said and Angie laughed.

"Halt!" A man in a black T-shirt with a bright yellow star on it, black fatigues, and black combat boots jumped in front of them. He assumed a fighter stance and was carrying what looked like a very large semiautomatic weapon.

Mel jumped. "What? What did we do?"

"I'm with the Department of Zombie Defense," the man barked. "And you look undead to me."

"Who? Us?" Angie asked. She looked like she was trying not to laugh as she played along. "No, no, we're very much alive."

"Yep, we have all of our body parts," Mel said. "See?"

She and Angie shook their arms and legs to prove that all their parts were still attached.

The man gave them a dubious look. "All right. I'll let you pass this time, but you may want to get some sun. You're looking a little pale."

"Will do," Mel promised. She and Angie hurried around him to go meet the cupcake van, which was slowly rolling towards them.

"And probably you should get that axe in your back looked at," the guy yelled.

Angie snorted. "Oh, yeah, this is going to be fun."

Two zombie cheerleaders scuffled past them with their pom-poms hanging low.

Mel grinned. "I think we need to work on our shamble."

"Agreed," Angie said. She pulled her veil over her face and then limp/shuffled towards the cupcake van, which had just pulled into its designated space near the amphitheater.

Tate leaned out the driver's window and let out a wolf whistle, which made Angie giggle.

"There was absolutely nothing zombie sounding about that," Mel said.

"Sorry," Angie said. "He's just so cute."

Mel looked at Tate, with the knife through his skull dripping fake blood all over his collar and down his shirtfront. He'd put in a pair of fake rotten teeth, and his makeup made his eyes appear sunken and his features gaunt.

"If I didn't know better, I'd think you were drunk," Mel said.

"I'm worse than that," Angie laughed as they approached the van. "I'm in love."

Mel studied her friend. Her eyes were bright, her smile wide, and even under her ghoulish foundation, she glowed. Yep, Angie had it bad.

"Have you two set a date yet?" Mel asked as Tate stepped out of the van to join them.

"Not yet," Angie said. "But don't you worry; as my maid of honor you'll be the first to know."

"Hold the phone," Tate said. "Mel can't be your maid of honor. She's my best man, well, woman. Yeah, that's right. She's my best wo-man."

"Um," Mel hummed as she glanced between them. Once they'd become a couple, she had thought she'd never have to choose between them unless they broke up, a thought she refused to let enter her head for fear she'd never sleep again.

"No, I have dibs on Mel," Angie said. "She's my best friend."

"She's my best friend, too," Tate protested. "I always figured when I tied the knot, she'd be at my side."

"Well, so did I," Angie said.

"Come to think of it, I thought you'd be there, too, as a groomsman, but that was before I fell in love with you."

"You mean before you noticed me." Angie glowered. Gone were the joyous sparkles from her eyes, replaced with sizzling lasers of seriously not happy.

"Yeah, I always figured the three of us would rock

matching tuxes, and the bachelor party would be the stuff of legends, maybe Vegas. You know, what happens in Vegas stays in Vegas," he said.

"Not helping," Mel whispered as she leaned towards Tate. He glanced at her and then at Angie, who looked like she might pull the axe out of her back and whack him on the head with it.

"Who do you want to stand up for, Mel?" Angie asked. "Me or Tate?"

"Oh, no." Mel shook her head and raised her hands. "I'm Switzerland. I am not stepping into the middle of this. It will be an honor to stand up for either of you, but that's for you two to decide, not me."

Angie glared at Tate and crossed her arms over her chest. He scowled back. Neither one of them looked like they were going to budge, until Oz poked his head out of the service window of the van and shouted, "Hey, how about a little help here?"

Together, Tate and Angie stomped towards the van.

"What's going on with those two?" Marty asked as he joined her.

"A stand-up standoff," Mel said.

"Huh?" Marty asked. "What the heck does that mean?"

"It means, 'Houston, we have a problem,' " Mel said.

Three

"*Apollo 13*," Marty said.

Mel looked at him.

"What?" he asked. "I don't watch movies? Anyway, it's wrong."

"What's wrong?" Mel asked.

"The quote," Marty said. "I was older than you are now in 1970 when *Apollo 13* launched and what Jack Swigert, the pilot, really said was, 'Houston, we've had a problem here.'"

Mel tried to wrap her head around the fact that Marty had been almost forty in 1970. She couldn't make it compute. The world events he'd seen and the things he'd done in his lifetime boggled her mind.

"Wow," she said, finally. "You're pretty smart for an undead guy."

Marty shrugged. "Meh. You pick stuff up along the way, you know, if you're paying attention."

"Nice outfit, princess."

Mel and Marty spun around to see Olivia Puckett standing there with her arms crossed over her chest, not an easy feat with a knife sticking out of her ribs, and a frown marring her zombified features. Like Mel, she had gone with the undead chef thing, which did not make Mel happy for a variety of reasons—not the least of which was that Olivia's fake blood looked more real than Mel's. Annoying.

Mel glared. Olivia Puckett was the owner of Confections, a rival bakery, and had been the bane of Mel's existence since the day she opened her shop. Their enmity had gotten pretty heated right up until Marty had decided to venture into the online dating world and had inadvertently hooked up with Olivia.

Mel told herself that this was one of those the-universe-works-in-mysterious-ways sort of situations, but it still felt like a cosmic ass kicking, which was usually what she wanted to do to Olivia.

The relationship was complicated for Mel because she was afraid if Marty were forced to choose between working at Fairy Tale Cupcakes and his girlfriend, he'd choose the girlfriend. Losing Marty to Olivia would be even worse than losing a bake-off, and so Mel was forced to play nice, but it was an effort.

"I could say the same to you," Mel said. She crossed her arms over her chest, mimicking Olivia's stance. "You make an okay zombie chef."

"Okay?" Olivia bugged her eyes at her. "I am so much better than okay. And who are you to judge since you didn't even bother to dress up."

"Why you—" Mel took two steps towards her nemesis, when she felt someone grab her arm and spin her around.

"All rightie then, all kidding aside," Marty wheezed, looking slightly panicked at the catfight that was about to ensue. "Mel, I think they need you at the cupcake van. Liv, how about you show me your setup? I'd like to see where my girl will be during the shindig."

"Your girl?" Olivia tittered and blushed. "Oh, Martin, you are a charmer."

It took everything Mel had to keep her eyes from rolling back into her head. Then again, given that she was at a zombie walk, it was a look that would work, and she could always say it was part of her shtick.

She let her eyeballs roll. Sadly, the effect was wasted on Marty as he had linked arms with Olivia and was now strolling through the undead vendors over to her spot in the festivities. Mel was just relieved that it was not right next to theirs. She didn't think Angie would manage her temper near as well as Mel had.

She circled the van and glanced in the back door to see how things were going between Tate and Angie. Judging by the way Angie was keeping her axe, rather her back, to him, Mel assumed not well.

"We need to put the eyeball cupcakes where people can see them," Oz said. He was fussing with the display case beside the service window. Both Tate and Angie were ignoring him. "Hey! A little help here, please."

"Oh, I'd love to help but I'm sure Tate already has dibs on the eyeball cupcakes," Angie said.

"Now is that nice?" Tate asked.

"Just as nice as you claiming my best friend for your own," Angie said.

Mel backed away from the truck. She was not going in there until they resolved their issue. She supposed it was lame of her to abandon Oz, but since they were fighting about her, she felt her presence would only make things worse.

She spied their chalkboard sandwich board. Angie had doodled their zombie specialties on the board with prices. Mel lugged it out to the front of the van and propped it up where she figured it would be most visible.

She wanted to wheel the coffin out front, too, as she figured it would give the undead a nice photo op and bring them in to buy cupcakes. She knew she wasn't strong enough to carry the coffin herself, but she really didn't want to get into the bride and groom scuffle again.

She glanced up to see if there were any festival workers that she could ask for help. Then again, how would she know who was working the zombie walk if they were all dressed as zombies?

"Yo, Mel, over here!"

Mel turned at the sound of her name. She squinted at the crowd, trying to see who was calling her. It took her a few seconds to recognize the two zombies shambling towards her. Al DeLaura, who was dressed as a redneck zombie complete with John Deere cap and grubby white tank top, and Paulie DeLaura, who was wearing a torn suit with one sleeve empty, which made perfect sense when Mel realized he was carrying his "missing" limb in his other hand. Ew.

"Al, Paulie," she greeted them as she hugged them.

Paulie patted her on the head with his fake arm, and she straightened her toque and frowned at him. "Stop that."

He grinned, showing some blacked-out teeth.

"Do I look as awful as you two?" she asked.

"No one looks as gruesome as me," Al declared. "There's a cash prize for best zombie outfit, and I'm betting on Bubba the redneck zombie to bring it home for me."

"Since you're here, how about a favor?" Mel asked. The brothers nodded and Mel gestured for them to follow her.

When they rounded the cupcake van and saw the coffin, they both went wide-eyed.

"That's bringing it to all new levels," Paulie said in approval.

"Agreed," Al said. He ran his hand over the blue satin lining. "It's so plush."

"Can you help me wheel it to the front?" Mel asked. "I want to prop it up to help lure the zombies in."

"Great idea," Al said. "Where'd you get it?"

"Dom knew a guy," she said. The brothers nodded. Among the seven DeLaura brothers, Dom, Sal, Ray, Joe, Paulie, Tony, and Al, they always "knew a guy." Mel knew Joe kept tabs on his brothers and their flirtations with breaking the law. Although some of the DeLauras bent the rules a bit, for the most part they stayed within the law, mostly out of respect for Joe since he was a county attorney and all.

When Mel went to grab a side of the coffin and help, Paulie and Al shooed her away, making it clear that they had it under control. Paulie popped out his real arm and handed her the fake to hold for him. *Ish!*

Mel followed them, directing them to the spot where the coffin would get the most traffic. They locked the wheels on the little trailer, keeping the coffin safely propped up.

"Is it stable enough?" Mel asked. "Marty is going to hang out in it and let people take pictures in it."

"Let me try," Paulie said. He took his fake arm back and climbed into the coffin. He rested against the satin, clutching his fake arm to his chest. "How do I look?"

"Horrible," Al said. He screwed up his ghoulish features with a look of distaste. Then he reached forward and slammed the door shut on the coffin.

"HEY!" Paulie shouted from inside, making it muffled but still discernable. The banging coming from inside started slow but quickly became panicked.

Mel shot Al a reproving look before she lifted the lid on the coffin. Paulie came staggering out and fell to his knees. His free hand was clutching his throat and he was gasping for air.

"I can't breathe," he wheezed.

"Oh, Paulie, are you okay?" Mel asked and she hunkered beside him. "That was not nice, Al. You scared your brother half to death."

Al had the grace to look slightly abashed and he hung his head and mumbled, "Sorry."

Paulie snapped up straight. "I was *not* scared, not even a little. It was the lack of oxygen."

"Yeah, right," Al said. He pushed his John Deere cap back on his head and gave his brother a skeptical look.

"It was!" Paulie insisted.

The two looked ready to brawl so Mel figured a change of topic was in order.

"Have either of you heard from Joe?" she asked.

If she'd hit them with a spray of ice water, she was pretty sure they wouldn't have clenched up as much as they did at the name of the brother who had ripped her heart out.

They exchanged a worried look and Al said, "Nope, haven't seen him."

"Me neither," Paulie said. He waved his fake arm at Mel as if to emphasize his words. "And you need not to be asking about him."

"Why not?" Mel asked. "His trial is in all of the papers and on the news. It's not like I can avoid it."

"Well, you need to try," Al said.

"Yes, Joe was very clear that we need to keep you safe," Paulie said. "And to do that, we shouldn't talk about him with you at all ever."

"Oh, he said that, did he?" Mel asked.

Al reached over and snatched Paulie's fake arm and then whacked him over the head with it.

"You are an idiot," Al said. Then he handed the arm back.

"*Ouch!* What did I say?" Paulie asked.

"You just admitted that you've been in contact with him," Mel said. "Now spill. When did you see him? What did he say? How does he look? Is he all right?"

The brothers exchanged another look, and she was afraid they were going to clam up on her. She was desperate for news about Joe, as he'd cut ties with everyone at the bakery in order to keep them safe from the mobster case he was presently working on. It had been an excruciating few months for Mel, and she wasn't about to let the brothers hold out on her now.

"Please," she said. She gave them her best sad puppy look. "Please just tell me how he is."

Four

Paulie opened his mouth and then closed it. He didn't know what to say and it showed.

Mel tried to juice up her eyes a little. It wasn't hard to do given how much she'd missed Joe over the past few months. In fact, the sob that made her throat constrict was barely manufactured at all.

"Please . . ." she said.

Al groaned and Paulie nodded. She knew she had them.

"Brains! Brains! Brains!" Chanting voices interrupted Mel's plea and she was shoved back when one particularly large zombie pushed her aside to get to the cupcake van. She was separated from Paulie and Al as the horde of zombies shambled forward.

"Sorry, Mel, gotta go," Al cried as he and Paulie dove into the horde, hiding from her.

Mel glanced over her shoulder to see that the park was filling up with the undead. It appeared the walk was over and the festival had begun.

Marty came shuffling back to the van, not that much of an act for him, and took up his post beside the coffin.

"I got this," he said as he climbed back into the coffin.

When a group of teen zombies walked by, Marty reached out with a curled hand and grabbed one on the shoulder. The adolescent boy let out a yelp, which his friends thought was hilarious. Marty gestured for the youth to take his spot and prank the next group that came along. The teen jumped at the chance. Seeing that Marty had the front under control, Mel went back to stalking the brothers.

If Al and Paulie thought they had escaped her, they were so very wrong. Mel circled the cupcake van where Tate, Angie, and Oz were doling out chocolate coffins, mummies, eyeballs, and brains. Judging by the crowd, it appeared even zombies would forgo brains for cupcakes. Good to know, if there ever was a true zombie apocalypse.

She figured Paulie and Al had decided to blend with the crowd in an effort to hide from her. But she knew them too well. The lure of buttercream was their downfall, and sure enough, she found the two brothers hunkered down behind the van's engine, trying to get Angie's attention so they could score some cupcakes. Did they really think this wasn't the first place Mel would look for them? Honestly, did they not know her at all?

Mel strode forward and braced an arm on each side of the zombie brothers. "All right, you two, start talking."

Al hung his head while Paulie let out a yip of fright.

"Mel, we can't," Al said. "First, Joe would kill us. Second, it really is too dangerous for you to have any contact with him. We love you like a sister; we can't risk anything happening to you."

"Save it," Mel said. "If you've seen him and nothing has happened to any of you, then I'll be fine, too."

"Now we haven't actually seen him," Paulie said. "He won't see any of us. He says it's too dangerous."

"Then how have you been in contact with him?" Mel asked. The brothers were quiet. "Tony rigged something, didn't he?"

Al pursed his lips and began to whistle while studiously not looking at her. Paulie examined his fake arm as if he were a surgeon trying to figure out how to reattach it.

"Angie!" Mel yelled.

Angie poked her head out of the passenger side window of the front of the van. "Hey, there you are, we were wondering where you went. We could use a hand in here, you know."

Paulie held up his fake arm. "Here you go, Sis."

"You've been waiting for someone to open that door all day, haven't you?" Al asked.

Paulie nodded and grinned. "I can't believe she said that. It was beautiful."

"I need two chocolate coffins," Mel said. "Stat."

Angie frowned. "Why?"

"I need to loosen some lips," Mel said.

Angie looked back at her brothers. Her eyes narrowed and she disappeared back into the van. Instead of handing them through the window, Angie climbed out the driver's side door and walked around.

"Chocolate cake with chunks of chocolate mixed into the batter, a dark chocolate buttercream with a milk chocolate coffin perched on top," Angie said as she studied the two cupcakes in her hands. "I think we should rename these the Rest in Peace cupcakes."

"Oh, I like that," Mel said. "Did you know that chocolate releases endorphins? Studies show that even the smell of it makes you feel better."

She and Angie both took a sniff of the cupcakes and sighed.

Al and Paulie looked as if they'd taken a punch to the gut.

"Too bad we don't know anyone with a weakness for chocolate," Mel said.

"Yeah, it's a shame," Angie agreed. "I'm sure they'd really enjoy these."

"Hey, now, you're not playing fair," Paulie protested. "We took a brothers' oath, a vow that we can't break. You have to respect that."

"You're right," Mel said. "You should put those back, Angie."

"Wah," Paulie sniveled. "Come on, have a heart. It's not our fault we can't tell you that Tony has rigged up the bakery so Joe can monitor—"

"You did not just say that!" Al interrupted.

"Say what?" Paulie asked. Mel held out the cupcake to him, and his eyes lit up as he chomped a bite of cake and frosting. "Oh, man, this is your best cupcake yet."

"Details," Angie said. She waved the cupcake under Al's nose. "We need details."

"All right, all right," Al said. "Paulie pretty much blabbed it all out anyway. Tony rigged up a camera system at the bakery so that the brothers could communicate with Joe and he could keep an eye on who came and went at the bakery in case there was anyone suspicious."

"Suspicious how?" Mel asked.

"Like someone sent to do a hit," Al said.

He grabbed the cupcake from Angie and took a bite. Mel and Angie exchanged a look, and Mel wondered if she'd just gone as pale as Angie had.

"What do you mean 'sent to do a hit'?" Angie asked.

Al looked at her while he chewed. "What do you think I mean?"

"What about Mom and Dad and the rest of the family?" she asked. "Is he having all of us watched?"

"Maybe," Paulie said, which meant yes. "Oh, Joe did say that you make an adorable zombie chef, Mel, really cute."

For a moment Mel felt the same schoolgirl gushy mushy feeling inside that she always felt when Joe DeLaura's name came up in conversation. Then like a soap bubble it popped.

"Explain to me how this spying on me works exactly," she said.

Al and Paulie shook their heads.

"We can't," Paulie protested. "Joe would kill us. Dead."

"Deader than dead," Al said.

"That's nothing compared to what I'll do if you don't tell us," Angie said.

"What could you do?" Al scoffed.

Angie took her cell phone out of the bodice of her dress and opened the images file. She tossed her veil back from her face as she studied the small screen. Finally, she found what she was looking for and she opened the picture, making it bigger.

Mel glanced over her shoulder and bust into a belly laugh. "Is that . . . ? Oh, wow, that's hilarious."

"So, help me, Alfonso DeLaura, you tell us how the system works, or I go live on your social media files and share this picture of you with the world."

"What picture?" Al asked.

Angie turned the camera so he could see it. When he tried to grab it, she smacked his hand away.

"No!" he cried. "Where did you get that?"

Paulie looked over his brother's shoulder and burst out laughing. "I remember that. Virginia Beach, summer of '95. Ange wanted someone to play dress up with her, and she was so pitiful that you volunteered. Dude, you look horrible in a bikini and makeup. And, wow, your chest was hairy even when you were fourteen."

"Shut up!" Al yelled at his brother. Then he turned on Angie. "Delete that!"

"Yeah, no," she said. "I found it in Mom's box of old photos and took a quick snap of it for exactly this reason."

"Blackmail?" Al asked. "That's just heartless. You're a cold woman, Angela Maria Lucia DeLaura."

Angie shrugged. "I can live with it. Start talking."

"Fine," Al said. He gestured to Paulie. "Tell them."

"Why me?" Paulie asked. "She's not blackmailing me."

"Everyone knows you're the weak link in the DeLaura chain," Al said. "Besides, you understand Tony's gizmo better than I do."

"When the front window of the bakery got smashed a couple of months ago and we were doing cleanup, Tony took the opportunity to install some security cameras, monitoring the interior of the building and the perimeter. We've all been taking turns watching the feed. It's not that hard when there are seven of you. Less than three and a half hours per day."

"You've been spying on us?" Angie accused.

"No, just monitoring," Al said. "The cameras don't have

sound, so it's not like we could hear your conversations or anything."

"So let me get this straight," Mel said. "Joe has been watching all of us for the past few months, even while telling us it was too dangerous to have any communication with us. How is it that he can communicate with you all?"

"That was the ingenious part," Al said. "Tony has us communicating using aliases on the Deep Web."

"The what?" Mel asked.

"Tony would be better at explaining it," Al said. "But essentially for the past ten years, searching the Internet is sort of like skimming the cream off of fresh milk. There is a lot more to the bottle of milk below the surface in the Deep Web, but it's very tricky to access, so that's what we've been using to communicate."

Mel looked at Angie. "Tony is like scary smart, isn't he?"

"Criminally," she agreed. She looked back at her brothers. "So, is that all of it?"

"Yeah," Paulie said. "Ange, I think I deserve a second cupcake for spilling my guts."

Angie studied him for a second and then hoisted up her poufy skirts and climbed back into the van to get him one.

"One of the brain ones, please," Paulie called after her.

"Why didn't Joe tell us?" Mel asked. Her feelings of betrayal ran deep and right into rage. "He had no right!"

Her mind was spinning. What if she had started dating? He would have seen it. If the bakery was wired, was her home as well? Was he watching her most intimate moments? Which had been a horrifying amount of midnight pizza eating and Carmen Miranda movies, because really, how could a gal not be cheered by a woman dancing with a basket of fruit on her head and a sausage and green olive pizza?

"Relax," Al said as if reading her mind. "It's just the inside of the bakery and the exits. He was very clear that Tony stay out of your personal space. He's only checking to make sure that whoever threw that brick through the front window a few months ago—you remember, that one that caused you to get four stitches—yeah, he wants to avoid that again."

Mel blew out a breath. Joe cared. That wasn't a bad thing, right? She still cared, too. Then why was she hopping mad? Because he wasn't playing fair. She had to worry about whether he'd be gunned down by bad guys day and night, but he was sitting back monitoring her every move.

How much easier would the past few months have been if she could have checked a computer screen to see that he was okay? Lots. And why was it okay for him to communicate with his brothers on the Deep Web but not with her? No, this was unacceptable. Completely unacceptable.

Angie came back bearing brain cupcakes, but Mel stepped in between her and the brothers, blocking Angie's path.

"You can have the cupcakes," Mel said. "But you have to make me a promise first."

Al and Paulie exchanged nervous glances.

"That sort of depends upon what the promise is," Al said.

"It's simple," Mel said. "You tell Joe I want to talk to him. I don't care if it's on the Deep Web or in person, but tell him, I am going to talk to him or I am going to rip the cameras out of the bakery. Am I clear?"

"Aw, man," Paulie whined. "Joe's going to kill us."

"That shouldn't be a problem," Mel said as she gestured to their outfits. "Since you're already dead."

Five

Looking decidedly morose, Al and Paulie took their cupcakes and disappeared into the crowd. Mel didn't feel sorry for them. For the first time in weeks, her heart didn't feel as if it were made out of lead, and she knew it was because one way or another she was going to get to talk to Joe.

"You look entirely too happy to be dead or undead or whatever we are," Tate said as he joined Mel and Angie.

"I know, right?" Mel asked. She grinned at them, but they were not sharing her joy. Instead, they glared at each other, still caught up in their argument from earlier. Mel shook her head. "Oh, no. You are not going to keep squabbling about the maid of honor–best man wedding sitch. We'll figure it out."

Angie and Tate did not look as if they were ready to unbend, but Mel was having none of it.

"Come on," she ordered. She looped an arm through each of theirs and tugged them together. "I can hear the band is starting up. Let's get into the spirit of things, yes?"

"Fine," Angie grumbled.

"Sure," Tate said.

"Marty, will you help Oz out in the van?" Mel asked as she moved around the van and peered into the coffin. "We'll be right back. We're just going to check out the band."

Marty was reclined against the blue satin, looking horrifyingly at home. Mel was afraid he was getting a wee bit too attached to the wooden box as he looked to be nodding off again.

She coughed and his eyes popped open at the sound. He stifled a yawn. He stretched as he climbed out of the wooden box, and Mel noted that he gave it a loving pat. He closed the lid and when Mel frowned, he gave her his most innocent look.

"What?" he asked. "We can't have people climbing in there unsupervised. They could get trapped and suffocate."

"Uh-huh," Mel said. He didn't fool her, not one little bit.

Marty made a shooing motion with his hands, and Mel turned and left the van, dragging Angie and Tate with her. She marched on, dragging the bride and groom with the relentlessness of a mama determined to see her baby girl married off. Mel was certain that some good music was just what Angie and Tate needed to take their mind off their wedding dilemma.

Mel squinted at the stage across the park. She had only met Chad Bowman once, when Fairy Tale Cupcakes had signed on to be a vendor at the zombie festival. Her impression of Chad was that of a twenty-something hipster as evidenced by his skinny jeans, white Converse high-tops, paisley shirts, and well-worn tweed trilby. Marty had observed that Chad looked as if a thrift store had vomited on him. Hard to argue.

As he stood on the stage getting ready to announce the band, Mel noted that even Chad's zombie persona was a hipster, with a trendy blue scarf wrapped around his neck and smart-looking black-framed glasses accentuating the gash in the side of his head.

Mel parked the three of them under a tree as close to the stage as they could get without being on it. She was hoping the entertainment was something upbeat and fun, maybe an eighties cover band that would get Angie and Tate feeling nostalgic about all of their eighties movie nights.

As they watched, Chad strode out to center stage and took the mic out of its holder. His grunt of welcome was magnified across the park and the horde of zombies grunted back.

"Welcome to the first annual Old Town Zombie Walk," he said. "We have a last-minute surprise for you. One of Scottsdale's own is in town to do a promotional photo shoot for their latest album, and they agreed to play here today because they're just that cool."

A rumble of excitement whipped through the crowd. Mel wondered who it was. She really hoped it was someone good and not some lame one-hit wonder has-been.

"Oh, no," Angie murmured on Mel's right. She clutched Mel's arm in a grip that pinched. "We have to get out of here—now!"

"Why?" Mel asked. "What's the matter?"

Angie was scooping up her wedding dress skirts and looking to find a way out, but the crowd of zombies behind them was pressing forward, trapping them at the front of the stage.

"So without further ado, put your undead hands together for . . . the Sewers!" Chad yelled into the mic, and the crowd went nuts.

Mel felt Tate stiffen beside her as the first one to run out onto the stage was Angie's old boyfriend Roach. At six foot three, his tall, lanky frame commanded the stage. Per usual, he was shirtless, showing off his many tattoos as he jumped behind his enormous drum kit and began to snap out a rhythm as the rest of the band followed him out onto the stage.

"Did you know he was going to be here?" Tate asked Mel.

"No!" Mel shook her head. "I'm just as surprised as you."

Angie was trying to fight her way out of the crowd, but they weren't budging. If anything they were pushing the three of them closer. She dropped her skirts and wailed, "It's no use. We're trapped!"

Just then the band kicked in, playing one of the singles that had hit the top of the charts a few years ago. Despite herself, Mel felt herself getting swept up into the music. She had been a fan of the Sewers before Angie started dating Roach, and secretly she still was.

"What are you doing?" Tate hissed in her ear.

"Huh?" Mel asked.

"Stop singing," he hissed.

"I can't help it," Mel said. "It's catchy."

"So is the flu," he grumbled.

Mel glanced at him and Angie. They looked to be the picture of misery. Seeing Roach while they were in the middle of their skirmish was obviously not helping the already tense situation.

She grabbed Tate by the arm and pulled him into her spot while she maneuvered around him. It was best if the two of them faced Angie's past as a united front. At least, she hoped they'd manage that.

Mel bobbed on her feet in the tiny square foot of space that the press of bodies allotted her to dance in, and watched her friends out of the corner of her eye. Tate was leaning down and whispering in Angie's ear. She looked irritated, and then she looked up at him with her big brown, sunken eyes, and a smile parted her black lips.

Angie grabbed Tate's hand in hers and began to dance to the band. Mel wondered what he'd said to her. She wondered if he'd given in and told Angie that she could have Mel for her maid of honor. Mel was okay with that. She was okay with whatever they chose, although she did dig the idea of wearing a tux and being Tate's best wo-man, but that was just the lure of men's fashion. The truth was, Mel was just as divided as Angie and Tate about which of them she should stand up for. Who'd a thunk?

The band blasted through three more raucous songs before they turned it down to play a ballad. Mel got a nervous flutter in her stomach when she realized this one was to be sung by Roach. Oh, no, he wouldn't. He couldn't.

"This is a song I wrote about a girl who stole my heart and then smashed it," Roach said into the mic. "It's called 'Angie.'"

He did!

Mel felt the acid in her stomach bubble and gurgle. Where was her Uncle Stan and his ever-handy roll of antacid tablets when she needed him?

Roach paused and scanned the crowd as if he knew Angie

35

was out there. His light blue eyes turned their way, and Mel's breath stalled out in her lungs when Roach spotted Angie in her zombie wedding dress! Oh, this was not going to end well.

The guitarist must have been thinking the same thing, because he stepped forward when Roach jumped up from his seat behind the drums, and put his hand out, gesturing for Roach to stop. Roach looked like he wanted to argue but the bass player joined them.

Roach shot Angie a desperate look, which she missed since she was staring at her shoes, but Tate didn't. He threw an arm around Angie's shoulders and hugged her close. Roach narrowed his eyes and Mel was afraid he was going to launch himself off the stage and crowd surf over to them if he had to.

Thankfully, the band manager Jimbo had the presence of mind to grab Roach by the back of his sparkly belt and haul him back into his seat. He seemed visibly shaken, but, ever the performer, Roach shook his head of long black hair and kicked into his ballad about Angie.

Mel had heard the song a million times; sort of hard to avoid a chart topper. As Angie said, she felt like the song was bird-dogging her in the grocery store, the gas station, the mall, truly, it had been a megahit. But in all those times, Mel had never heard Roach's voice sound so plaintive. He sang the song right to Angie, and Mel almost felt like an intruder on their moment.

Tate must have felt the same way, because with a heavy sigh he took his possessive arm off of Angie and stepped behind her, letting Roach sing just to her.

"That's awfully nice of you." Mel stood on tiptoe and whispered in his ear.

"How can I not feel bad for the poor bastard?" Tate whispered back. "He lost *her*."

Mel gave Tate a half hug. This was one of the many reasons why she loved him so much. He was good all the way down to his core. He was going to make a wonderful husband for Angie.

After glancing at Tate and getting a small nod of approval in return, Angie lifted her face and watched Roach play with a small, bittersweet smile on her lips. Mel assumed that now that Angie was engaged to Tate, perhaps she could forgive Roach for writing a song about their relationship, which had turned into the monster breakup song of the past year. Perhaps.

When the song ended, the crowd went nuts and the band broke into a thrasher of a tune that had all of the zombies dancing on their feet. Mel glanced behind them to see if she could work her way out of the crowd. She didn't like the idea of leaving Marty and Oz on their own in the van for this long.

She began to wind her way out, glancing back to let Tate and Angie know she was going. To her surprise, or maybe not, they were following her. When they cleared the crowd, she studied Angie's face, trying to determine her state of mind. The heavy gray makeup made it impossible.

"You all right?" she asked.

"Yeah, I'm good," Angie said. She sounded unsure and must have known it as she added, "I think that was surprisingly good closure."

Tate looked at her. His gaze was direct as if it killed him to ask, but he had to anyway, so he said, "No regrets?"

Angie stopped walking and looked at him. Her brown eyes glowed with warmth when she smiled up at him.

"Not a one," she said and jumped into his arms.

Tate laughed. He didn't hesitate but snatched her close and planted a kiss on her that made Mel blush.

"Well, then, I'll just . . . yeah." Mel turned and strode back through the crowd, unable to stop the smile that creased her lips. There was something magical about Tate and Angie's relationship, and she couldn't help but be happy for them.

Back at the cupcake van, she saw the undead were circled around the vehicle. She climbed up into the back, taking Oz's place at the window.

"Go out and open up the casket; it'll give them all something to do while they wait," she said. Oz nodded.

"I'll go," Marty volunteered.

"No," Mel said. "Oz needs out of the van for a bit." Marty made a sour face and Mel added, "Relax. Tate and Angie should be back shortly to spell you both."

Two boys in green coveralls with a nuclear emblem on the front were next up at the window.

"What can I get you?" Mel asked.

"Have you witnessed any paranormal activity, ma'am?" the taller of the two asked.

"Excuse me?" Mel said.

"We're the Bonehead Investigators," the boy said. He looked at Mel as if this should mean something to her.

"We're ghost hunters," the smaller one said as if Mel were too stupid to live. "I'm Atom and this is Leo. Our specter meter clearly indicates that you have a paranormal presence here. Please confirm."

He gave her a severe look and Mel blinked. He was holding a small gadget that looked like an iPhone, and it was flashing with blue lights and making a whistling noise.

"What's the holdup?" Marty groused from behind Mel. "Order some cupcakes, kids, or move along."

The meter in the boy's hand went berserk, the flashing intensified, and its whistle became a screech that had both Mel and Marty covering their ears.

"Shut it off!" Mel cried as she saw the costumed people behind the boys cover their ears and back away.

The two boys looked from the meter to Marty and then at each other. In unison, they cried, "It's him!"

Six

Leo dropped to the ground and began fishing through his backpack. For what, Mel could not imagine and she really didn't want to find out.

"Time for you to take a break, Marty," she said and she shoved him towards the back door.

Atom, the smaller boy, had grabbed the window ledge and was trying to hoist himself into the van.

"Oh, no you don't, short stack!" Mel said.

She hustled Marty out the back and then grabbed two of her brain cupcakes. She gently nudged the boy off of her window and held out the cupcakes.

"Here you go," she said. "These are on me. Probably, you shouldn't be chasing people with your . . . uh . . ."

"Specter meter," Leo said.

He and the smaller one exchanged a look, and Mel

realized, judging by their matching nose and chin, that they were brothers. They ignored her proffered cupcakes and Leo jerked his head in the direction of the back of the van. Atom nodded. They took off running in opposite directions.

The next person in line stepped up and Mel went to take their order, when she heard a yelp. She glanced up and saw Marty hotfooting it through the crowd with the two boys on his tail. If she was a betting woman, she'd lay odds that Marty was beating feet over to Olivia's booth.

Mel had no doubt that Olivia would scare the two hooligans away from her man. She just hoped Olivia didn't do any permanent psychological damage to the boys.

"What's the haps?" Tate asked as he climbed back into the van.

"You wouldn't believe me if I told you," Mel said. Luckily, the crowd surged forward and Mel was spared from trying to explain about Marty and the sawed-off Bonehead Investigators and their specter meter.

She figured they'd see Marty again as soon as he lost his newly acquired shadows, er, shadow hunters? She was unclear on the proper nomenclature for ghost hunters or whatever it was those two boys thought they were.

"So, are you and Angie okay?" she asked.

"Yeah, we're good," he said. "Seeing Roach like that, well, it made me realize how lucky I am. Anything Angie wants for our wedding she gets, so it looks like you're going to be hers."

Mel smiled. "Works for me, but you know I would have been happy to stand up for you, too."

"Yeah, I know," he said.

They grinned at each other.

"Where is Angie?" she asked.

"Bathroom," he said.

Mel nodded. She turned back to the next customer, and she and Tate double-teamed the window, getting the cupcakes out as fast as the zombies could order them.

When there was finally a lull, Tate nudged her towards the back door. "Take a break," he said. "I can handle the horde."

"Thanks," Mel said. She didn't admit it to Tate, but she was eager to find Angie and hear her side of the Roach encounter. It had to be a little weird to have your ex sing a song about you to a crowd of, well, monsters.

Mel circled the van and found Oz taking pictures of people as they climbed into the casket. Some went for the grisly fresh-from-the-grave look while others pretended to be dead, and the last two girls had fits of the giggles and could barely stay in the coffin long enough to have their picture snapped.

"Where's Angie?" she asked.

Oz handed the cell phone back to the girls, who were still giggling. One of them cast Oz a look of longing, which Mel noted he was oblivious to, no doubt because he was utterly smitten with his girlfriend Lupe.

Oz glanced around the area, looking for Angie as if he'd misplaced her. Then he frowned.

"I haven't seen her," he said.

Mel assumed Angie must still be in the restroom. She didn't envy her the problem of trying to maneuver into a public stall in her big poufy dress. Then again the bakery was only a five-minute walk at best; maybe she'd gone there.

"Why don't you take a break?" Mel asked. "I can manage the coffin for a spell."

"Are you sure?" he asked. "Some of these people are sort of scary."

"Nothing can be scarier than a real dead body," Mel said. "Sadly, I've had enough experience with those to tell the difference. This is nothing."

Oz nodded and said, "Point made. I'll be back in five."

"Take your time," Mel called after him as he stepped into the crowd.

Oz hadn't been gone more than a few seconds when Mel heard a shout coming from the direction he'd taken. She stood up on her tiptoes and tried to see over the crowd. A man, a very large man, with a scraggly beard that ended in a braid in the middle of his chest had grabbed Oz by the shirtfront and was shaking him. This was no small feat given that Oz was a big boy, having several inches and many pounds over Mel.

"Tate!" Mel stuck her head in the open window of the truck. "Tate, come quick! Oz is in trouble."

Tate shoved a cupcake at the ghoul in front of him and hunkered down to look out the window. Immediately, he slammed the window shut and jumped out of the back of the van.

"Lock it up!" he yelled at Mel as he threw himself into the melee.

Mel grabbed her keys and hurriedly closed the windows on the van before locking it up. Then she stuffed her keys in her pocket and raced after Tate.

"I saw you touch her, man," the thug growled into Oz's face while still holding him by the shirtfront.

"Hey, now," Tate said as he moved in between them. "I'm sure it was just an accident. Right, Oz?"

Oz was glaring at the man who held him. "Like I already said, I got shoved into your girl. I said I was sorry. What more do you want?"

"Your blood," the man sneered. Then he pulled out a very large switchblade and snapped it open.

"Whoa!" Tate shouted. "Are you nuts? Put that away before someone gets hurt."

Mel cringed. That was the voice of the old buttoned-down power-suit-wearing Tate. While that voice might make administrative assistants scurry and junior execs cower, it wasn't going to do jack on a guy who looked like he snacked on bats and spiders for milk and cookie time.

"Not helping, Tate," Oz choked out as the man's fist wound tighter into the fabric of his chef's coat.

Mel stomped forward. Enough was enough.

"Put him down. Now," she said. The man looked down at her as if she were no more than a mosquito buzzing in her ear.

She could sense a crowd was forming around them, and she had a flash of annoyance that no one else was stepping up to help them out.

"Is this your girl?" the man asked Oz. "Maybe I should grab her tits and we can call it even."

"Oh, hell no!" Tate and Oz cried together. Then Tate looked at Oz and said, "Do it!"

Oz raised a knee and nailed the man in the junk with it. Mel heard every man in the crowd wince in sympathy. The ogre dropped Oz and with a primal roar, Tate lowered his head and charged the man. The two of them went down with a thump against the pavement.

Just then, Marty came running up. He clapped his hands to his bald head and cried, "What the hell is going on here?"

"He started it!" A buxom redhead, wearing a zombie maid's outfit complete with cheesy fishnet stockings, pointed at Oz. "He grabbed my breasts!"

"I did not!" Oz protested. His voice cracked and his face turned bright red, visible even under his thick gray makeup. "I tripped and fell on . . . er . . . you."

Mel glanced back at Tate and the big man. They were rolling across the ground. Tate had his arms and legs wrapped around the giant man, making it almost impossible for the guy to get a solid punch in. That didn't stop the ogre from rolling until Tate was on the bottom, where the man tried to head butt him.

"A little help here!" Tate yelled as he dodged the cranial smack-down.

Mel, Oz, and Marty moved in to help, when three Scottsdale police officers on bicycles rolled up.

"Uh-oh," Marty said.

Seven

The officers wasted no time in grabbing the big guy off of Tate. The skanky girlfriend immediately got into the officer's face, pointing at Oz and shrieking about how he had jumped her, and her boyfriend was just protecting her.

Mel recognized one of the officers as being friends with her uncle, Stan Cooper, who was a detective on the Scottsdale PD. She gave him a little wave and he came over.

"Mel, I almost didn't recognize you with your brains coming out of your forehead like that," he said. "Not your best look."

"No, I don't suppose it is," she said. She fingered the latex on her forehead that was beginning to itch. "Good to see you, Henry. How are Jackie and the kids?"

"Good, everyone is good," he said. They were quiet for a moment and then he gestured to Tate, who was talking to another officer. "Friend of yours?"

"Yes, Tate Harper," she said. "Uncle Stan can vouch for him. He's a good guy, but that thug accused our employee of trying to feel up his girlfriend, and Tate was forced to intervene."

"I didn't!" Oz protested.

The officer smiled at Oz's genuinely alarmed face.

"Officer Henry Dodge, this is Oscar Ruiz," Mel introduced them and they shook hands.

"Can you tell me what happened from the beginning?" Henry asked Oz.

Marty stepped forward, looking like he wanted to add to the conversation, but Mel gestured him back. He made a huffy sound but held his silence.

Oz explained how he was going on a break and got jostled in the crowd. He accidently brushed up against the mean girl, and the next thing he knew her crazy boyfriend had him up in the air by the front of his shirt.

"Stay put," the officer said. "I'm going to check in with my partners."

"You don't think they'll arrest me, do you?" Oz asked as Henry walked away.

"Nah, you didn't do anything wrong," Marty said. "And look at that guy. I bet he has a rap sheet as long as his beard."

"Let's hope," Mel said. "Some outstanding warrants would be nice, too."

It wasn't long before Tate, looking a bit rumpled and missing the dagger that had been lodged in his skull, came back over to them.

"It's going to be just a few minutes," he said. "They've got some witnesses that are telling them exactly what happened, how the guy jumped on Oz and that I backed him up."

He and Oz paused to knuckle-bump each other while

Marty thumped them both on the back. The testosterone was so thick in the air, Mel was pretty sure she caught a whiff of it on an inhale.

"Why don't you and Marty head back to the van," Tate said to Mel. "We don't want anyone messing with the coffin, and we still have a lot of brain cupcakes to move."

"Really? I thought they'd be the most popular. No, huh?" Mel asked.

"The Dark Chocolate Demise with the coffins on top are definitely the favorites," Tate said. "We should remember this for when we open our franchise."

Mel heaved a sigh. Tate had been working on expanding her business for the past few months, ever since he quit his high-powered investment job. It had caused some friction between them, mostly for her, as he was trying to take the bakery to the next level, while she was content with things just as they were.

"Yeah, sure," she said. "Look, if the officers need us, let them know we're over there."

"Got it," Tate said. "Hey, has anyone seen Angie?"

He was scanning the crowd for his zombie bride, and Mel knew he was wishing she'd been there to see him take down the big baddie. Probably, because it was usually Angie who led with her fists and punched out the bad guys.

"No, but if I see her, I'll send her over," Mel promised.

Together she and Marty worked their way through the crowd to the van.

Halfway there, she saw some uniformed members of the Zombie Defense Squad. All role-playing had apparently been suspended during the fight as the squad and zombies all mingled and stood up on their toes, trying to see over the crowd to find out what the ruckus was about. This reminded Mel of Marty's earlier departure from the van.

"What happened to your two new buddies?" she asked.

Marty scowled. "Nothing."

Which Mel took to mean he didn't want to talk about it. Silly Marty. Had he not known her for over a year?

"When you say nothing, you mean . . . ?" she prompted him.

"You're just not going to let it go, are you?" he asked.

"No," she said.

"Fine." Marty stepped around a family of undead, and Mel had to move quickly to keep up. "If you must know, they tried to capture me."

Mel stifled her laugh enough to ask, "How?"

"They had a whosiwhatsis in their backpack. Sort of looked like a humane mouse catcher. Not sure how they thought they were going to stuff me in there, but I got Olivia to run interference while I escaped."

Now Mel did laugh. Marty gave her an outraged look, which only made her laugh harder.

"I'm sorry," she said. "Really, it's just, why you?"

"Danged if I know," Marty said. "Every time they pointed that goofy gizmo at me, it started flashing and beeping like all get-out."

"Well, obviously, it's faulty," Mel said.

"Yeah," Marty said. "Unless . . ."

"What?"

"Unless I died and now I'm a ghost, like in that movie Tate made us watch that scared the snot out of me."

"*The Sixth Sense*?" Mel asked. When Marty nodded, she

shook her head. "No, because that would mean that everyone who comes into contact with you has the ability to see dead people. You. Are. Not. Dead."

Marty nodded, looking relieved. "You'd tell me though, right?"

"I promise," Mel said. "The minute my hand passes right through you, I'll be sure to scream and let you know."

She patted the sleeve of his suit just to reassure them both that he was very much alive and kicking.

They pushed through a group of rowdy teens dressed like dead rock stars to reach the van. It stood deserted with no line as everyone had rushed over to see the fight.

As they unlocked it and climbed into the back, Mel said, "Push the brains."

"Okay, in all my eighty-plus years, I never thought anyone would say that to me," Marty said. "What about the coffin? Shouldn't one of us be out there with it?"

"Oh, I forgot," Mel said.

Marty made to back out of the van, but Mel put her hand on his arm.

"Not you," she said. "No more napping."

"Aw, but I'm tired," he said. "And it's all plush and sound-proof."

"Yeah . . . no," Mel said. "I'll go out until the others get back."

Mel hopped down from the van and circled around to the front where the coffin was propped. She noted the lid was open, which was a surprise since she was sure they'd closed it. Then again, there were thousands of people here. It would have been easy for someone to open it while they were away.

She hurried forward and noticed the big poufy white dress hanging out the side. Of course!

"Very funny, Ange," she said. "While you're napping in the coffin, your fiancé was getting his butt stomped. Oh, but don't tell him I said that. If he asks, tell him I said he was whuppin' the big hairy beastie."

Mel peered over the side. Angie was wedged in the casket on her side with her hair and veil covering her face. Her dress was crammed in around her. It had never been a sparkling-clean gown, given the fake blood and all, but now it seemed even more dingy with dirt streaks and rips and even more fake blood.

"Angie, did you hear me?" Mel asked. "Tate was in a brawl."

Angie didn't move. She didn't even twitch at hearing that Tate had been in a fight. That was odd. Mel had expected Angie to explode out of the coffin and go kick some butt on behalf of her man, which was normal Angie-operating procedure. Maybe she really was asleep.

"Angie!" Mel reached into the casket and shook Angie's shoulder. It felt wrong. "Angie!"

Mel began to shove aside the veil and hair, trying to see what was wrong with her friend. One of Angie's arms flopped out of the casket. Mel started and then smiled. Obviously, Angie was having fun with her and playing the zombie bride to the hilt.

"All right," Mel said. "You win. You startled me. Now come on, we have cupcakes to schlep."

She grabbed Angie's arm to help her out of the coffin. Her skin was cold to the touch. Too cold. Instinctively, Mel put her fingers over the pulse point on Angie's wrist.

There wasn't one. Angie was dead.

Eight

Mel dropped Angie's arm. She tried to push aside the veil and Angie's thick dark hair to see if her friend was breathing. Her hands were shaking too hard to function, and she was whimpering like a wounded animal as tears clouded her vision.

"Damn it, Angie," Mel cried. "You're freaking me out. Quit the act!"

Angie didn't move, and Mel knew. She knew it was true. Her friend was dead.

Hysterical, Mel spun around and faced the crowd. "Help! Please somebody, help!"

As if this was a part of the event, no one moved at first. Terror and frustration made Mel charge the crowd. She grabbed the first normal-looking person she could find and yanked them back towards the coffin.

"My friend is . . ." She couldn't say it. "Help me!"

The man stared at her as if he suspected a con. He approached the coffin as if fully expecting the body in it to jump out at him. She didn't.

He reached forward and took Angie's arm. He gave Mel a bug-eyed glance and then shouted over his shoulder.

"Oh, my God! She's telling the truth—this woman is dead!" he shouted to the friends he'd been walking with.

At that, his friends hurried forward and began to help him get Angie out of the coffin. Mel dashed around the side of the bakery truck and pounded on the window. Marty glanced up and before she could say a word, he was rocketing out of the back of the van.

"What is it?" he asked.

"We need to find Tate," Mel gasped. Snot and tears were coursing down her face, making it hard to talk or breathe. "It's Angie."

"Is she hurt?" He grabbed her arms and gave her a little shake. "Where is she?"

Mel choked; she couldn't form the words. She pointed to the coffin in front of the van. "She's d—"

"What?" Marty dropped Mel's arms and raced to the front of the van, where the three men were trying to maneuver Angie's body in its voluminous gown out of the casket.

Marty darted forward yelling, "Call an ambulance!" to a woman nearby

Mel followed in a stupor. Her ears were ringing. Her vision was blurry. She couldn't breathe. Her brain was refusing to register anything in front of her, and she felt as if someone had reached inside and yanked out all of her innards.

Someone took her arm, and yelled, "I think this woman is in shock."

The world tilted sideways and Mel felt woozy. She blinked and tried to suck in enough air to stay conscious. She couldn't faint. Angie needed her. Tate needed her.

Her legs gave out and she leaned heavily on the person who'd taken her arm. People were shouting and she was jostled as someone grabbed her other arm.

"What's going on?"

"What's happening?"

"Mel!"

She glanced up and saw Tate and Oz running towards her. She shoved away the person who held her and stumbled forward.

Tate caught her as she wobbled on her feet.

"Mel, are you all right?" Tate cupped her face and checked her eyes as if looking for signs of an injury or illness.

Mel's voice sounded garbled even in her head. She gestured behind her and finally managed to say, "No. Go. There."

Tate looked over her head, and his already pale face went deathly white. He let go of Mel and bolted towards the bride being lifted out of the coffin.

"Angie!" His shout was hoarse and so full of terror that Mel felt her own heart clench hard in her chest.

Oz grabbed her arm to steady her, and they hurriedly followed in Tate's wake.

"What's happening?" Oz asked. His voice sounded scared and vulnerable, and Mel wished she could lie and tell him everything was okay, but it wasn't, and she knew it never would be.

"Angie!" Tate shoved his way through the men who'd

lifted Angie out of the coffin. He knelt beside her and began to push back her veil and dark hair.

Mel got a glimpse of the front of Angie's dress. It was saturated in blood, not the artistic splatter she and Tate had flicked onto each other with paintbrushes and laughter, but rather a full-on soaking of blood. Mel felt bile splash the back of her throat, and she gagged.

"What's going on?" someone demanded, but Mel couldn't look away from her friend's body. Her throat felt as if it had hardened, and no words were able to pass. "Never mind, I'll see for myself."

Mel felt someone brush past her and she watched as a woman in a gown knelt beside Tate. He turned to look at her once, twice, and then he yelled. He stood up and grabbed her and crushed her to him.

"Are you real?" he cried. Then he kissed her face all over. Angie was blinking and smiling and—

Angie!

Mel glanced from the body to her friend and back and back again. She grabbed Oz and hugged him hard. Relief hit her like a brick to the temple, and she didn't pause to stop and think but instead launched herself at her two friends.

"You're alive! Oh, thank god, you're alive," she said.

She wrapped her arms about both of her friends and squeezed them in the tightest hug she could manage.

"Can't breathe," Angie cried.

Mel quickly let go and stepped back. Oz reached around her to give Angie a bear hug before giving her back to Tate.

"I love you guys, too, really, but what's going on?" Angie asked.

Just then Officer Henry bustled through the crowd. He

was talking into his radio and he knelt beside the body of the woman on the ground. The sound of a siren in the distance alerted them to an arriving ambulance.

Henry pushed aside the last of the woman's hair and veil. She was young and pretty, like Angie, but not Angie. He checked her over and with a sad shake of his head, he stood and began talking into his radio again. Mel didn't need to hear him to know that he was reporting that the woman was dead.

"Oh, wow," Angie said. "She's dressed as a bride like me." Then she put it all together. She looked at Tate and then at Mel. "You thought that was me."

Mel nodded, still not really sure she was up to talking. The men who had helped to lift the woman out of the coffin began to back the crowd up to make room for the other bicycle officers who arrived.

"What happened?" Angie asked. "How did she get here?"

Tate looked at Mel as if he was wondering the same thing. Mel cleared her throat and started to explain.

"She was in the coffin. When I saw her, I thought you were pranking me," she said to Angie. "I couldn't see her face, because she was on her side, but her dress looked like yours so I just assumed . . ." Mel pushed back her toque with a shaky hand and saw a smear of the woman's blood on her hands. "I think I might be sick."

"Come on," Tate said. "Let's move to the side, where you can get some air."

They circled around the van, where Marty and Oz joined them. Marty borrowed a folding chair from the T-shirt vendor next to the van and helped Mel sit down.

"Put your head between your knees if you need it," Marty said. "I'm going to keep an eye."

Mel wasn't sure if he meant he'd watch the body or the coffin, but she suspected he meant the coffin.

Oz went into the van and came back with a cold cloth that he put on the back of Mel's neck. It helped a bit.

Marty stood by the corner of the cupcake van. He was peering around the corner, reporting the goings-on.

"Ambulance guys are here," he said. "Oh, no."

"What is it?" Tate asked. He was standing with an arm around Angie's waist as if afraid to let her out of his sight again.

"There's a commotion," Marty said.

"I guess an actual dead body at a zombie walk would do that," Oz said.

"No, this, ah." Marty stalled out of words and rubbed the back of his head as if he could generate the right explanation with a good scalp massage.

"Marty, what is it?" Mel asked. She felt her anxiety spike. Was the dead woman reanimating like a real zombie? What?

"Angie!" An anguished cry reached their ears, and they all glanced at one another.

"Yeah, Roach just arrived," Marty said.

Angie glanced at Tate and said, "I have to go to him."

He gave her a quick nod.

Angie hurried around the van while the rest of them followed.

Roach was flailing and fighting the officers who were holding him back, trying to keep him away from the body.

"Roach!" Angie cried. "I'm here. I'm okay. I'm fine."

But the crazed rock star couldn't hear her over the shouts of the crowd. He was bucking and fighting, and it wasn't until Angie jumped right in front of him and yelled, "Stop!" that he finally heard her.

"Angie!" He blinked and then he grabbed her. He hauled her up tight against him and then planted a kiss on her that made every woman in the crowd wilt at the knees.

Angie melted up against him for just a second before she wrenched herself out of his arms. She was breathless when she straightened her veil and said, "Easy there, cowboy, I'm spoken for."

The officers stepped back just as Tate rolled up to stand beside Angie. His eyes were hard and Mel wondered if he was going to punch Roach in the mouth. He didn't. Instead he crossed his arms over his chest, probably to keep himself from doing exactly that.

"I don't think I've ever seen T-man lose his cool," Oz whispered.

"Emotions are running high," Marty said. "He'll be okay."

"It wasn't you," Roach said. He was staring at Angie in wonder. "I heard that a zombie bride had been found dead. Oh, man, I think I just aged five years."

"I'm sorry," Angie said. She patted his arm. "It wasn't me. It was another bride."

Roach glanced from her to where the officers and EMTs were examining the body of the other woman. His face paled and he turned back to Angie as if to make sure that she was just fine.

"Are we good here now?" Tate asked. He took Angie's arm to lead her away.

"You! Todd!" Roach stomped forward, blocking Tate's way and shoving his face right in front of his. His voice was a low, menacing growl when he asked, "What did you do?"

"Excuse me?" Tate asked. "I know your feeble brain can

only retain drumbeats, but my name is Tate, as in Tate Harper, the man who is going to marry Angie DeLaura."

"Todd, Tim, Turnip, who cares?" Roach seethed. "I know what you did."

"Really? What's that?" Tate asked. He looked completely unfazed in the face of Roach's fury, which Mel knew he was doing just to make Roach even more furious. It worked.

"You know what you did!" Roach shouted. "What happened, Tom? Were you so afraid that you were going to lose Angie to me that you decided to stop her by any means possible?"

Now Tate was getting angry. Mel could tell by the red flush that crept up the back of his neck and the way he bunched his fists and leaned forward like he was ready to take a swing and put some weight behind it. Judging by the way the police officers took a few steps closer to the two men, they sensed it, too.

"What are you talking about, you narcissistic jackass?" Tate yelled.

"Guys, stop!" Angie scolded them. "A woman has been killed." She gestured to the body behind her, which was now being photographed by the crime scene unit. "Show some respect. Whatever issue you two have, it does not need to be worked out right here and now."

"That's where you're wrong," Roach said. He glared at Tate before he looked back at Angie and continued. "Don't you see, baby girl? He found out that we were together after the show, and in a jealous rage he killed that woman thinking she was you."

Nine

"Now hold on!" Tate yelled. "First, I didn't kill anyone."

Officer Henry gave him a scrutinizing glance, and Tate gave it right back.

"I'm a witness," Oz said. "T-man and I were in a fight."

"You were in a fight?" Angie squawked, noticing Tate's scraped knuckles for the first time. She grabbed his hand and studied it more closely.

"That's not the issue right now," Tate said, pulling his hand away with a wince. "What exactly does he mean you were together after the show? I thought you went to the bathroom."

"I did," she said. "But I didn't want to try and cram all of this"—she gestured to her poufy skirt—"in a stall, so I went back to the bakery. On my way back, I ran into Roach and we talked."

Roach made a scoffing sound and Tate frowned at him. Mel had a feeling fists were going to fly at any moment. She suspected that Oz and Marty were getting the same feeling as they inched closer to Tate, as if to be in grabbing range.

"Oh, no you don't," Angie said to Roach. "Don't you try to make something out of nothing. We talked. It was very nice. Don't ruin it."

Roach let out an impatient sigh, and Mel noted that Tate's shoulders seemed to ease down just a little bit. Then they snapped back up as Tate studied Roach more closely.

"You know, given that you've been accused of murder once before, I'd say that of the two of us, that makes you the more likely suspect," Tate said. "That and the fact that *I* got the girl. What's the matter, you couldn't sweet talk her back to you so you decided to kill her?"

This time Roach did lose his cool. With a gruff shout, he lowered his head like a bull about to charge. Tate shoved Angie into Oz's arms and braced himself. The hit never came. Roach took only three steps forward, when he was grabbed by the back of his expensive leather jacket.

Mel glanced around him to see Detective Manny Martinez holding on to Roach but looking at her.

"It's been a long time, Mel," he said.

Caught off guard by the handsome detective, Mel nodded.

"Five weeks, four days, and a handful of hours to be exact," he said.

Mel raised her eyebrows in surprise. He'd been counting?

Manny passed Roach off to Officer Henry. "Walk him around until he cools off." Then he turned to Tate and said, "Really?"

"Sorry, it's been a rough afternoon," Tate said.

Manny nodded. "So, I heard." He glanced over his shoulder at the crime scene techs working around the body. "If you'll excuse me, I need to be briefed."

He left without waiting for a response, and Mel felt her insides pinch. She and Manny had been friends, maybe even a little bit more than friends, given that he had saved her life and all, but he had wanted more, and she could never be more. She was in love with Joe DeLaura, and she always would be.

"I think I liked it better when he thought he had a chance with you," Angie said. "This feels . . . awkward."

"Tell me about it," Mel said.

Uncle Stan came tromping through the crowd. He had his usual roll of antacid tablets clutched in his fist, and Mel could see he was clearly unhappy about being called to the scene of a homicide in the middle of all of this chaos.

"Back up!" he barked at a pair of zombies who were crowding him. He stopped in front of Mel and company and stared at them. "Oh, for the love of Pete, not you, too."

"We're working it," Mel said by way of explanation. Then she gestured to the van as if to prove they had not been having any fun of any kind.

"Stan," Officer Henry called his name, and Stan turned to face him. "Did Mel tell you that she's the one who found the body?"

Stan turned back to Mel with a look of disbelief. She gave him a sheepish shrug.

"She was stuffed in our coffin," Mel explained. At his sympathetic look, the words came tumbling out in a rush. "She's dressed like a bride and I thought she was Angie and then I couldn't get her out and then there was so much blood . . ."

Mel started to hiccup and Stan opened his arms and pulled her into a bear hug, so much like the ones her father, Stan's older brother, used to give when she was little that Mel's hiccups turned into sobs, and she gooped all over his suit jacket. Stan didn't care. He patted her back and shushed her while she cried even harder.

Coming from sturdy Irish stock, the Cooper men were built big. They gave the best hugs in the world, and there wasn't a day that passed that Mel didn't miss getting squeezes from her dad. She was so grateful to have Uncle Stan in her life to help fill the void. She hugged him back as hard as she could.

"You all right?" he asked when her sobs began to slow.

"Yeah, I'm good," she lied. "It's just been . . . awful."

Stan let her go and stepped back to study her face. They both knew she wasn't just talking about finding the body. Heck, she'd found enough bodies to have developed the requisite gallows humor as a coping mechanism.

No, she was talking about the relentless stress and worry she'd been enduring since Joe had begun his trial a few months before, and Stan knew it.

"He's okay," Stan said. "We've had protection on him since day one, and don't discount the brothers. They're excellent guard dogs."

Mel snuffled and nodded. "I know. I'll just be really glad when this trial is over."

"Hang tough, kid." Stan patted her shoulder. Then he straightened up and Mel knew he was bracing himself for what he was about to go do. She didn't envy him the grisly task.

One of the crime scene investigators was cordoning off the area with yellow tape. Mel was relieved that they didn't loop the van, although she was certain there was no way they'd be selling any more cupcakes today. The mere thought made her sick to her stomach.

"I feel sort of disgusting in this getup," Angie said. "Do you think Stan will mind if I leave?"

"I don't think so," Mel said. "I mean, you weren't here, so it's not like you're a witness or anything."

"Kristin!" a man yelled as he charged towards them.

Mel only had a moment to register that he was dressed in a tuxedo and looked an awful lot like Tate, the zombie groom, before he was upon them. He grabbed Angie's arm and spun her around.

"Kristin! Where have you been? I've been looking all over for you," he said. He hugged her close. "Did you hear a woman was killed? When I couldn't find you . . ."

His voice trailed off and he let go of Angie as he noticed Mel standing beside them. Mel glanced at Tate, who looked as sick about the situation as she felt. This had to be the dead woman's boyfriend or husband. Mel closed her eyes for a second and dug deep, looking for strength. This could have played out so differently.

"Sir, I'm so sorry, there's been a . . ." she began but he interrupted her.

"Mel? Mel Cooper?" he asked.

Mel looked at him. She couldn't see past the ghoulish makeup or the fake gash on his neck. If he was a regular at the bakery, she couldn't place him.

"It's me, Scott Streubel; I'm a law clerk in your . . . er . . . in Joe DeLaura's office," he said.

Ding! The light went off and Mel remembered Scott and his wife, Kristin. They'd gotten married about six months ago.

She and Joe had attended the service and reception. Joe had even toasted them, wishing them a long and happy life together.

Mel felt bile splash up into the back of her throat. She desperately hoped that she was wrong, please, please, please, but on the off chance she wasn't, she figured it was better if she was the one to tell Scott what was happening.

"Oh, Scott," Mel said. Her voice must have registered her distress, because he gave her a wary look.

"What is it, Mel?"

"This isn't your wife," she said, gesturing to Angie. "This is my friend Angie."

Angie faced him so he could really see her, and Scott blinked. "Oh, I'm sorry. I thought . . . then . . ."

Mel hadn't thought he could get any paler than the white pancake makeup he had on his face. She was wrong. So wrong.

Scott whipped his head in the direction of the police. He lurched forward as if he'd forgotten how to walk and was forcing his feet to move by sheer will.

"Kristin!" he cried.

Mel hurried along beside him. Manny met them at the yellow tape. He held up his hands to hold them back, but Mel shook her head at him. Manny's eyes darted to Scott's wedding suit. Manny looked pained. He lifted the plastic tape and gestured for Scott to follow him. Mel followed, hoping against hope that this was all just a horrible mistake.

The crowd was silent as they watched the groom kneel by the bride. Mel hovered behind Scott, not knowing what to do or how to help. Manny stood beside her as if offering his strength. She appreciated it more than she could say.

The tech moved aside, and Scott slowly crawled forward. It took him only a second. He took the woman's hand in his, and the anguished cry that left him as he bowed his head to the ground made the hair on the back of Mel's neck stand on end.

It was the sound of a man's heart being ripped out of his chest and squeezed by the mean fist of grief until it stopped beating completely.

Ten

There was nothing she could say. She felt like a voyeur watching Scott smooth away the hair from his bride's face with trembling hands. The zombie makeup she wore made a sick joke of the vicious crime that had befallen her. Standing this close, it was easy for Mel to see that the blood on her gown came from one bullet hole right through her heart.

Uncle Stan knelt beside Scott. It was a few moments before Scott realized he was there. He looked like an abandoned child, dazed, bewildered, and crushed. Stan spoke softly to him in a calm, reassuring voice that made Mel want to cry because it was the tone Stan used when he had to deliver the worst possible news. She knew because the day her father had died, Stan had used that voice on her.

Manny leaned close to Mel and whispered in her ear. "You know him?"

She nodded and cleared her throat. She turned towards him and said, "His name is Scott Streubel, and that's his wife, Kristin. He's a law clerk in Joe's office."

Manny rocked back on his heels. Mel could tell the news was a surprise. Manny took her by the elbow and dragged her away from the crime scene.

"I want you out of here," he said. His expression was dark and a little scary. "Have Tate, Marty, and Oz take you back to the bakery. You don't stop anywhere; you don't split up. You stay together and when you get to the bakery, you call me."

"What?" she asked. "What's going on?"

"Just do it, Mel!" he snapped. "For once in your life don't argue with me, and do what I say."

And then Mel knew. "You think it was a hit, don't you? She was shot. You think one of Tucci's thugs did it, don't you?"

"Not here, not now," Manny hissed. He turned and stomped over to Tate, dragging Mel behind him. He said the exact same thing to Tate, who met his intense stare with one of his own.

"We'll leave right now," Tate said.

"What about the cupcakes, and the van?" Angie protested. "And the coffin?"

"The coffin is evidence and is going back to the crime lab," Manny said. "Angie, I really can't emphasize enough how much I want you out of here. Right now."

Angie met his gaze and then her chin went up. Her face was pale and her voice shook when she spoke. "You think they meant to shoot me, don't you? You think because she and I are both dressed as brides that they meant to kill me."

"It's a definite possibility," Manny said. His tone was gentle but grim. "You need to go."

"Come on, Ange," Tate said. "We can pack up and get out of town for a while."

"Leave town?" Angie sounded outraged. "I can't leave. Not while Joe has this huge trial going on."

"How is you being at risk helping your brother?" Manny asked. His voice was exasperated now.

"I'm supporting him," Angie argued.

Mel felt her neck get hot. Manny and Angie had always had a tenuous relationship. Primarily, because Angie tried to be accepting of Manny's interest in Mel, even while hoping that Mel and Joe got back together.

"He doesn't need your support," Manny said. "He needs you to be safe."

He looked at Mel when he snarled this last bit, and she nodded. She agreed with him completely. Besides, he was right.

"I am safe!" Angie snapped. "You don't know that this was meant for me."

"I don't," Manny conceded. "But guess what I do know? Frank Tucci is one sick bastard, and he's going to do everything he can to rattle Joe's cage until he can't think straight, never mind argue his case in front of a judge and jury. Killing you sure would destroy your brother, wouldn't it?"

Angie blew out a breath. "You're trying to scare me."

"Damn right I am," Manny said. He shoved a hand through his hair. "Tucci is an animal. He'd think nothing of shooting you; hell, this is a guy who cut off his goomah's right hand when she refused to make him a sandwich."

Mel felt dizzy, and when she glanced at Tate he seemed to wobble on his feet, too. Angie didn't even blink. She nodded as if she'd heard it before, and Mel realized she had probably gotten an earful from her brothers.

"Fine, I'll leave the festival," Angie said. "But I still don't believe that this was about me. She doesn't even look like me."

Manny looked at Mel. His black eyes were intense when he said, "Go and be careful."

"I will," she said. "I promise, but what about Scott?"

"I'll take care of him," Manny said. "I promise."

Tate signaled to Marty and Oz to fall in, and the next thing Mel knew, she and Angie were being escorted out of the park.

It wasn't a walk back to the bakery so much as it was a jog. The only time Mel had been pushed this hard was when she'd signed up for fitness boot camp, in a not-very-well-thought-out plan to work off some excess buttercream. When the vein in her forehead had gone 3D and throbbing on her, she'd quit.

They circled an in-ground fountain near the edge of the park and stopped as two men squared off in what was obviously an altercation. The bigger of the two men had arms the size of hams. Mel could tell just by looking at him that he was a gym rat, the sort of guy who checked his muscle definition in every reflective surface he passed.

Tate tried to usher them around the men, but Angie stopped him. "We might be needed."

Tate opened his mouth to protest, but the two men shouting drowned out whatever he might have said.

"Do you have any idea how much I spent on this?" the bigger man shouted as he grabbed the smaller man by his scarf. "You're going to give back every dime!"

"Hey! Let me go!" Mel recognized Chad Bowman, the coordinator of the zombie event, by his scarf and his rectangular glasses. "Listen I can't be held accountable for something like this. How could I possibly know a woman was going to be shot?"

"I don't know and I don't care, but you'd better be insured, because I want every cent I spent on promo, swag, and merch back. I mean who the hell is going to want a souvenir T-shirt from an undead event where a woman was actually killed?"

"You might want to let him go," Tate said as he approached the duo. "There are cops everywhere."

Muscles, as Mel had started to think of him, glared at Tate as if he was ready to engage in another fight, but then he shook his head and shoved Chad away from him. He ran a hand through his close-cropped blond hair in exasperation, making it stand up on end in aggravated tufts.

"You're right, it's not worth it," the man said.

"You know who is behind this, don't you?" Chad asked.

They all looked at him in surprise.

"Chad, if you know something, you really need to go to the police," Mel said.

"They won't believe me," he said. "But just so you all know, it's the government."

"The government killed that woman?" Tate asked, clearly thinking he had missed something.

"Yes," Chad said.

"Why?" Marty asked, his voice full of derision. "Why would the government kill her?"

"To break up the event, because it's too close to the truth. The dead being reanimated, it's going to happen," Chad said. He smacked a fist into his open palm as if to emphasize his point.

"You're crazy." Muscles just shook his head and walked away. Apparently, he'd heard enough.

"I'm not. There's a gas that if unleashed on the masses would render us all zombies," Chad said. "The government is keeping it a secret."

"Oh, brother," Marty groaned and began to walk, pulling Oz and Mel with him. Tate and Angie fell into step behind them and, undeterred, Chad walked with them.

"It's true," Chad said. "They don't want the people to have zombie walks, because then we might know how to deal with the real thing when they attack us with it. They want to keep us stupid."

"They don't need to help with that," Marty muttered under his breath, and Oz snorted.

"Only the government has the cure, man; I'm telling you unless we figure out a way to stop them, we're going to become brain-eating crazies," Chad exclaimed. He spread his arms wide to emphasize his point.

"One of us is already there," Oz said and this time Marty guffawed.

Marty, Oz, and Tate closed ranks around the girls, making it very clear that they were leaving and Chad was not welcome to come along.

"Lord-a-mercy, that boy is dumber than dirt," Marty said as soon as they were out of earshot.

"Conspiracy theorist," Tate said. "I hear they have issues."

He glanced around at the mass of people pressing their way out of the park with them and then exchanged a cautious look with Marty. The three men became abruptly serious. Tate picked up the pace as they continued walking back to Old Town.

Once inside the bakery, Tate hustled the remaining customers out of the building and closed and locked the door.

He was pulling the shades closed when Joyce, who'd been behind the counter, looked at them all and asked, "What on earth is going on?"

No one answered. Joyce glanced at their faces and then clutched her chest.

"Oh, no, not again," she cried. She looked at Mel as if she just couldn't believe it. "You found another body, didn't you?"

"Not just a body," Tate said. "A body that looked just like Angie."

"No, she didn't," Angie protested. "If you looked beyond the wedding dress and the long brown hair, we really didn't look much alike, and I bet after all of the makeup is off, you'll find we looked nothing alike."

"Angie." Tate's voice was impatient. "We're not arguing about this. You and I are leaving town."

"Again with this?" Angie asked. "Where exactly are we going to go?"

"I don't know," he said. "But we're out of here. I want you out of Frank Tucci's reach until this case Joe is trying is over."

"You have lost your mind," Angie said. She looked at the others as if expecting backup.

Oz and Marty both looked up as if the ceiling's paint job suddenly needed a visual inspection.

"I think he's right," Mel said. She braced for Angie's rebuttal, which predictably came out of her like cannon fire.

"Aw, come on," Angie argued. "Not you, too. How can you agree with this?"

Mel looked at her friend and gave her a sad smile. "It's simple, really. When I thought that was you in the coffin, I died a thousand deaths. I never, ever, ever want to feel that way again. Ever."

"But—" Angie started to protest but Tate cut her off.

"No, this is not negotiable," he said.

Angie turned to look at him, and something in his fierce expression must have tipped her off that this was not the time to argue.

"My clothes are up in your apartment," she said to Mel. "Okay if I grab a quick shower and change?"

"Go for it," Mel said. She felt the tension in her shoulders ease. Angie was going to be smart about this. It was going to be all right.

"I'll walk you up," Tate said. Angie nodded.

"I'll lock the back door behind you," Oz said. He followed them into the kitchen. As soon as the door swung shut behind them, Mel and Marty collapsed into seats at a center table.

Joyce went into the kitchen and came back minutes later with a steaming pot of coffee and three mugs. Oz came in behind her and joined them.

"You three look like you could use a pick-me-up," she said. "Now can you tell me what happened exactly?"

Marty gestured to Mel. "You saw more than I did."

Mel nodded. She told her mother everything, only pausing when Joyce gasped and covered her mouth with her hand as if to keep from crying out. When Joyce nodded, Mel continued right up until they arrived at the bakery.

"What did your uncle say?" Joyce asked. "Does he think Angie was the target?"

"I didn't get a chance to talk to him," Mel said. "Manny pretty much threw us out of there. I don't even know when we'll be able to go and get the van."

"We'll go back and get it," Marty said, gesturing between himself and Oz.

The door to the kitchen opened, and Tate and Angie reappeared. Gone was any trace of their zombie makeup, Mel noted with a prick of jealousy. Her own skin felt shrink-wrapped, as if it couldn't breathe through the heavy makeup, and she felt greasy and grubby all over.

A knock on the front door made them all jump. Mel rose to go answer it, but Joyce grabbed her arm.

"Mom, if it's a hit man, I'm pretty sure he's not going to knock," she said.

Joyce let her go with a quick nod.

Marty and Oz both stood and crowded Mel all the way to the door.

"Really?" she asked. Having them breathe down her neck was not helping her nerves in the least.

"Yes, really," Marty said. "Until we know who it is."

"Mel, it's us, Al and Paulie, open up," a man's voice shouted.

"How do we know it's them?" Joyce asked.

"Paulie, if you hit me with that fake arm one more time, I swear I'm going to shove it right where the sun—"

"It's them," Mel said. She unlocked the dead bolt and pushed the door open. "Hey, guys."

Al and Paulie jostled their way into the room. Mel glanced past them out onto the street. Could she really afford to close the shop just because they were all on edge about a murder?

What if it had been Angie in the coffin? Her heart felt like a lump of ice in her chest. She slammed the door and locked it. She'd figure out what to do when all of the facts were in.

"We came as fast as we could," Al said. He crossed the room to where his sister stood, looked her over, and then hugged her hard. Paulie did the same.

"We ran into Stan and Manny," Paulie said. "They told us what went down. I'm sorry you had to go through that, Mel."

He doubled back and gave her a quick hug. Al took his place when he was done.

"We were on the other side of the park when word came that there had been a shooting," Al said. "At first no one believed it, but when the crime scene van arrived people started to freak out. It's chaos over there."

"I said to Al right away, 'I bet Mel and Angie are in the middle of this,'" Paulie said.

He helped himself to one of the mini sample cupcakes Mel put out on the counter every day; today's flavor was the strawberry banana, a strawberry cake with banana-infused buttercream. He popped it into his mouth in one bite and reached for another. Angie smacked his hand away.

"He did," Al confirmed. Then he looked at his sister. "And you were, weren't you?"

"Only because the body was stuffed into our coffin, and Mel happened to find it," Angie said.

"And because we thought it was you," Tate added.

He sounded breathless at the mere idea, and Mel felt bad for him. She knew exactly how he was feeling: relieved and yet still terrified that the hit had been meant for Angie. Then she felt horrible because Scott didn't get to feel the same relief about his wife, Kristin. Instead, he was left with just grief.

"Uncle Stan and Manny will figure it out," she said. "Whoever killed Kristin Streubel won't get away with it."

"You knew her?" Joyce asked.

"I met her just once," Mel said. Then she sighed. "At her wedding."

A thumping knock sounded on the front door. Again,

they all jumped. Marty was closest to the front window and he peered out behind the shade.

"Holy bananas!" he cried.

"What is it?" Mel asked.

"Looks like the undead are preparing to storm the place," he said.

Mel glanced out the window. If she were in a horror film, she would have started screaming. A mob of zombies ten rows deep was standing on the front patio.

Marty turned to look at her. "What do we do?"

Eleven

Mel saw a mother with two little girls dressed as princess zombies. They all looked traumatized and Mel realized that what had started as a fun family outing for them had taken a nasty turn. They needed some comfort stat.

"Tate, take Angie home and stay there," Mel said.

"But—" Angie started to protest but Mel cut her off.

"No," Mel said. "Until we know for sure that you weren't the target, I want you out of sight." When Angie looked about to protest again, Mel gave her a pleading look and said, "Please."

"Fine, but only until we have more information," Angie said. "I'll be back at work tomorrow."

Tate looked relieved and flashed Mel a grateful look.

"We'll go out the back and I'll lock up behind us," he said.

He gave her a quick hug and Mel took the opportunity to whisper, "Keep working on her."

Tate nodded when he let her go. As soon as they disappeared into the back, Mel crossed to the door. She glanced at Al and Paulie.

"Are you two willing to stay on as cupcake bouncers?" she asked. "Anyone acts up, you take them down, no questions, no hesitation."

"With pleasure," Al said. He cracked his knuckles, looking a little too eager.

"Dial it back a little," Mel said. "I'm not looking for a lawsuit. I just want to contain any crazy."

The brothers nodded and assumed their positions by the door.

Mel nodded at Marty and he flipped the CLOSED sign to OPEN and she unlocked the door. She could only hope that among the living dead that poured into the bakery, no one was a killer.

The next three and a half hours passed in a blur of buttercream. The zombies were ten deep at all times, and other than the fifteen minutes she escaped to go shower, Mel was on duty for all of it. And for the first time since it had opened, Fairy Tale Cupcakes ran out of cupcakes.

After the last customer had departed, taking Mel's last Blonde Bombshell with them, she closed and locked the door even though it was still two hours until official closing time.

Joyce and Marty collapsed into a booth while Oz lay down on the counter, looking like he might never move again. Mel surveyed the wreckage of the shop with weary eyes. Good thing they'd closed early, because it was going to take her a few hours to clean up the crumbs, paper liners, wadded-up napkins, and used glassware that had been left behind.

Al and Paulie had gone outside to do a sweep of the

building. They came back in through the back door and collapsed in another booth.

"The building is clear," Al said. "And with Tony's surveillance system in place, if anything funky happens, we'll know."

Mel wondered why she didn't find this as reassuring as he meant it to be.

"I'm going home and taking a hot bath," Joyce said. "Do you want to come with me, Melanie?"

"No, I can't," Mel said. "Not until I know what's going on. Besides, I need to do some serious baking."

"We'll keep an eye on her, Mrs. Cooper," Al said.

"Thank you," Joyce said. "You're good boys."

"Marty and Oz, why don't you two call it a day, too?" Mel asked.

The two men exchanged a worried look.

"I'll be fine," Mel said. "I've got these two and apparently a camera all spying on me."

"Not spying," Paulie protested. "Surveilling."

"Is that even a word?" Al asked.

"Sure it is," Paulie said. "As in, 'I'm surveilling the sitch.'"

"Another made-up word," Al said.

Mel rolled her eyes and then made a shooing gesture with her hands at the others. "Go before I change my mind and make you suffer with me."

"Come on, Joyce, we'll walk you to your car," Marty said.

Joyce paused beside Mel to give her a fierce hug. "Be careful. If you change your mind, come over no matter how late."

"I will," Mel promised. She followed her mother through the kitchen, locking the door behind Joyce and her escorts.

Mel turned around and found Al and Paulie raiding the walk-in cooler.

"Uh, Mel, I don't want to alarm you," Paulie said. "But you've been robbed."

"What?" Mel asked.

"See for yourself!" Paulie said. "There are no cupcakes in here. None."

Mel relaxed against the steel table that sat in the center of her kitchen.

"I haven't been robbed," she said. "We sold out."

"Ah!" he gasped, looking horrified.

"That's a good thing, dummy," Al said. "It means business is good."

"Yeah, but I'm hungry," Paulie whined.

Mel was about to offer to make him some eggs, when a noise sounded from the front of the bakery.

"Get down!" Al ordered.

Mel dropped to the ground behind the table.

"Don't move," Paulie said. "We got this."

She peered under the table as the two brothers scuttled their way to the swinging door that led to the front of the bakery.

Al eased the door open and Paulie rose up behind him and leaned on his back so they could both peer through the crack.

"Do you see anyone?" Al asked.

"No, open the door a bit wider," Paulie said.

"Ugh, I would but I can't support you and open the door," Al complained. "How much do you weigh, anyway?"

"It's all muscle," Paulie snapped.

"Really?" Al asked. "'Cause it feels like a lot of baby fat pressing on me."

Bam! The kitchen door was shoved open, smacking the

brothers back onto the ground. Paulie clutched his forehead. Al moaned and grabbed his nose.

"Who's there?" Mel grabbed a cooking pot from the rack under the table and jumped to her feet. She was not about to let anyone cut off her right hand over a sandwich or anything else.

"Me, it's just me," a voice answered, sounding forlorn.

Mel glanced at the kitchen door to find Chad Bowman standing there, still in his zombie hipster getup, looking lost and confused.

"I was in the bathroom," he said. "The next thing I knew the lights were off and the front door was locked. I couldn't get out."

Mel lowered the pot and blew out a breath. Her closing procedures had been shot to heck tonight. No one had checked the bathroom.

"I'm so sorry," she said. She walked past Chad and led the way back into the main bakery. "We forgot to check the customer bathrooms. I'll let you out."

"Not your fault," Chad said. "I'm sure it was the feds. They probably have a gadget that locks people in rooms so they can snatch them. They're trying to stop me, you know. They have me under constant surveillance."

Mel couldn't help but glance at the camera in the corner of the shop. She gave it a sour look. Maybe Chad wasn't just a conspiracy nut. Maybe he could sense he was being watched even now.

"You'd better hurry on home then," Mel said. "I imagine you're safer there."

Chad glanced out at the dark street. He shivered and when he looked at Mel, his fear was palpable.

"*They* did it, you know," he said. "They killed her and I know why."

Mel felt her heart thump hard in her chest. Did Chad know something? Had he seen something at the zombie walk?

"What do you know, Chad?" she asked.

"She really was a zombie," he said. "The dead woman was infected with the chemical gas that could make us all zombies, and they killed her because they didn't want anyone to know."

Okaaaay. So Chad was crackers and not too tightly wrapped. Great.

"Go home, Chad," Mel said. "Get some rest."

"You believe me, don't you?" he asked.

Mel hesitated. If she said no, he would stand there badgering her all night. If she said yes, he might think they were allies or friends and start hanging around. Hmm. How was she going to get rid of him?

"I believe that you believe it," Mel said. Then she gave him a pat on the back that was more of a shove, and she shut and locked the door behind him.

On that peculiar note, Mel decided to call it a night. She'd get up early to clean and bake. She had no stamina for it now. All she wanted at the moment was a glass of wine, her leftovers from last night's meat loaf at her mom's house, and a snuggle with Captain Jack, her mischievous cat.

It took an ice pack and the promise of future cupcakes to get rid of Al and Paulie, but she was feeling very determined. She loved her friends and family, truly. She even had great affection for many of her customers, but right now she just wanted to be alone, completely and utterly alone.

As she climbed the steps to her apartment above the shop,

she thought about her longing for quiet, and then she felt a heart-pinching pang of terrible because she knew that Scott Streubel was going to be facing an awful lot of alone, too, and she knew he'd give anything for it not to be so.

It seemed a sick sort of irony to her now that she'd only seen Kristin twice, and both times she'd been dressed as a bride. Mel remembered the first day she'd seen her, with her bridesmaids all dressed in bright yellow. At the time she'd thought they all looked like brilliant butterflies as they hovered around Kristin and her bright bouquet of sunflowers.

When had that been? Six months ago? Kristin and Scott had had less than one year of wedded happiness before it was cut short. How was that right? How was that fair? And just like that, the sadness Mel had been feeling was squashed, hammered down by a meaty fist of rage that made her wish she could do some damage to the evil bastard who had done this to the young couple, especially if it turned out that they were really gunning for Angie.

She unlocked the door to her studio apartment and stepped inside. She'd forgotten to put a light on and it was dark, so she braced herself, not knowing where her favorite fur ball was going to attack from. Captain Jack's greetings were always an enthusiastic combination of yay-you're-home and here-are-my-claws-digging-into-your-skin. Mel figured it was his passive-aggressive way of telling her he'd missed her, too.

She waited for a beat but he didn't greet her, which was odd, but didn't explain the hair rising on the back of her neck. In an instant, Mel knew that something was wrong. She wasn't sure how she knew, but she did. Someone was in the room with her.

Twelve

She stood frozen. She couldn't leave unless she had Captain Jack, but she really didn't want to stay and end up shot dead like Kristin Streubel.

Could she just leave the door open and run down the stairs? Then if Captain Jack was in there he'd be able to escape. What if the person inside harmed Captain Jack? She couldn't bear the thought.

Wait, she chided herself. This was ridiculous. Surely Jack had just gotten himself shut in the bathroom. It had happened before. She let out a long breath. She was just nervous because of all the talk about the mobster Frank Tucci gunning for Angie. It was making her imagine things.

"Jack," she called. She was determined to prove to herself that she was just being an idiot. "Where are you, buddy?"

She was just reaching for the lamp on the table behind

her futon when she spotted the little fur ball curled up on the couch. In the dark she could make out his coat of soft white fur, and she reached out to scratch his head, filled with relief that her baby was fine.

When he felt her hand, he pressed his head against her fingers to encourage more love. Mel smiled and rubbed him right behind the ears where he liked it best. Captain Jack uncurled and stretched, and Mel realized that he wasn't curled up on her dark chenille throw, but rather he was napping on the chest of a man, a big hairy man with a broad chest and a beard.

Ack! Mel let out a squeak and snatched Captain Jack off of the man. In her haste she lost her balance and landed on her butt on the floor. The noise woke the man and he sat up. Mel scrambled away. She had to get out of here.

She rolled to her knees, keeping Jack in a football hold with her right arm. She half stumbled half crawled towards the door. Captain Jack let out a yowling protest, wiggled free, and darted towards the kitchenette, where normally she would be fixing his supper at this time.

"No, Jack! Damn it!"

Mel snatched her cordless phone from the holder and was trying to dial 9-1-1, but her hands were shaking and she was still trying to scuttle away.

"Mel, wait!" the man said.

Mel glanced up. She knew that voice. She felt the world contract and then spring back, or maybe that was just her heart.

"It's me," he said. Then he reached over and switched on the same lamp she had been trying to turn on when she came in.

Joe!

He stood while Mel crawled onto the lone armchair in the room. She felt all of the blood rush to her head, and she could do no more than stare at him like an idiot. He took the opportunity to lock the door.

"Hi," he said.

"Hi?" she asked. She grabbed a pillow from behind her back and hurled it at him with the force of a closing pitcher in a pennant race.

Joe caught it before it connected with his face. He lowered it and smiled at her. It was his knee-wilter, Joe DeLaura patent-worthy grin, the same one that had been turning her to jelly since she was twelve and he was sixteen.

"It's been a while," he said.

"Seven weeks, five days"—she paused to glance at the clock on the wall and then added—"and one hour. Not that I've kept track."

When he grinned, his teeth were a white slash against his scruffy beard. Mel wondered when he had acquired that. She wondered if it was soft or bristly; then she reminded herself that she didn't care.

"The brothers said you wanted to talk to me," he said.

"Yeah," Mel said. But now that he was here and since so much had happened, she had no idea what to say to him. She'd thought she'd have more time to prepare.

"I've missed you," he said. His chocolate brown eyes looked as miserable as she felt. And the way he was staring at her made her feel as if he was trying to reacquaint himself with every bit of her.

"Well, then perhaps you shouldn't have rejected my proposal," Mel said. She was pretty sure she was spitting out icicles with her words.

Joe looked pained. They hadn't spoken since the night he had told her that things had changed between them, no explanation, just a rejection of her proposal of marriage. Then he had disappeared into the night like a fugitive.

"Mel, I'm sorry, I know I could have handled it better," he said.

"You think?" she asked. She rose to her feet. This had been a bad idea. She'd thought she wanted to talk to him just to see how he was doing and reassure herself that he was okay, but too many old feelings were bubbling to the surface. It was time for him to go.

Joe tossed the pillow onto the futon, and they stood staring at each other. The four feet between them might as well have been filled with hot coals. There was no crossing this chasm.

Mel was a potent cocktail of angry, sad, scared, confused, you name it. She was practically vibrating with the combustion of emotions inside of her, and she had no idea which one was going to explode out of her first. If Joe had a functional fight-or-flight response going on, he would be smart to run for cover, because she was a little bit crazy right now.

Captain Jack had leapt up onto the counter. As if sensing a squabble brewing between his kitty parents, he let out a long, pitiful yowl and then knocked his plastic dish off the counter. Mel had no doubt that it was to remind her that no matter her personal issues, it was dinnertime.

She heaved a sigh and strode over to the counter. Retrieving his dish from the floor, she crossed over to her pantry, which was little more than a narrow floor-to-ceiling cupboard.

As she filled Jack's bowl, she glanced at Joe, who was still watching her with the intensity of a laser beam. She swallowed past the sudden dryness in her throat. She shook off any misguided attraction she might be feeling and reminded herself to cling to her rage.

"I'm going to need my key back," she said. She was pleased that her voice sounded even, almost casual in fact.

"No," Joe said.

"Excuse me?" She placed the food bowl in front of Captain Jack, who commenced chowing down.

"I'll need it to keep an eye on the place," he said. "I spoke to Tate. I know what happened today. You're leaving town with Angie."

Mel thought it was a darn good thing all of her pots and pans were well out of reach, otherwise she might have been tempted to pick one up and brain him with it.

"That's not happening," she said. She turned to face him, crossed her arms over her chest, and raised one eyebrow in challenge as she stared him down.

Joe mimicked her stance right down to the eyebrow, and she knew it was game on.

"I'm sorry," he said. "Did I make it sound like it's optional? Because it's not."

"You are not the boss of me," Mel said. "I have two weddings, a bar mitzvah, and three baby showers to bake for in the next two weeks. I am not going anywhere."

"Oz can do the baking," he said.

"He's still in culinary school," Mel said. "He doesn't have time."

"Then cancel the orders," he said.

"No!" Mel said. "My business reputation will be destroyed."

"Fine," he said. "Subcontract Olivia to fill the orders for you. You know she'd do it."

"And have her steal my customers?" Mel argued. She

uncrossed her arms and spread them wide in the universal gesture that asked, *Are you a moron?*

Joe scratched the beard on his chin as if it itched. Mel stepped closer to get a better look at his whiskers. There was something not right there. She reached out and grabbed the edge of his beard, and then she yanked. With a sound like Velcro separating, Joe's beard peeled off of his face.

"Yow!" he yelped and clapped a hand to his chin. "What did you do that for?"

"Why are you wearing a fake beard?" she asked. She wanted to cling to her fury, but he looked so ridiculous that she was having a hard time not laughing at him.

"I didn't want anyone to recognize me," he said. "I didn't want to come anywhere near you until this case is over."

"And you think this piece of roadkill"—she paused to dangle the faux face hair in between them—"was a decent disguise?"

"You have to see the whole thing," he said.

"Go on then," she said.

Joe turned away from her and scrounged around on her futon. He fumbled with his back to her, and when he turned around she had to admit he looked nothing like Joe DeLaura, assistant district attorney and snappy dresser. Instead he had a pillow-enhanced gut and a ratty NASCAR baseball hat, and when she handed over the beard and he stuck it back on his face, she knew she wouldn't have recognized him if they'd passed each other on the street.

Then she met his gaze, and his disguise unraveled like tugging a loose thread on a sweater. The long dark lashes that surrounded his warm brown eyes were so pretty they were almost feminine, and when he looked at her with equal parts worry and want, she felt the impact like a fist to the chest.

Mel spun away from him. She didn't want to do this anymore. It hurt.

She went to check on Captain Jack, who kept his face in his food bowl and ignored her.

"Good disguise," she said. She heard Joe rustling behind her and she assumed he was removing the hat and pillow. "How is Scott doing?"

The sounds behind her stopped. She would have turned around to look at him, but she didn't want to. Maybe it was best if Joe stayed in disguise. Then she could pretend he'd gone to seed and try to get over him.

Joe was silent for so long she wondered if he'd heard her. When she glanced behind her, she found him beardless, hatless, and pillow-less standing right behind her. He braced his hands on the counter, one on each side of her, caging her in. He was so close, Mel could feel the heat coming off of his body. The desire to lean against him and seek comfort after such a horrible day was almost more than she could resist.

She stiffened her spine. She knew Joe was not above using her attraction to him to manipulate her into doing what he wanted. This was the problem with letting someone wholly into your heart; they knew exactly which buttons to push to get what they wanted.

"He is beyond devastated," Joe said. His voice was a low, gruff rub. "Kristin was his other half. At the medical examiner's office, noises were coming out of him that I've never heard before. It sounded like someone was ripping his heart out of his chest with their bare hands."

Joe paused and ran his hand over his face as if he could wipe away the memory.

"It is exactly how I would feel if anything happened to you. Don't you see? You have to go," he said.

Mel felt herself soften under his pleading like wax under a flame. She broke eye contact. She shook it off.

"Stop it," she said. "Frank Tucci isn't coming after me. He went after Angie—maybe. She's the one who has to leave town, and I trust Tate to make sure that she does."

"And when she does, who do you think he'll go after next?" Joe persisted. "Even with us being . . . apart, you're still a target as my last girlfriend."

Last? Mel told herself she didn't care, but the way her heart banged around in her chest, she knew she couldn't deny that she was happy that Joe wasn't dating anyone else. So stupid! As if the man had time to date while trying the biggest case of his career.

"Do you really think that one of Tucci's thugs killed Kristin thinking she was Angie?" Mel asked.

Joe winced. He ran his hands through his thick black hair and blew out a breath. "I hate it, but yeah, that's what I think. I can't let him win, Mel. I'm going to get that son of a bitch, and I'm going to make him pay."

Thirteen

His voice came from deep in his chest and sounded like the menacing growl of a wild dog. Mel had never seen him so furious or so determined.

She nodded. She could only imagine how he must feel. The guilt that she felt after realizing that Angie was okay only because Scott's wife was killed in her place had been the emotional equivalent of getting backslapped by a wrecking ball. She knew Angie and Tate felt the same.

"Tate will convince Angie to leave," she said. "But Joe, I can't go. I would lose everything."

"Not your life," he said.

Mel saw his jaw jut out. Oh, boy. The DeLaura stubborn streak was rearing its blocky head.

"I could always call your mother," he said.

"You wouldn't dare," she protested.

One of Joe's eyebrows twitched, and she knew that he would tell Joyce and he wouldn't even feel bad about it.

"No, just no," she said. "My mother does not need that kind of stress and worry. You could give the poor woman a heart attack."

"Not if you leave town," he said.

"Let me be very clear," Mel said. "I. Am. Not. Leaving."

"But—" Joe began but she cut him off.

"No," she said. "Listen, if there had been an attempt on my life or any indication that I was in danger then sure, I'd consider leaving, but there hasn't been. You should be happy. Dumping me really worked out for you."

It was a cheap shot to the man junk, and she knew it. Still, she didn't take it back or apologize.

"Mel," he said. "You know it wasn't like that. Listen, I'm sorry. I know I hurt you, but it was to keep you safe."

"Because I am just an idiot cupcake baker who can't take care of herself, right?"

"You know it's not that simple."

Mel knew he was right, but she had a couple of months of stored-up hurt and resentment, so even knowing he was right, she kept on arguing.

"Oh, I think it is that simple," she said. "You think I am too dumb to handle myself in your world, so you just cut me loose."

Okay, now she was just needling him. She knew it. He knew it. She knew he knew it, and yet she couldn't stop herself.

"Mel." Joe knuckled his eyes as if trying to get everything back into focus.

He looked so tired that she almost relented, but then she

remembered that he had walked away from her proposal without even telling her why. Manny had been the one to tell her what was up; for that alone, Mel harbored a chip on her shoulder with all the density of a pound cake.

"Don't you 'Mel' me," she said. She pushed around him, snatched his things up, and shoved them at him. "Time to put on your fugitive outfit and git."

She didn't wait for him but strode to the door and unlocked the dead bolt and the door handle. She gave him a pointed look, making her expectation of his imminent departure clear.

He shook his head as if he knew he would get no further with her. He pressed on his beard, stuffed the pillow in his shirt, and slapped on the cap. He took a moment to scratch Jack's ears and exchange a head butt. Jack purred deep and long as if pleased that the members of his human-cat pack were all here.

Mel wanted to hustle him out the door, but the sight of her two boys together took her out at the knees. She'd missed Joe so much. She'd missed this, the three of them together. She missed being a part of a "We be" instead of an "I be," as in "We be doing this" instead of "I be doing this."

And it wasn't that she couldn't be alone. Mel did alone alarmingly well. In fact, since she worked with customers all day long, most nights she was more than happy to spend her evenings with no one to talk to except Captain Jack. But Joe, well, she missed him. She missed knowing that at the end of the day there was someone waiting for her. And yeah, she could go out and find a new man, but he wouldn't be Joe.

Joe straightened up from snuggling Jack. He turned to look at her, and Mel didn't like the look in his eyes. It didn't bode well for her winning the argument.

He strode towards her, his lanky form well muscled

despite the pillow stuffed into his shirt. He stopped right next to her, and his chocolate brown gaze was warm as it studied her face as if trying to memorize the shape of her lips, the length of her eyelashes, and the curve of her cheek. It also made her brain turn to goo.

Before Mel could register his intent, she was hauled up against him, and he planted a kiss on her that made her light-headed and weak in the knees. She had only a second to note that the rough feel of his faux beard against her skin was kinda hot before he pulled away to look at her.

"Do you want to know when the first time I noticed you *that way* was?" he asked.

Mel swallowed. He was still holding her pressed up against him, and she found her language skills were lost somewhere amidst the sensory overload she had going on. She tried anyway.

"A year and a half ago," she guessed. It came out breathier than she intended, but he didn't seem to mind. She tried to make light of it and added, "Right after we opened the shop, and your sweet tooth led you to your doom."

"Wrong," he said. "The very first time I knew Melanie Cooper was going to cause me a whole lot of trouble was on the family vacation to Cabo. The second night there you and Angie dressed up and snuck out to go clubbing."

Mel's eyes went wide. "I was seventeen. That was back when I was a chunk."

Joe cupped her face and stared into her eyes. "You were as beautiful then as you are now, and I almost had a heart attack when you smiled at me from across the club, wearing that too-tight and too-short dress and flirting with men who had bad intentions."

Mel was stunned, then she frowned. "You grabbed us and hauled us out of the club and then yelled at us all the way back to the hotel. You tortured us for days, threatening to tell your parents about what we'd done."

"I had to keep you in line somehow, didn't I?" he asked. "Besides, I found the thought of you smiling at any other man the way you smiled at me in the club—disturbing."

"You spent the rest of the vacation bird-dogging us," Mel said. "Angie was furious."

"You didn't seem to mind," he said.

She knew what he was doing. He was reeling her in the way he always did, reminding her of how long she had loved him from afar. Per usual, it was fruitless to deny it.

"No, I didn't mind," she said. "Because you already had my heart; I'd been crushing on you for five years by then. Why didn't you say anything or do anything in Cabo?"

"Because you were my little sister's best friend," he said. "Because right up until Cupid snuck up and shot me in the behind that night, I had always thought of you as another sister. But once I didn't, I found I couldn't anymore."

"Then you went back to college," she said.

"And then you went to college while I was off to law school," he said.

"But you never said anything the few times I saw you," she said.

"I convinced myself it was just a phase, some temporary Mexico vacation insanity that would pass," he said. "And then you had that boyfriend. He was a toad."

He sounded jealous. Mel smiled.

"And you had a girlfriend," she said. "Sal said she looked like a giraffe."

"She did," Joe admitted. He laughed and then he grew serious. "You moved to Los Angeles."

"But then I came home."

"And I was waiting."

Mel leaned forward and rested her head against Joe's chest. The hurt and anger she'd been hanging on to over the past few weeks was yielding under the old Joe DeLaura razzle-dazzle. Damn him.

"You're asking me to wait," she said.

"Just one more time, if you're willing," he said.

Mel straightened up and met his gaze. How long could she wait for this man? She felt as if she'd been waiting her whole life, but then, from what he'd told her, she wasn't the only one. He'd been waiting, too. And didn't that just charm her stupid.

"Maybe," she said.

Joe raised his eyebrows in surprise. She supposed he'd expected her to be more resistant. Silly man.

"But things have to change," she said. "You can't just shut me out of the information loop. If something is going on, like a dangerous case, you have to tell me about it and not just walk away. And you can't order me to leave town."

He nodded as if he was really listening to her. Mel had her doubts, but she was willing to give him a chance. One more chance.

"All right," he said. He hugged her close, picking her up off of her feet, and Mel had to fight the urge to wrap herself around him in a hold that strangled. He set her down and added, "You do realize that since you refuse to leave town, I'm going to have to deploy alternate measures to keep you safe."

"Huh?" Mel braced herself against the wall as her thinking was still a bit fuzzy from being so near him.

"You leave me no choice," he said ominously. He cupped her face and kissed her one more time. It was equal parts tender and possessive, a thorough debauching of her senses, and it left Mel dazed and bewildered and hopeful. "Be careful, cupcake."

He looked like he wanted to say something more, but he didn't. Mel fought to get her moorings as he opened the door and with one last soulful look, he left.

Mel reached out and locked the door behind him, realizing as she did that he had never handed over her key. She noticed her fingers were shaking and her breath was coming in shallow hiccups. Her throat was tight and she was trying not to cry. Now that there was a new understanding between them, she realized how much she hated that he was leaving her—again.

As if sensing her distress, Captain Jack hopped off of the counter and padded to where she stood by the door. He wound himself around her ankle and let loose a yowl that told her he wasn't happy with Joe's departure, either. Then he stood on his hind legs and placed his front feet on her knee, slowly extending his claws to hook into her jeans.

"Okay, okay," Mel said. She reached down and scooped up her boy, snuggling him close. As he purred and rubbed against her, Mel sighed. Then she straightened up and looked at him. "What do you suppose he meant by 'alternate safety measures'?"

Captain Jack didn't say, and the sinking feeling in her stomach was not reassuring.

Angie slammed through the back door the next morning. She was muttering under her breath, and Mel glanced up from the steel table in the bakery's kitchen and watched as her friend yanked open the door to their tiny office, threw her purse into the room, and slammed the door shut. The force of her slam caused the door to pop back open and bang off of the wall and slam shut again. This time it stayed shut.

"Finished?" Mel asked.

Angie sucked in a breath. It sounded to Mel as if she was trying to take in all of the air in the room. She had known Angie for over twenty years, and she knew that when Angie stood with her shoulders back and her head high, she was in the grip of a powerful temper.

Mel put down the tiny cookie cutter she'd been using to punch out gerbera daisies in the bright yellow fondant she had rolled out. She considered her friend with the same respect she'd give a wild javelina, should one come barreling into the bakery.

When it looked like Angie was successfully calming herself down, Mel offered, "Want to talk about it?"

"No," Angie snapped. "Yes. Oh, what's the point?"

"You might feel better," Mel said.

"No, and in about five minutes you're going to feel as livid as I do," Angie said.

"What are you talking about?" Mel asked. "Is something wrong with Tate? Are you two okay? What aren't you telling me?"

Angie glanced over Mel's head at the imperceptible camera

her brother Tony had installed in the shop. She stomped towards it, glared up at it, and then made a rude hand gesture.

"Angie," Mel said. "What has gotten into—"

"Hello, ladies," Sal DeLaura said as he stepped through the door. "Hey, Ange, I did not appreciate the hand gesture you just sent to the camera."

"Aw, what?" Angie asked. "How'd you know I did that so fast?"

"Tony and I were on the phone," he said and wagged his cell phone at her. "Now, look, I'll try and stay out of your way, but Joe said I was to monitor every person who comes into the shop. Tony has them on camera surveillance but we figure if there is trouble, I can jump in."

Mel stared stupidly at Sal. "I'm sorry, what are you doing here?"

"I'm your bodyguard," Sal said. "But don't go all Whitney Houston to my Kevin Costner. Joe still has dibs."

"Dibs?" Mel said. "Like I'm the front seat of a car?"

"Or the last Pringle in the can," Sal agreed.

"Don't worry," Angie said. "Mel won't go near you. Aside from the fact that you're not Joe, your girlfriend would skin her alive and probably enjoy it."

Mel knew the DeLaura clan had yet to warm up to Sal's girlfriend. She was a Jersey girl with the big hair and attitude to match and, yeah, Mel was afraid of her.

"Carla is a little possessive like that," Sal said. He looked pleased by the observation. "So, I'll check back here. We'll be keeping it locked and then I'll go sweep the front."

Mel was still gaping as Sal locked the door, searched the kitchen, including the walk-in cooler, and then headed out front. She looked at Angie, who was still looking peeved.

"Wild guess here," Mel said. "Your scary face this morning is because Joe is having the brothers monitor the shop."

Angie put one index finger on her nose and then pointed at Mel with the other. "Bingo."

"Well, now I know what he meant by alternate measures," Mel said. She saw Angie looking at her, but she didn't explain. "I'm guessing we have no choice."

"I tried to ditch him," Angie said. "Tate is at the lawyer's office, working out some franchise stuff, so he was thrilled to have Sal keep tabs on me. I think Tate was actually going to cancel his meeting just to follow me around all day. So dumb. Believe me, I have tried to shake Sal loose, but he clings like a wart."

"We'll just have to make the best of it," Mel said. "Maybe if we humor them, they'll go away."

Angie gave her a dubious look. "Have you not known the brothers for twenty-plus years?"

Mel shrugged. "I know, I know, but we're not twelve anymore. Maybe it won't be as bad as we fear."

It wasn't. It was worse.

Fourteen

Sal utilized his time by intimidating every customer who entered the bakery. He was so into his task that Mel was surprised he didn't frisk them as they came through the door.

In fact, when one of her favorite customers, Dawn Frazier, a cute brunette with a powerful love of dark chocolate cupcakes, popped in to order a dozen for a party she was going to, Sal followed her to the counter and stared at her as if he expected her to pull out a gun or a bomb or a very large knife.

As he loomed over her, Dawn turned to face him. Her blunt-cut bangs gave her a no-nonsense look and she lowered her sunglasses and glanced at Sal over them. In a voice that did not invite an argument, she said, "Back up."

Sal's eyes widened as if this was proof that Dawn was there to cause them bodily harm. Mel blew out a breath of exasperation.

"You heard her, Sal," she said from behind the counter. "Give her some space."

"But she could be a cold-blooded killer," Sal protested. "What if she's armed?"

"Sal, you numbskull, Dawn's a regular," Angie said as she joined Mel behind the counter. "She always pops in when she blows through town."

"Oh," Sal said. He looked disappointed.

As Mel handed Dawn the big box of cupcakes, Dawn leaned over the counter and whispered, "You might want to consider buying him a leash."

All three women looked at Sal in disapproval but he was too busy to notice, staring at the two teens who had just entered the bakery.

"Duly noted," Angie said.

They waved good-bye to Dawn, and Mel turned to Angie while the teens debated flavors, and said, "We're going to have to do something."

"Agreed," she said. "Pants him?"

"Um, no, how would that go over if Carla found out?"

"Good point." Angie nodded. "Well, what can we do?"

"I don't know but it'll come to me," Mel said. "Maybe we can put him to work."

"Doing what?" Angie asked. "The brothers are only good at plowing through our walk-in cooler on a cupcake-eating bender. They wouldn't know a spatula from a PEZ dispenser."

Mel raised her eyebrows. "You might be onto something there." She gestured to the kitchen. "Marty should be here shortly to take over the counter. Let's get to work. I'm thinking we need to bulk up our supplies."

Marty clocked in while Mel and Angie scrambled to start baking for the display counter. As Angie was covering a just-cooled batch of chocolate cupcakes with peanut butter frosting, Sal strolled into the kitchen with his nose twitching like a bunny sniffing a carrot.

"Do I smell peanut butter?" he asked.

Angie shoved a peanut butter cup into the top of the cupcake and gave her brother her most innocent look.

"Do you like peanut butter?" she asked.

"Ange, come on," Sal said. He put his hand on his hips. "You know it's my weakness."

"Oh, you should have one then," Mel said. "In fact, eat as many as you want. It's the least we can do for you since you're looking after us and all."

She didn't have to insist. Sal's eyes lit up and he licked his lips as he debated which one to pick. Torn between two, he grabbed both. Mel noticed Angie had lowered her head to hide her smile.

Sal scarfed down his cupcakes in a blink, and then he offered to deliver the tray of cupcakes Angie was working on to Marty, so he could put them in the display case. Sal had been gone thirty minutes when Marty popped his head through the swinging door.

"Ange, we're going to need a twelve-step program or a stomach pump if you don't come out here and stop Sal from eating his body weight in cupcakes."

"Oh, really?" Angie asked innocently. "Gee, I wonder what's gotten into him."

"Aw, don't try to bamboozle me," Marty grumped. "You gave him carte blanche and, boy howdy, is he going for it."

The door was pushed wider from behind Marty, and Sal

staggered into the kitchen, looking pasty and sweaty. He sat at the metal table and groaned.

"I'm sorry, Ange, I had to call in a backup," he said. "I don't know what happened. I think I have the flu."

"More like frosting poisoning," Marty grumbled.

"Go home, Sal, you look like garbage," Dom, the oldest of the DeLaura brothers, said as he entered the kitchen.

"Dom!" Angie cried.

She gave Mel a concerned look over Dom's shoulder as she hugged him. Not only was Dom chronologically the oldest DeLaura brother but he was born an old soul, too. In his mid-forties, with his thick head of hair just starting to go gray, he looked the part of the conservative husband and father that he was. Conning him into eating too many cupcakes was going to be near impossible.

Mel shrugged and moved in to hug Dom, too. She didn't mind if Dom stayed to keep an eye on them. She didn't think he'd go the way of Sal and try to intimidate everyone who entered the bakery.

"You're looking as lovely as ever, Mel," Dom said.

"Oh, thanks," Mel said. "Can I get you anything?"

"No thanks," he said and patted his middle. "The wife has me on a diet."

"Ha!" Sal scoffed. "You'd never catch me being told what I can and can't eat."

Dom lifted a brow as he studied his brother. "Is that chocolate frosting on your lip?"

Sal hastily wiped at his mouth. "Peanut butter, and so what if it is?"

"How many cupcakes have you eaten?" Dom asked.

"A few," Sal said, not meeting his brother's eyes.

"Uh-huh," Dom said. "Looks like you need to go home and purge."

"You're not the boss of me," Sal protested.

"Tell me about it," Angie muttered under her breath.

"Go," Dom ordered, making it clear he did think he was the boss. "Mel, is it okay if I sit out front?" He gestured to the laptop bag he carried. "I have some work to do."

"No problem," Mel said. "If you need anything, let me know."

"Thanks," Dom said. He pushed through the swinging doors and disappeared.

"He thinks he's such a hotshot," Sal said. His stomach made a horrible grumbling noise and he quickly slipped out the back door, looking decidedly green.

"Should we feel bad about that?" Mel asked.

Angie shook her head. "We didn't make him eat all of those cupcakes. Life is choices, and Sal tends to make bad ones."

Mel nodded. She'd known him long enough to know this was true.

The kitchen door swung open again, and this time it was Tate. He was grinning from ear to ear, which Mel thought was pretty amazing given that his fiancée was being targeted for murder.

Tate beelined it for Angie, picked her up, and swung her around in circles until she was breathless and clinging to him for fear of falling.

"What has gotten into you?" she asked.

"Millions," he said.

"Millions of what?" Angie asked as he set her down on one of the stools around the worktable.

"Cupcakes," he said.

Mel smiled. "I think that's how many Sal ate, but he's not looking as happy as you."

"That's because he ate those cupcakes instead of franchising them," Tate said. "Check this out. After extensive research and cost analysis, I have determined that the best price to buy into a Fairy Tale Cupcake franchise would be two hundred and fifty thousand dollars."

Mel rolled her eyes. She might have known this had to do with Tate's franchise idea. Then she smiled. No way was anyone ever going to pay that to start up a sister bakery to her original store.

Angie bit her lip and said what Mel was thinking, "No one is ever going to pay that."

"You're right," Tate said.

Mel almost jumped up and down and clapped with joy. She was so tired of having the same argument with Tate.

"No *one* is going to pay that," he said. Then he grinned. "However, five some *ones* have already filed the paperwork to buy in. My dears, we are going to be rich!"

Angie cheered and launched herself into Tate's arms. "You are a financial genius!"

Mel twisted her apron in her hands. She truly did not want to be the flat can of pop at the picnic, but all she could hear in her head was her hysterical baker voice screaming about the quality of the franchised baked goods.

Tate must have sensed she was starting to hyperventilate, and he quickly turned and grabbed her hands in his and said, " 'If we're not pioneers, what have we become? What do you call people, who when they're faced with a condition or fear, do nothing about it?' "

"Charles Bronson in *Death Wish*," Mel said with a smile. Leave it to Tate to pick that movie to quote, such a dude's pick. "But let's not forget that is a movie and not my bakery."

"Mel, you'll have the authority to oversee operations and make sure that everything is up to scratch," Angie said.

"Nice wordplay," Tate said and kissed her.

"I know, I know that's what we agreed on, but until I see it in action, it's very stressful," Mel said.

"On the upside, one of the strongest applicants is in Vegas," Tate said.

"Road trip?" Angie asked. "Oh, man, we have to watch *Viva Las Vegas* before we go."

While a fan of all things Elvis, Mel felt a little hurly at the thought of her cupcakes trying to hold their own on the Strip.

"It'll be okay," Tate said. "I promise."

Mel nodded. She believed him. She did. Really.

"So where is your chaperone?" Tate asked.

"Oh, yeah, that sounds so much better than bodyguard," Angie said. "Not."

"Sal went home ill," Mel said. "Dom is out front keeping an eye on things. Didn't you see him when you came in?"

"No," Tate said. He turned and strode through the swinging doors to the front. Mel and Angie followed him.

Dom was in a corner booth. His laptop was open and he was on his cell phone. His face was a mottled shade of red, and his low voice boomed through the bakery when he growled, "Put your sister on the phone. Now."

Fearless, Angie approached her brother, looking concerned. "What's going on?"

In answer, Dom spun the laptop so that she could see.

Angie's eyes went round and she backed away. She rejoined Mel and Tate and said, "We may want to clear the area. Big brother is about to go vol-freaking-canic."

"Why?" Tate asked. He looked nervous and Mel knew it was because his status as fiancé was still under scrutiny by the brothers.

"My niece, in a singular lack of good judgment, posted a pic to her social media page of her swigging a beer at a party," Angie said.

"She's sixteen!" Mel said.

"Yeah, and I'm not sure she's going to see seventeen," Angie said.

"Are we having a staff meeting?" Marty asked as he joined them.

"More like watching a DeLaura implosion," Tate said.

"What's the hullaballoo?" Marty asked.

"Niece. Beer bottle. Internet."

Marty shook his head, clearly confused. "What's the big stink?"

"You are grounded!" Dom thundered into the phone. "You will not be going anywhere this weekend, no parties, no friends, nada. Do not sass me, young lady."

There was a pause. Dom gasped. Then he pulled the phone away from his ear and stared at it as if it had bit him.

"She hung up on me."

"Oh, that's not going to go well," Angie said.

Sure enough, Dom began throwing all of his things into his laptop bag. He paused beside their gawking group and looked at Tate.

"You got this?" he asked.

Tate put his arm around Angie. "With my life."

"If necessary," Dom said. He left the bakery at a run.

"Parents these days," Marty said.

"Don't you mean 'kids these days'?" Angie asked.

"Nah, it's the parents," he said. "They give 'precious' a participation trophy just for showing up, and they wonder why the kid thinks they don't have to do squat but should still get a trophy."

"I don't think I ever got a participation trophy," Mel said.

"That's because you didn't join anything," Tate said. "I got a few. They were lame."

"Agreed," Angie said. "They never meant as much as the awards I knew I'd earned. How does that factor into my niece being an idiot?"

"No consequences," Marty said. "You think she would have posted that picture if she knew her dad was going to take a hammer to her phone if she did anything that dumb? No, instead he grounds her. What's that going to teach her when she's still connected to her friends with her phone?"

"Good point," Angie said. "I'm going to text him your suggestion."

She pulled out her phone and fired off a text to her brother.

"So, it's about respect," Tate said. "And a little fear."

"Exactly. Your kids aren't your friends until they're grown-ups. People just don't get that," Marty said. "How many times do we have moms come in here, and if we don't have the cupcake flavor little Johnny wants, she starts negotiating with him. You've heard it. Mom bends down to the squirt's level while he's pitching a stink and she says, 'How about vanilla? You like vanilla,' and on and on it goes while the little runt gets meaner and meaner. What she should do is order what she wants and let the wee one go without. Once is all it would take."

Mel nodded. She'd played out this scene just the other day. The whining kid had been like fingernails on a chalkboard, and the mother coddled the mini-monster because she was so worried about his feelings she didn't give a hoot about his manners.

"Sometimes you don't get the flavor you want," Tate said.

"And you learn how to deal with it," Angie said.

"I actually had a dad offer me a fifty if I could just make a carrot cake cupcake appear for his little princess," Marty said. "All I could think was that poor little girl is screwed for life."

"Sad but true," Mel agreed. "Hopefully, your niece is about to have her rude awakening right now."

"It's overdue," Angie said. "Marty's right about how Dom has been with her since she was born. In fact, I've never liked spending time with her. Hey, this might be kind of fun to watch."

"Promise me when we have kids, we won't ruin them," Tate said to Angie.

"Sure, if Marty will work in an advisory capacity," Angie said.

Marty grinned. "So, we're going to have a baby?"

Fifteen

"What?! Who's having a baby?" Ray strode into the bakery, looking like he was gearing up to crack some skulls, namely Tate's.

"Relax," Angie said. She stepped forward and hugged her brother. "We're talking someday, not right now."

"That's good, very good," Ray said, giving Tate the hairy eyeball. It was definitely a look that said the jury was still out.

He then shook Marty's hand, not Tate's, and hugged Mel and said, "And you, you're saving yourself for Joe, right?"

Angie slapped a hand to her forehead. "Really? Just like that you're going there? You're not even trying to finesse it a little?"

"What's to finesse?" Ray asked. He turned and bumped knuckles with Marty. "Am I right, Z?"

Angie glanced between Marty and her brother. "You two seem awfully chummy, Z?"

Marty's bald head turned a faint shade of pink. Ray was the DeLaura family wild card. Sal liked to think he was it, but really as a used car salesman, not so much. But Ray was the one who was "connected." He lived at Turf Paradise during the horse-racing season, and he was the one who usually "knew a guy" when something needed to be done quickly and quietly. Mel knew that of all the brothers, Joe lost the most sleep over Ray.

"We've taken in some horse races together," Marty said. "NBD."

"No big deal?" Ray exclaimed. "Z, are you telling me that you didn't tell them about your big win?"

"I didn't want to brag," Marty said. Mel noticed he was not making eye contact with any of them.

"Brag? My friend, you should have been headlining the nightly news. This guy," Ray poked Marty in the chest and shook his head before he continued, "this guy put three hundred down on a thirty-to-one horse just because"—Ray stopped to laugh—"because"—he laughed again—"the horse evacuated its bowels on the way to the gate, and Z figured he'd lightened his load enough to win."

Ray slapped Marty so hard on the back that Marty lurched forward, stopped only by Tate, who was quick enough to catch him.

"It was epic," Ray concluded. "And that's not his only amazing win. I swear you must have some psychic abilities, Z."

"Of course he does—he's from another dimension."

Mel turned around to see two boys standing just inside

the entrance to the bakery. They were dressed in green coveralls, and each had a bulky backpack on. Mel thought they looked familiar, but she couldn't place them.

"There he is!" The smaller one pointed at Marty while the older one dropped his backpack, opened it, and went digging inside.

"Don't let him disappear this time," the bigger one said. "He's a sneaky specter."

It all came back to Mel in a flash. The Bonehead Investigators, the two brothers from the zombie walk who thought Marty was a ghoul. In all the commotion that day, she'd never found out how Marty had managed to ditch them.

"You're the two ghost hunters, right?" Mel asked. "Leo and Adam?"

The smaller one rolled his eyes. "Wrong. It's Atom A-T-O-M, and we're paranormal investigators."

"Of course," Mel said. She didn't look at any of the others for fear she'd burst out laughing.

"Oh, for gosh Pete's sake!" Marty said. "I told you two before I am not a ghost."

"My specter meter begs to differ, ghoul," the younger one said. He was holding his phone at Marty, and the thing was flashing and whistling.

"Did we miss something?" Angie asked.

"No!" Marty said. "Just two dopey kids playing a prank."

The taller of the two, Leo, looked offended. "This is no prank. Look."

He took his specter meter and aimed it at Mel. It went quiet and blank. He did the same with Tate, Angie, and Ray. Then he turned it on Marty, and it went berserk just like his brother's.

"See?" Leo said as if it was all perfectly reasonable. "He's a ghost."

"I am not, you little mongrel," Marty said.

"Surely, there is a logical explanation," Tate said. "Maybe your meter is picking up Marty's belt buckle or something."

The little one gave Tate a look of utter disdain. "It's not a metal detector. Honestly, do you know *anything* about the denizens of the netherworld?"

Ray moaned and Mel looked at him in concern. "Are you all right?"

"No, I hate this stuff," he said. "Ghosts and scary movies, possessions and hauntings, it all just freaks me out."

"It's true," Angie said. "He tried to watch *Halloween* when he was sixteen and scared himself so bad he had to sleep with Mom and Dad for a month."

"Aw, man, thanks for sharing my shame, Ange," Ray snapped.

"Sorry." She shrugged. Then she gave Mel a knowing look. "You know, it might not be Marty that they're picking up on. Maybe we have a ghost."

The young brothers exchanged a look of excitement while Ray turned a puke shade of gray.

"What ghost?" Tate asked.

"You remember?" Angie said. "The one the Realtor told us about when Mel first looked at the place."

Tate scratched his head. "No, it doesn't ring a bell."

"Or maybe we're being haunted by that guy who was murdered in the alley," Marty offered. "You know, the cranky reporter from the magazine. I mean if you had to spend eternity hanging around, wouldn't you rather be in a pretty bakery than a stinky alley?"

"There was a murder here?" Atom's eyes went wide.

Mel felt bad talking about the tragic event, but maybe it would scare the daring duo away, which for Marty's sake would not be a bad thing. She didn't know how long he could put up with the two stubby shadows without losing his cool.

"Do you think there was a transference?" Leo asked Atom. "Maybe the specter is now inhabiting the body of the old man and that's why we're getting a reading off of him."

Atom scratched his head in thought. "I suppose it's possible. It would explain why he appears alive with such a high specter reading.

"I don't appear alive," Marty snapped. "I am alive. And I am not possessed by some ghostie. Don't you think I'd know if I were possessed?"

"We'd better check," Leo said. He pulled out a miniflashlight and shone the beam in Marty's eyes.

"Hey, knock it off, I have cataracts," Marty said and pushed the boy's hand away from his face.

"Any periods of blackout?" Atom asked. "Unexplained memory loss."

"Of course; I'm old, aren't I?" Marty asked. "Hell, five times out of seven I can't remember why I enter a room."

"Blackouts?" Ray yelped. "OMG, he is possessed! That's why he can pick the winning horses!"

"That does make sense," Angie said, looking thoughtful. "Maybe we need to have an exorcism."

"No, it does not make sense," Marty argued.

"I . . . I . . . I have to go," Ray stammered. He was texting on his cell phone as he backed to the door. "Tony or Al will be here shortly."

"Huh, he looks like he's seen a ghost," Leo said to Atom, and they both cracked up. Mel and Angie joined them, but Tate looked irritated. "Your brothers are here to keep an eye on you," he said to Angie. "Scaring them off is not funny."

"He's right," Atom said to Leo, looking serious. "We have a mission to contain the ghost."

"Roger that," Leo said. They began digging in their backpacks again.

"What are you looking for now?" Angie asked, clearly charmed by the brothers.

"A containment unit," Leo said. He pulled a glass jar out of his backpack with a twist-off lid.

"Looks like a pickle jar to me," Tate said.

"Pickles, poltergeists, it's multifunctional," Atom said.

"What are you going to do?" Mel asked. The thought of broken glass in her bakery was not wowing her.

"Contain him," Leo said.

"You can't contain me," Marty said. "I'm not a ghoul or possessed by a ghost or anything else. I am, however, closer to the gateway of death by about sixty-plus years. Maybe that's why you get a reading on your spookameter."

"Specter meter," Atom corrected him.

Leo looked thoughtfully at Marty. "He might be onto something."

He reached out and pinched Marty's forearm.

"Yow!" Marty cried and yanked his arm back. "What did you do that for?"

"The subject does have a human response to pain and feels very fleshy."

"Fleshy?" Marty looked outraged. "Are you calling me fat?"

Leo ignored him.

"Perhaps we need to study the subject more in his natural environment," Atom suggested.

"Agreed," Leo said. Together they commandeered a booth in the corner.

"Hey, tables are only for paying customers," Marty said.

Leo produced a twenty from his pocket. "Two cupcakes, please."

Marty rolled his eyes so far back, Mel was afraid they might get stuck.

"What flavors?" Marty asked.

"What do you have?" the boys asked together.

Marty glared. "Ectoplasm in a jar."

"Are you mocking us?" Atom asked, looking annoyed.

"Now why would you think that?" Marty asked. "Just because you want to stuff me in a pickle jar?"

"How about I take over the order?" Angie offered. She gave Marty a shove towards the kitchen. She gave Mel a pointed look.

"Come on, Marty, you can help me restock the supplies," Mel said. "Tate, you're good out here?"

"No one gets in without me checking them over," he said.

With one nervous glance at the front window, Mel nodded. There was nothing they could do, really, if Frank Tucci decided he was going to come after Angie. If he could kill Kristin Streubel in the middle of a crowded festival, what would he be able to do to Angie here in the bakery? The thought was unpleasant, and she wondered if it was such a good idea to chase the brothers off.

Of course, Ray and Dom had left of their own accord. But Sal was definitely their fault. Then again, no one told him to eat his body weight in cupcakes. Mel could only wonder which brother would show up next. She knew it was impossible, but she really wished it would be Joe.

Sixteen

It wasn't Joe. Al arrived wearing sunglasses and a black leather overcoat that looked like it could hide a wide array of weapons but did not look particularly cupcake friendly.

" 'Never send a human to do a machine's job,' " Tate muttered in Mel's ear as they watched Al case the joint.

"*The Matrix*," Mel said, identifying Tate's movie quote. "You could have gone with one from *Men in Black*."

"No, he is Neo all the way," Tate said.

Angie shook her head. "I think he'd make a better Spoon Boy."

Tate laughed and gave her a squeeze. "Either way, I'm glad he's here to help me keep you safe."

"I'm not in danger," Angie said. She sounded mad. "And the damage those idiots are doing to the business is not good for any of us."

"They're not damaging . . . okay, maybe Al's hulking presence is a bit off-putting," Tate said.

"A bit?" Angie asked. "Five people saw the Terminator there in the door and turned away. Honestly, we'll be lucky to have a business left after this."

"Hmm." Tate watched as another couple caught sight of Al and passed by the bakery. "I'll talk to him. Maybe if he stations himself in the corner . . ."

"I think we should sic the terrible twosome on him," Angie said as she gestured to the ghost hunters, who were watching Al with more than a little interest.

"I don't know, Ange," Mel said. She led the way into the kitchen. She had to start working on her special orders, and she could feel her stress level rising with every interruption in her day. "Maybe we just need to let the brothers be here and do what they do. I mean, what if you're wrong and what if Frank Tucci is targeting you to get to Joe?"

"Don't you start," Angie said. "I am not a target. I am not in danger. This whole thing is stupid."

"Maybe, but what's wrong with taking a little vacation?" Mel pressed. "You and Tate could get away for a while."

"Only if you come with me," Angie said. Her chin jutted out with her trademark stubbornness.

"Yeah, that's romantic," Mel said. "And I can't. I have too much work."

"Sure you can," Oz said as he stepped out of the walk-in cooler with a tray full of cupcakes to be decorated. "You know I can handle it."

"I have no doubt you'd do a fine job," Mel said. "But I can't ask you to do that while you're still in school."

"You're just making excuses," Angie said. "If I'm not here, what makes you think Tucci won't then go after you?"

"So you admit he's after you," Mel said. She was trying to outmaneuver Angie in the verbal arts, which was always a dicey proposition.

"No! I'm saying no such thing," Angie said. "I'm just pointing out that if it's true that Tucci is looking to get to Joe, you would be pretty high on his list, don't you think?"

"No," Mel said. "Joe and I have been apart for a while now, which is why it is highly possible that Tucci targeted you as his sister, and poor Kristin got hit by mistake."

Angie shuddered and Mel narrowed her eyes. "Are you okay?"

"I'm fine," Angie said.

"You don't look fine," Oz chimed in while loading up a pastry bag with buttercream.

"Who asked you?" Angie said. She pointed to his tray of bare cupcakes. "Just get with the frosting magic there."

Oz shrugged and set to work. "It's not your fault, you know."

Angie was halfway to the kitchen door when she turned around. "What did you say?"

"It's not your fault," Oz said. He paused and lowered his pastry bag. It was hard to see his pretty eyes through the thick fringe of bangs that hung over them but whatever Angie saw, it kept her frozen in place. "It would be understandable if you felt guilty that a woman who was dressed like you and bore a small resemblance to you was killed because a bad man thought she was you. But you're not the bad man, you did nothing wrong, and it's not your fault."

The kitchen was so quiet, Mel could hear the clock ticking and the hum of the small refrigerator in the corner.

"I don't . . ." Angie began to protest but she broke off with a sob. "That poor woman. If only she hadn't dressed like me. None of this ever would have happened."

Mel gave Oz a wide-eyed stare. How had he known that Angie was so wracked with guilt when Mel hadn't even picked up on it? She glanced at him and he shrugged.

"It just makes sense," he said. "Especially with her being so resistant to protection like she's trying to prove that Tucci wasn't after her. It's sort of like survivor's guilt, you know?"

Mel nodded. "Listen, Angie, you don't know that it was supposed to be you. None of us do. Think about it. Scott is working on the case against Tucci, too. It could very well be that Kristin was the target all along."

"Then why does everyone keep saying she looked like me and that Tucci was really out to get me?" Angie asked. "If that poor woman died because of me, I can't bear it. I just can't."

She slumped onto the table and sobbed. The sound was horrible and it made Mel's chest clutch in sympathy. Poor Angie, what a burden she'd been carrying since the zombie walk.

Tate pushed through the swinging doors. "Angie, what's wrong? Did something happen? Are you hurt?"

He crouched beside her and pulled her into his arms. Angie hugged him hard and buried her face in his shirtfront.

"She's hurting pretty bad," Mel said. "She thinks it's her fault Kristin was killed."

"What?" Tate asked. He reared back and cupped Angie's tear-streaked face. "No. No. No. You are not responsible for someone else's evil. That's on them. Not on you."

"But if I hadn't dressed as a bride," Angie blubbered. "If I'd gone as something else . . ."

Her voice trailed off and Tate said, "Then someone else would have been killed, possibly you, or someone else if they got mixed up with you. What if you had gone like a baker? It could have been Mel or Oz that they killed instead."

Angie blanched. Tate pulled her close and whispered soft words in her ear. Mel couldn't hear what he was saying, but judging by the way Angie's sobs calmed, it was working.

"We'll just leave you two alone for a bit," Mel said. She took Oz by the elbow and steered him out front.

"T-man will take care of our girl," Oz said. He patted Mel on the shoulder. "Don't worry."

"I feel as if that's all I do lately," Mel said. Her voice sounded more despondent than she'd meant so she forced a smile, trying to make light of it.

"Nice try," Oz said. He stopped abruptly and said, "Whoa!"

The bakery was empty, not a good thing in Mel's opinion, aside from Matrix Al, Marty, and the two ghost catchers.

The two boys were standing in the booth, aiming what looked like a jerry-rigged Nerf gun at Marty.

"Again with this?" Mel asked. She strode forward. These two were about the same age as her nephews, so she put on her unhappy-aunt voice and barked, "Get. Down. Now."

The little one looked like he was going to ignore her but the older one yanked him down with him as he jumped from the booth.

"Sorry, ma'am," the older one said. The younger one repeated him, but it sounded grudging.

"Stop trying to contain my employee," Mel said. She put

her hand on the plastic gun and pushed the muzzle down so that it faced the floor.

"Our specter meter went bonkers," Leo said. "We were just being cautious in case he morphed on us."

"Morphed into what?" Marty asked. "A spanking machine? Because you could use one!"

"Marty." Mel's voice was full of warning. She did not want the wrath of the boys' parents unleashed on her head.

"There was a real dead person at the zombie walk," Marty grumbled. "Why didn't you contain her ghost so we could figure out who murdered her?"

"Marty!" Mel reached out and pulled the boys against her while clapping her hands over their ears to keep them from hearing anything. "Ixnay on the urdermay alktay."

"It's okay." Atom wriggled out of her hold while the older one leaned against her, seemingly content. "We already know about it. Oh, and we're fluent in igpay atinlay."

Marty wheezed out a laugh. "He's good; knows his pig latin, too."

Mel frowned and then looked at the boys, gently pushing Leo away from her so she could study them both. "You know about the unfortunate . . ."

"Murder," they said together.

"Yeah, we were hoping to catch her ghost, but we couldn't get near her with all of those ambulance guys and cops," Leo said. He sounded put out about it.

"You really need to stay away from situations like that," Mel said. "Whoever hurt her—"

"Oh, we know who killed her," Atom said. Leo gave him a sharp elbow to the ribs. Atom grimaced and rubbed his side.

"What do you mean?" Mel asked. "Did you see something?"

Leo blew out a breath. "Only the man who was crying over her, her husband, well, he was kissing another woman earlier."

"No, that can't be. I'm sure it wasn't him," Mel said. "Probably just someone who looked like him."

"No, we remember the tuxedo," Leo said. "He had a pink pocket square, very memorable."

Mel concentrated. She couldn't remember if Scott had a pink pocket square or not.

"Maybe he was just greeting an old friend or . . ." The boys weren't looking at her or each other. Mel felt her skin get tight. "What exactly did you see?"

Leo looked too embarrassed to speak, but Atom was grinning and he busted into a preadolescent boy's rendition of making out, which basically meant he made loud kissy smacking noises and stuck his tongue out.

"I can't take him anywhere," Leo confessed, looking pained. Atom was too busy laughing to care that he'd mortified his sibling.

"Are you sure you saw that sort of . . . er . . . behavior?" Mel asked.

"Quite sure," Leo said.

Mel fretted her lower lip. "What did the other woman look like?"

"A zombie," Atom said. "But with blue hair and wearing a lab coat. They were hiding out behind one of the vendor booths."

"Have you mentioned this to anyone else?" Mel asked.

"God, no," Leo said as if the mere thought was too embarrassing to endure.

"Then don't," Mel said. "I'm going to talk to my uncle, who is the detective in charge, and if he needs to talk to you about it, he'll be in touch. Okay?"

The brothers exchanged a look and nodded.

"Do you live in the neighborhood?" she asked.

Again, the boys nodded.

"Oz is going to walk you home," she said.

"Aw, what?" Oz protested. "Now I'm a babysitter?"

"Think of it as a lesson in containing chaos," Mel said. "When you own your own business, it'll be an invaluable skill."

"Fine, but if anyone shoots a Nerf dart at me, I consider it an opening shot to full-on warfare," he said.

Oz ushered the two boys out, and Mel propped open the front door, hoping it made the shop more welcoming. Then she turned on Al.

"Lose the jacket and glasses," she said.

"But that's my intimidation technique," he said.

"Tough," Mel said. "You're killing business. No one wants to buy a cupcake from a man who looks like walking death."

Al smiled.

"That was not a compliment," Mel said.

Al frowned.

"Come on, big guy." Marty put his arm around Al and led him into the back. "If you're going to loiter around the shop, you may as well put on an apron and get to work."

"I think I just felt my manhood shrivel up," Al said with a sigh as he followed Marty into the back room.

Mel glanced around her shop, with its black-and-white

tile, pink vinyl furniture, and atomic accents, it was a slice of retro-fifties Americana, and she loved it.

She closed her eyes and took a deep breath. The smell of frosting and cake and all things yummy and lovely filled her senses. It was going to be okay. Whatever was happening with Joe and his terrifying trial, with Kristin's murder, with the ghost hunters and all of it, one way or another, it would end.

Of course, if Leo and Atom were right and they had seen Scott with another woman on the day of the zombie walk, well, things could get very dicey. It meant Scott had more of a reason to kill his wife than Tucci did. The thought made Mel shiver, especially because she had no way to let Joe know what she had just learned.

The scary thought that it could end with Joe being dead destroyed all of her calming techniques, and she had to swallow back a sob of her own. For the first time since opening her shop, she felt as if everything she had worked so hard to build was about to fall down around her ears.

Tate stuck his head through the kitchen door and told Mel he was taking Angie home. Now that Angie had admitted to the burden of guilt she'd been trying to deny, Tate felt she needed some time to process her feelings about the situation. Mel was actually relieved to see them go. Angie would be safe and Mel could start to get some work done.

Oz returned from the boys' house, looking a bit ragged. Mel couldn't get any details out of him, but it seemed the boys had talked his ears off during the entire walk, and Oz wasn't sure if they were geniuses or sociopaths. Mel was afraid if they didn't stop fixating on Marty, they were going to find out where the boys stood whether they liked it or not.

Out of his scary outfit, Al worked diligently until closing.

Mel had told him he could leave since Angie was gone, but he gave her a funny look and refused. Of course, Marty gave him all of the grunt jobs, so Al's day passed in a blur of mopping the floor, wiping the tabletops, and refilling napkin holders.

When it was finally time to lock up for the night, Mel felt her shoulders suddenly drop from around her ears. She hadn't realized she'd been so tense all day waiting for something, something bad, to happen.

She stepped outside to release the front door from its open position. It was swinging shut when a foot wedged itself in the gap, stopping it.

Seventeen

"I'm sorry, we're closed," Mel said through the opening, not releasing the door.

"It's me, Mel, let me in."

Mel didn't need to look. She knew that voice. *Manny!*

She pushed the door open, and the detective stepped into the bakery.

"Go ahead and lock it," he said.

Mel turned the dead bolt and spun to face him.

"You here alone?" He sounded unhappy.

"No," she said. "Marty, Oz, and Al are in back."

"Where's Angie?" he asked.

"Tate took her home," Mel said. "She's struggling with the whole situation."

Manny nodded. Mel took a moment to study him. He was in his usual perfectly pressed khaki trousers and white dress shirt. His tie was loose and his sleeves were rolled up to his elbows. He was also carrying a duffel bag.

Mel pointed to it and asked, "Running away?"

"More like having a sleepover," he said.

She frowned at him but he gestured her forward and said, "Let's go release the troops."

They walked into the kitchen. Oz and Marty shook hands with Manny. They had warmed considerably to the detective since he had saved Mel's life six months before. Oz even banged knuckles with him. Al did not look nearly as pleased to see him.

"So, what brings you here?" Al asked after a grudging handshake.

"Joe," Manny said.

Mel felt all of the blood drain out of her face. She sucked in a breath and asked, "Is he all right?"

"Oh, damn, yeah," Manny said. "He's fine. I swear. He's totally fine."

"You might want to lead with that next time," Marty said.

"Noted," Manny agreed. "No, I'm here because Joe asked me to . . . watch over you."

"Oh," Mel said. "Well, you don't need to. I have the brothers coming in rotations. So, believe me, we're full up on testosterone around here."

"Yeah, well, Joe, Stan, and I agreed that I should take the graveyard shift."

Mel felt her pulse pound in her ears. "The what shift? Graveyard, meaning you're spending the night?"

"Hey there, roomie," Manny said. Then he winked at her.

Al whipped out his cell phone and began furiously tapping a text message with his thumbs.

Oz and Marty exchanged a glance.

"Well, I'll sleep easier knowing you're watching over our girl," Marty said.

"Me, too," Oz said. But with the unfiltered candor of youth, he added, "But what is Joe thinking?"

"Clearly, he's not," Marty said. "Now let's go mind our own business."

With a wave, he and Oz headed for the back door.

Al's phone beeped. His eyes scanned the screen. "This can't be right! He's says he knows Manny is here and, yes, he sent him. Obviously, this case has caused the man to crack."

"Come on." Marty grabbed Al's arm and pulled him out the back door. "If I know Mel, she's going to have something to say about this in five, four, three . . ."

The back door shut behind Al, and Mel turned to Manny and yelled, "No! Absolutely, not! This is ridiculous!"

"Tell it to your boyfriend," Manny said. "He and I agreed. You need watching by a trained professional."

"What am I, five?" Mel asked. As soon as the words were out of her mouth she realized she sounded as crabby as Marty. What was happening to her? She checked the appliances, shut off the lights, and led the way out the back door.

Manny looked her over and Mel swallowed. It was a look that scorched.

"Nope, you're not five," he said. "But you and Angie have managed to disable most of the brothers, haven't you?"

Mel refused to comment lest she incriminate herself.

"Look, I'm not thrilled with this assignment either," Manny said. "But you are in danger, and both Joe and I take that very seriously."

Mel was surprised by how much it smarted to hear that he didn't particularly want to be here, either. She ignored it.

"Listen, I appreciate the concern, I do," Mel said as she locked up the bakery and began to walk up the stairs to her apartment. "But shouldn't you be camped out at Angie's?"

"We have a squad car parked in front of her place," he said. "Plus she has Tate watching over her. You, however, are stubbornly not at your mother's."

"I'm not going to put her in danger," Mel said as she unlocked the door to her apartment.

"Aha!" Manny said as he followed her inside. "You admit it. You know you're in danger."

"I admit no such thing, but I would never put my mom in danger if there is even a remote, as in Antarctica remote, possibility that she could be harmed."

"Very noble of you," Manny said. He bent down and unhooked Captain Jack from his pant leg and kicked the door shut behind him. Captain Jack purred and rubbed his head against Manny's chest. Mel felt a fleeting moment of envy and then shook her head.

"Not noble," Mel said. "Just sensible. Speaking of which, this is not."

Manny leaned back and studied her. "Are you worried about being alone with me all night?"

His voice was a low, gruff growl and Mel felt it all the way down to her toes.

"No!" she protested. The denial was supposed to come out strong and sure like a heroine in a Jane Austen novel when she still hates the hero. Unfortunately, Mel's voice came out high and squeaky. Manny smiled.

"You. Can't. Stay."

"Have. To." He muscled past her into the living room. "I ordered takeout and it should be arriving any minute."

"You ordered . . ." Mel's voice trailed off as she stared at him. She was hungry. "What sort of takeout?"

"Vietnamese food from Noodles Ranch," he said. "I ordered plenty to share."

"Oh, I love how they use mint in their dishes. I didn't think they delivered," Mel said.

"They don't. Stan does," Manny said.

"Which of us is Uncle Stan checking up on, you or me?" she asked.

Manny crossed the room with Jack still in his arms. He sat at her small breakfast table and began to unpack his laptop while still holding the purring cat.

"You, definitely you," Manny said. "Stan knows I'll do what I'm told."

"So, he's afraid I'll kick you out?" Mel asked.

"Frankly, I'm surprised you let me in," Manny said. His dark eyes met hers in a questioning glance. Mel looked away, unsure of what he was looking for and not wanting to give him any mixed signals.

Mercifully, a knock at the door sounded and Mel went to answer.

"See who it is first," Manny ordered.

Mel glanced through the peephole. Uncle Stan stood waving at her with one hand while the other held a big white plastic bag.

She pulled open the door and gestured for him to enter. Uncle Stan buzzed her cheek as he passed her as if having two detectives over for dinner was normal for Mel.

She glanced around her apartment. It was a tiny studio with a futon that was currently in couch position, a small kitchen, a tiny bathroom, and a corner breakfast table that would barely fit the two men, never mind her.

"Uncle Stan, while I appreciate dinner . . ." Mel began but Stan interrupted her.

"Save it," he said. "In case you're thinking this is negotiable, I'm going to disabuse you of that notion right now."

"So, I don't even have any say over who sleeps in my house all night?" she asked.

"No, you don't," Stan said.

"Don't worry, I won't be sleeping," Manny said.

They both gave him a dark look, and he gestured to his laptop. "I meant I'll be working. Sheesh!"

Uncle Stan plopped his takeout bag on the table and shrugged out of his jacket, which he tossed onto the futon. Mel knew defeat when she saw it. Uncle Stan, for all his teddy bear hugs and unflagging support, was also as immovable as a mountain when he made up his mind about something.

Mel turned away from them and went to retrieve plates and silverware and napkins. While she banged around in the kitchen, she heard them talking. She couldn't make out what they were saying, so she suspected that they were talking in low tones for just that purpose. Well, too bad; if they were going to have a meeting in her house, they were going to pony up the info.

"So, what's happening with Kristin Streubel's murder?" Mel asked as she joined them. "Any suspects in custody?"

"We aren't at liberty to . . ." Uncle Stan started, but Mel cut him off with the universal hand signal for *stop right there, buster.*

"Save it," Mel said. "If you think I'm going to put up with being assigned a babysitter and not know what's going on, you need to rethink. Immediately."

"She might be able to help," Manny said. "She knows Scott and Kristin."

Uncle Stan popped open one of the brown takeout boxes. He seemed to be pondering his choices, but Mel knew better than that. He was trying to decide whether to let her into the investigation or not. Years of experience told her it would do no good to rush him.

He loaded up his plate with some of the grilled pork, noodles, and egg roll. The smell made her mouth water, and she peered over his shoulder into the box while Manny unpacked the rest of the boxes. By silent agreement they waited until everyone's plate was loaded. Mel sat down on the wooden trunk she used as a coffee table when the futon was in couch position.

Captain Jack yowled at her and she gave him a piece of the pork to occupy himself with. Being a fierce hunter, he had to pounce on it a few times before he'd even consider taking a nibble.

Mel waited until Uncle Stan had a mouthful before she said, "So it would seem pretty clear that Frank Tucci is responsible for Kristin's death, whether indirectly or not, so what have we uncovered so far that will lead us to an arrest?"

Uncle Stan finished chewing as if he hadn't even heard her. Manny glanced at her with a twinkle in his eyes.

"She's so cute when she's determined, isn't she?" he asked.

Mel glared at him. She was not going to be provoked. She was going to maintain constant steady pressure and bend them to her will.

" 'Cute' was not exactly the word I had in mind," Stan said.

Mel heaved a put-upon sigh. "Is there a reason I can't know what's going on?"

"The less you know the better off you'll be," Uncle Stan said.

"Has that really worked out for us in the past?" Mel asked.

"You know what Tucci looks like, right?" Uncle Stan asked.

"I'd have to live in Siberia not to," Mel said. "He's on the news every night. He's got a thick head of gray hair, he's short with a plug for a nose, and he wears oversized square glasses and really expensive suits."

"Good," Uncle Stan said. "If he comes into the bakery, leave."

"Given that he's locked up, I don't think he's going to be popping in for an Orange Dreamsicle cupcake any time soon," Mel said.

"I think he's partial to Red Velvet," Manny said. At Mel's questioning look, he added, "I know everything about him, even the brand of toilet paper he uses."

"Eating here," Uncle Stan said through a mouthful.

"Sorry," Manny said before he shoved two chopsticks full of food into his own mouth.

"What do his goons look like?" Mel asked. "Maybe I saw them at the zombie walk."

"Because they decided to have a cupcake before they iced Kristin Streubel?" Uncle Stan asked. "No, forensics did a sweep of the area. Kristin was killed on the other side of the park. They probably carried her while she bled out and then dumped her in the coffin a) because it was a great spot to dump a body and b) because they thought she was Angie and this was a clear message to Joe."

Mel felt her insides clench tight. Memories of Kristin and

how happy and beautiful she had looked on her wedding day flashed through Mel's mind. It hurt like a physical blow to the chest to realize she had died such a vicious and cruel death. Then she thought of what the boys had told her about Scott Streubel and the mystery woman with blue hair. She put her plate of food aside.

"Are we sure they thought it was Angie?" Mel asked. She thought about Angie's meltdown and wished they could prove that Kristin was the intended target, as awful as that reality was, for Angie's peace of mind. If Angie got wind of how cold and methodical Kristin's death had been, Mel really didn't think Angie could handle it, especially if she thought it was even remotely her fault.

Uncle Stan let out a weary sigh. "We're not sure of anything, and we have the feds crawling up our backside wanting in on the case."

"If we can tie the murder to Tucci, we can put him away for a much longer stretch or maybe even permanently," Manny said.

He had his detective face on. His square jaw was set and his black eyes were flat and bottomless with determination.

"What does Scott say? Does he think Kristin was the target?" Mel asked. "Joe said he was devastated, but what if he wasn't? Not really."

"You talked to Joe?" Stan asked.

"I assumed he told you," Mel said. She glanced from Manny to Stan. They were both giving her hard stares. "He stopped by last night."

"Damn it!" Uncle Stan cursed. "What was he thinking? He could have put you in terrible danger."

"Probably, that's why I'm here," Manny said. "I was

wondering why he was so adamant that I watch over you tonight. I might have known I'm cleaning up his mess."

"Um . . . thank you?" Mel said. Her voice was tart with sarcasm.

"You know what I meant," Manny said. "You only need me here tonight because someone might have seen him last night."

"I sincerely doubt anyone saw him, and if they did they wouldn't have recognized him. I sure didn't," Mel said. "He wore a disguise."

"Tell me it was something I can tease him about for the next fifty years," Manny begged. "Please. Did he dress like a woman?"

Mel smiled. "No, he went with more of a redneck theme."

"I thought you said it was a disguise," Manny said.

"Har har," Uncle Stan said. "Focus, people. Mel, did you get any sense of danger today?"

Mel thought about the two specter-hunting boys dogging Marty, the DeLaura brothers in all of their drama, and Angie's breakdown.

"Danger? No," she said. "Drama, yes."

Manny and Stan both watched her as if waiting for more of an explanation. She shrugged.

"Just the usual bakery chaos and mayhem," she clarified. She wasn't sure why she hesitated to tell them what the boys had told her about seeing Scott Streubel with someone other than his wife, but she found herself hesitating. If the boys were wrong, she couldn't bear the idea of causing Scott more grief. And really, how reliable were two boys who thought Marty was a ghost? If she could just contact Joe and tell him what she knew, she would feel so much better about it.

"Okay, so maybe Manny can show you some of the pics of Tucci's goons," Uncle Stan said. "Just so you have a heads-up if any of them come your way."

Mel nodded. This at least felt productive.

"Not that I expect any of them to come after you, but if they did, you would know not to engage," Uncle Stan said.

"Of course," Mel said.

"Scenario," Uncle Stan said. "One of Tucci's thugs shows up at the bakery; what do you do?"

"Call the police," Mel said.

"Wrong!" Manny said.

"Get the hell out of there," Uncle Stan said. "That is your first priority. Get out. Then call the police. Then call me."

"Got it," Mel said.

Stan gave her a worried look. His phone buzzed and he pulled it out of his pocket.

"The chief," he said to Manny. "I'm out. Watch over my girl."

"Will do," Manny said.

"I'll have a cruiser parked out front as a deterrent," Stan said. "And the patrol units will be doing constant sweeps."

Mel stood and walked him to the door. He gave her a bear hug and said, "Don't linger in front of any windows, and make sure someone is always watching the door. Do whatever Manny tells you to do when he tells you to do it."

"I'll be fine," Mel said. "Quit worrying."

"I just can't help feeling like I should talk to your mother about this situation," Stan said.

"Let's not do that to her," Mel said. "She hasn't put together the murdered bride at the zombie walk with Angie, and there's nothing to indicate my being in danger. Why cause her unwarranted stress?"

Jenn McKinlay

Uncle Stan patted his shirt pocket and pulled out his roll of antacid tablets. He popped one into his mouth and said, "Yeah, I've got that part covered by myself."

Mel hugged him tight. "Go see the chief, then go home and get some sleep."

Uncle Stan kissed her forehead, and Mel closed and locked the door behind him. When she turned around, it was to find Manny staring at her.

"And then there were two," he said.

Mel gulped.

Eighteen

As if to complain that he was left out of the count, Captain Jack gave a howl, and Mel realized she needed to feed her fuzzy feline.

"My mistake," Manny said. "Make that 'and then there were three.'"

Mel nodded. "Jack does make himself unforgettable."

While Mel set up Jack's supper, Manny cleaned up the refuse from dinner. She wasn't sure how she felt about him being so at home in her apartment, but since he appeared to be spending the night, she supposed it was only natural.

Except the entire situation wasn't natural or reasonable. To have him here while she slept, that was going to be weird. Good grief, she hoped she didn't snore. Then again, maybe it would be better if she did.

She had to fight a sudden urge to send Joe a text of her own. What was he thinking, putting her in this situation?

Manny moved behind her in the tiny kitchen, and Mel slid out of the way. She figured the only way this whole sleepover from hell was going to work was if she maintained a three-foot boundary zone away from him. Then nothing inappropriate could happen, right? Right.

"So, you were going to show me a lineup of thugs," she said.

"It's on my laptop," he said. "Come here."

He scooped up his laptop and sat on the futon. Mel perched on the nearby chair. He looked at her with one eyebrow raised.

"How are you going to see from over there?" he asked. "Come here."

Mel rose and sat on the end of the futon, maintaining her out-of-reach position.

"Really?" Manny asked. "We're so immature that we can't even sit next to each other? What do you think is going to happen?"

He sounded offended, and Mel felt her face grow warm with embarrassment. He was right. She was acting like an idiot. But the truth was she liked Manny, way more than she should in fact, and having him in her space was very confusing.

She slid across the futon until they were sitting side by side. His attention was on his laptop, and she was grateful because it gave her a chance to get used to the heat coming off of him. He smelled citrusy and masculine, and even after a long day at work, his chin was whisker free as if he enjoyed a really close shave.

Mel cleared her throat, which suddenly felt constricted like Captain Jack with a hairball. Speaking of which . . .

Where was he? He'd make an excellent buffer. She glanced over the back of the futon to see that Jack still had his face firmly planted in his food bowl; so much for that.

"Okay, here's our file on Tucci," Manny said. He propped the laptop on the wooden trunk in front of them, and they both leaned forward to see.

Mel saw a file full of pictures, and she leaned in closer to get a good look. She really hoped she saw someone she recognized. The thought of Tucci going away for longer or for good was all the incentive she needed.

Manny clicked on the file to open the pictures up. The image filled the screen, and Mel frowned. The man in the picture looked as buttoned down as a person could get, wearing a blue dress shirt, navy tie, and khakis with a belt and matching loafers.

"He looks like an accountant," she said. She turned to look at Manny and realized his face was only inches away from hers.

"That's because he is," he said with a laugh. He turned to look at her and he abruptly stopped laughing. His gaze flickered over her face as if he wasn't sure where to look exactly. He glanced back at the screen on his laptop.

Mel watched in fascination as the humor slid from his face, and his features resumed his stern cop mask. Now why was that? Because of the seriousness of the situation? Because he felt the same awareness for her that she felt for him? Because he'd remembered it was Joe who had sent him here tonight? She couldn't hazard a guess.

"Phil Terrazo," Manny said. "He's a certified CPA and while the FBI has been watching him, they've never been able to catch him cooking the books."

"Maybe he's legit," Mel said. She forced herself to look at the grainy picture on the computer and not think about anything but Tucci's thugs.

"No way," Manny said. "He just hasn't been caught . . . yet."

Manny scrolled through several more pictures. Each one of the men was an employee of Tucci's in some capacity or another. Mel desperately wished to see a familiar beak of a nose or bad comb-over, but no. She had never seen any of these men before.

Manny clicked the mouse, and another picture came up. This one showed a slick-looking young guy in a sharp suit beside a very expensive car. The way he was posed, looking over the top of his expensive sunglasses right at the camera, which Mel was pretty sure was supposed to be a surveillance camera, made her think he knew his picture was being taken and he didn't care.

"Who is that?" she asked. He looked familiar but she couldn't fathom why.

"Vincent Tucci," Manny said. "He's Frank's son. He apparently has taken over management of the family restaurant Frank and Mickey's."

"I know that place," Mel said. "I delivered cupcakes there once for a party. There was even talk about them carrying my cupcakes on their dessert menu. So, the Frank in Frank and Mickey's is Frank Tucci?"

"A restaurant or any cash-intensive business is a wonderful place to launder money," Manny said.

"Is Vincent a mobster, too?" she asked, looking back at the handsome man in the picture.

"By all accounts, he's legit, but we keep him on file just in case."

"So, that's why he looks like he doesn't care if he's being watched," she said.

"Yeah, the rookie who took that pic has taken a serious razzing for it," Manny said. "Undercover, my ass."

He clicked to the next picture. Mel glanced at it. It was a shriveled-up old man who looked like he couldn't harm a hamster, never mind a person.

"Don't let the geezer look fool you," Manny said. "That's Tommy the Knuckle."

"The Knuckle?" Mel asked. "Explain."

"He got his name because he was an expert at breaking the knuckles of people who owed him money—with his bare hands."

Mel curled her hands into fists and tucked them against her middle. "Please tell me he's retired."

"I wish," Manny said with a shake of the head. "He doesn't do the heavy lifting himself anymore, but he's still connected."

"A baker's hands are her livelihood," Mel said.

Manny gave her a sympathetic look, which he swiftly covered with a scowl.

"Then maybe you should consider leaving town like Joe asked you to," he said.

"He told you about that?" Mel said. "What else did he tell you?"

Manny glanced away. "What do you mean?"

"Is he going to win his case against Tucci?" she asked. "Or is he going to lose and then spend the rest of his life looking over his shoulder?"

"His case is strong; they've got him on racketeering, tax evasion, coercion, you name it," Manny said. "But the defense attorney is slippery and well connected."

"So no guarantee," she said.

"No, but I have to think Joe's got Tucci running scared," Manny said. "Otherwise why target Angie or Kristin or you?"

"There has been nothing to indicate that I am a target," Mel said. "And it could be that Kristin was the target all along, since Scott's working the Tucci case, too."

"Maybe, but why would he target a law clerk's wife?" Manny argued. "It's much better to go after the prosecuting attorney if he's out to disable the trial. Besides, it's too coincidental that both Kristin and Angie were dressed as zombie brides," he said. He gave a little shiver and Mel looked at him.

"Are you afraid of zombies?" she asked.

"No!" he said. He said it too fast and he didn't make eye contact.

"You are!" Mel accused and then laughed. "You're afraid of the undead!"

"No, I'm not," he insisted. "Do you have to call them that?"

Mel laughed. He frowned.

"You know my people celebrate Día de los Muertos, the day of the dead, so the whole zombie thing to me is a little too close to home."

"You really think the dead can be reanimated?" Mel asked.

"No, but I think their spirits don't always leave completely," he said. "And zombies remind me a bit too often that we aren't always as alone as we might think we are."

His words made Mel's skin tingle.

"Who?" she asked. She didn't have to explain; he knew what she was asking.

"*Mi abuelo*," he said. He stared across her small apartment, but she knew he wasn't seeing it. He was seeing his grandfather. "This is going to sound crazy, but the old man loved *Sábado Gigante.*"

"The variety show with Don Francisco?"

He nodded at her and she could tell he was impressed that she knew of the popular Latin American show.

"That's the one," he said. "My grandfather said it was for the comedy, but my brother and I were pretty sure it was for the hotties. Either way, after he passed, we stopped watching it. We were more sports guys. But a few times when no one was watching the television, it would turn on by itself and be tuned to that show. We knew it was him. We just knew it."

Mel felt the hair at the nape of her neck prickle. She shivered and Manny gave her a half hug.

"Sorry, I didn't mean to freak you out," he said with a chuckle. "But yeah, even the memory gives me the heebie-jeebies."

He kept his arm where it was, and Mel found herself leaning into his warmth. She didn't know if it was the talk of ghosts or knuckle-breaking mobsters that had her so jittery, but either way, Manny's strong arm across her back was very comforting.

She felt him go still and she turned her head to look at him. And there it was in his black eyes, that awareness between them that made it impossible to just be pals, or buddies, or friends.

He dropped his arm and Mel scooted back a few inches. They didn't look at each other.

"I've got two ghost hunting boys who'd love to hear about your *abuelo,*" Mel said. She knew she was babbling trying to get them back to normal, whatever that was, but Manny wasn't saying anything so she forged on. "They call themselves the Bonehead Investigators and have a specter meter and everything. Right now they're sort of locked in on Marty, but I think a real ghost story might divert them."

"This isn't working, is it?" he asked. His voice sounded a bit rueful. Mel pretended not to understand.

"What?" she asked. She decided to play stupid and hoped he would, too. No such luck.

"You and me," he said. "Specifically, me playing number two to Joe DeLaura, waiting and wondering if you're ever going to call it with him and give me a shot."

"I never—" Mel began but he interrupted.

"I know," he said. "You've never given me any reason to think that you were over Joe, but you didn't jump at the chance to marry him, either."

Mel closed her eyes. It hurt to know that she was giving Manny mixed signals. She'd never meant to. It was just that things were complicated with her and Joe.

"That was because of my own issues," she said. "That whole 'until death us do part' thing sort of tripped me up. So when Joe asked, I panicked."

"But you said yes," Manny said.

"Sort of," she said. "We kept it a secret and then I snapped. Too much grief and too many dead bodies were all around me. I didn't think I could handle it. Then when I finally got my head straightened out, I proposed to Joe, and he left skid marks. Well, you know, you were there."

She laughed but it was without humor.

"You know he did it to keep you safe," Manny said. "He walked away because he loves you, Mel."

Mel stared at her hands. She hadn't had anyone to talk

to about her and Joe. Angie, being Joe's sister, didn't really work as a confidant. And Joyce, Mel's mother, got too emotional about the whole thing. And Tate, bless his heart, had been too caught up in launching their first franchise and being engaged to Angie to really be the pillar of support that Mel had been looking for.

So, for the past two months, Mel had really been on her own with her mixed-up feelings, which had rocketed from anger to understanding back to anger to settle somewhere in confusion. And there she had remained, especially after seeing Joe last night and knowing that things between her and Joe were far from over. The irony that it was Manny she was talking about her relationship with did not escape her.

"So Joe says," she agreed. "But it feels more like being stuck. I can't go backwards and I can't go forward. And so I wait."

Manny was quiet for a while. When he spoke his voice was low, almost as if he didn't really want to ask the question but he couldn't help it, and so he said it softly in a half voice as if he weren't really asking. "How long?"

Mel didn't need to clarify the question. She knew he was asking how long she would wait for Joe.

"I don't know," she said. "Until it's over."

Manny didn't ask if she meant the trial or the relationship, and she was relieved, because she honestly didn't know what she'd answer.

Nineteen

Manny excused himself to walk the perimeter of the building. Mel figured it was an excuse to put some distance between them, and she was grateful. Not for the first time, she wondered what would have happened if she had met Manny before Joe had taken an interest in her.

Then again, after her talk with Joe last night, she wondered if Joe was simply her fate. How could he have noticed her at seventeen and not done anything about it? She had been such an insecure, emotional wreck during her teen years. Capturing Joe's attention could have changed everything for her. But she probably wouldn't have handled it well. They'd have broken up, and she'd have been heartbroken and probably started stalking him. Yeah, it was probably for the best that he'd done nothing.

Mel had spent more than a few hours last night rethinking

that long-ago trip to Cabo. Had she gotten any feeling of more than friendship from Joe? No. Whatever he'd been feeling, he'd managed to contain it. Sort of like now. She sighed.

Probably, even if she had met Manny first, she would have left him for Joe because they were just meant to be together. Or at least, she'd always thought so.

Now, she was beginning to wonder. Fate certainly seemed to be testing them. Then again, she remembered her first weeks of culinary school. It had been harder than she'd thought, and she'd debated quitting, but her father in one of their last heart-to-heart talks before he died had told her that getting what you want involved sacrifice, and if you weren't willing to make the sacrifice then you would never get your heart's desire and be truly happy.

If getting through this dark time with Joe meant that they got happy ever after in the end, then surely she could suffer through this time apart. Right?

She moved Manny's laptop to the small table and started to turn the futon into her bed. She was so tired, so emotionally drained, she realized that she didn't even care about her relationships right now. It could all get figured out tomorrow. She yawned.

She took her jammies into the bathroom and changed. Her oversized black Rolling Stones T-shirt and plaid flannel bottoms were about as sexy as tofu, so she figured she was safe from engaging Manny in anything other than brotherly affection. She pasted up her toothbrush and began to scour her molars, when she heard the door open.

She had a spasm of nerves but shook it off. This was Manny. Yes, he was good looking and had saved her life and he was also very clear that his feelings for her were more than that of a pal, but still he was a professional and her uncle's partner. She knew she could go out there butt naked and he wouldn't lay an unwelcome hand upon her. He was a good man.

She glanced down as she scrubbed the last of her teeth. She was covered from neck to toe with nothing tight or revealing, because good man or not, she didn't want Manny to get any wires crossed. Not if he was staying here all night.

She spit and rinsed her brush. She could hear Manny moving in her apartment and wondered if he was trying to figure out how to work around her bed. That was going to be weird having him working while she slept. She wondered if she should try to reason with him one more time. There really was no need for him to stay. She was fine, especially if there was a cruiser out front. No one, not even one of Tucci's thugs, was going to tempt that sort of trouble.

"Hey, Manny," she said as she opened the bathroom door. "I was thinking you don't have to—"

Mel's words stopped in her throat. She'd been prepared to see Manny in his khakis and dress shirt, holster on his shoulder and badge on his belt.

The man standing in her living room holding Captain Jack had none of those things. Tall with long black hair and a wiry build, he was dressed in black leather pants and a white tank top that showed off his colorful sleeves of tattoos. In other words, he was not Manny.

Without pausing to think, Mel opened her mouth and screamed. The man jumped and yelped as if she'd scared him. Captain Jack jumped out of his arms and scampered behind Mel. The door to the apartment burst open and Manny dove into the room, taking the man down at the knees.

They slammed onto the floor with a grunt and thwack. On the way down the man's eyes met Mel's, and recognition finally kicked in.

"Roach?" she cried. She dropped to her knees to see his face. "Oh, my god, what are you doing in my apartment?"

"I needed to talk to you," he said. At least that's what she thought he said.

Mel frowned and looked up. Manny had his knee in Roach's back and had secured Roach's hands behind him, causing his face to be mashed into Mel's fluffy area rug.

"Stop! Manny, stop!" she cried. "It's Roach."

"He broke into your apartment," Manny argued. "I'm not letting him blink an eyelash until I know just what the hell he thought he was doing."

"He's a friend," Mel said. She leaned forward and put her hand on his arm. "It's okay."

"This is why you're always in trouble," he snapped. Manny loomed over her. He looked a little wild-eyed and crazy, and she figured Roach's appearance in her apartment had triggered every one of Manny's cop instincts to protect and serve.

"I am not always in trouble," she snapped back.

She leaned forward, refusing to be intimidated by him. The unfortunate part of this move was that they were now inches away from each other, and their emotions were running pretty high. Mel wondered if he was going to kiss her. He looked like he was thinking about it. Then she wondered how she'd feel if he did. Time seemed to have stalled.

"If you're going to kiss her, get it done, because your knee in my back is beginning to warp my spine," Roach said from below them.

Both Mel and Manny jerked back from each other, and Manny yanked Roach up by his elbow and shoved him onto the edge of the futon.

"So, no kisses then?" Roach asked, glancing between them.

"Shut up!" Manny and Mel said together. Roach smirked.

"If you don't behave," Mel threatened him, "I'll let him take you in for trespassing."

"Aw, I thought we were friends," Roach protested.

"Friends knock before entering," Mel said.

"I did knock," Roach protested. "No one answered, I swear."

"Why are you here, Malloy?" Manny asked using Roach's real surname. "How did you get in?"

"The door was unlocked," he said.

"I told you to lock it after me," Manny said to Mel.

"I forgot." She winced.

Manny slapped a hand to his forehead and muttered something in Spanish that Mel couldn't understand, but she was pretty sure was not a compliment.

"Listen, I'm sorry I freaked you out, but I'm worried about Angie," Roach said. "I stopped by her house to give her some VIP passes to my CD release party, but her fiancé wouldn't let me see her. Since I'm being shut out, I figured Mel would be my next best source for information."

"I can't talk to you about Angie," Mel said. "She would skin me, especially since you wrote that song about her. I know she was working her way towards forgiving you, but I'm not sure she's there yet."

"That song went platinum," Roach said with a shake of his head. "Most girls would fall in love with a guy for that."

"Angie is not most girls," Mel said.

"Don't I know it," Roach said.

The look of sadness and longing in Roach's eyes made Mel glance away. She looked at Manny and noticed he was looking at Roach with an understanding that made her distinctly uncomfortable.

"Is there a specific reason you're worried about Angie?" Mel asked.

"You mean other than the fact that she's the target of a murderer?" Roach asked.

"We don't know that for sure," Mel said.

"Oh, come off it, Mel," Roach chided her. "She was dressed as a zombie bride"—he paused as if choking on the words before continuing—"and the woman who was killed looked just like her."

"That woman's husband is working a high-profile case with Joe DeLaura," Mel said. "She could have been the target just as easily as Angie."

"Unless it was a crime of passion and the murderer is living with Angie right this very minute," Roach said.

"Don't, Roach," Mel said. "You know Tate is not the murderer."

"I know no such thing," he said stubbornly. "Taylor could have been so enraged that I was going to win Angie back that he shot her."

"His name is Tate and you know it. And it would have been hard for Tate to shoot anyone as he was busy having a fistfight trying to protect Oz," Mel said.

"Details." Roach waved a dismissive hand, and Mel rolled her eyes.

"While we're on the subject," Manny said. He turned and glared at Roach. "You could have been so mad that Angie

tossed you over for Tate, that you lost control of your emotions and shot Kristin thinking she was Angie."

Mel studied Manny's face. He was definitely baiting
Roach, trying to get a rise out of him.

"Why would I shoot the woman I'm trying to get back?"
Roach asked. "Kind of defeats the purpose, doesn't it?"

"So, you are trying to get her back," Mel said.

"Not that it's working," Roach said. "But yeah, I'd like to
have her back. What does she see in the buttoned-down suit?
He's got such a stick up his a—"

"Tate is funny, kind, and hardworking," Mel said. "And
she's been in love with him for years. Don't mess this up for
them when they are finally getting it together."

Manny cleared his throat, and Mel realized her little speech
could have been to him about her and Joe. Did he think it was
about her and Joe? She felt her face get warm. Was it possible
to die of embarrassment? Sadly, she had never heard any such
reports on the news.

"I don't want to mess it up for her," Roach insisted. "But
I'm worried. Jimbo my manager said that the case her brother
is trying involves Frank Tucci. That guy is bad news."

"What do you know about him?" Manny asked. He had
his cop face on.

"Same as everyone else," Roach said with a shrug. "He's
a made guy with the mob, an untouchable."

"Not for long," Mel said. A burst of pride flooded her as
she thought about Joe putting it all out there to take on the
notorious mobster.

Roach tossed back his hair and looked at her. "Joe has to
win, Mel."

"I know," she said. Suddenly, she regretted all of the

things she hadn't said to Joe last night, like how proud she was of him, and she couldn't help but wonder if she'd ever get the chance.

"Will you do me a favor?" Roach asked.

Mel looked at him. Gone was his rock star veneer. Instead he just looked like a guy hung up on a girl. Boy, could she relate.

"Sure," she said.

"Tell Angie I said to be careful," he said. Then he paused and blew out a breath. "No, tell her I *asked* her to be careful."

"I can do that," Mel said with a smile.

"She really loves him?" Roach asked.

"Completely," Mel said.

Roach stood, letting out a heavy sigh. The others rose as well.

"Come on, I'll walk you out," Manny said.

Roach nodded. He opened his arms and Mel didn't hesitate. She gave him a big hug. Roach kissed the top of her hair.

"Be careful," he said.

"Hard not to be when I've got my own security detail," Mel said.

She watched as the door shut behind Roach and Manny. She wondered if she should text Angie about Roach's visit. She glanced at the clock. It was late. There wasn't much point in bothering her friend right now. Plus she didn't want to be the cause of friction between Angie and Tate; better to tell Angie in person when Tate wasn't around.

If Tate had sent Roach packing when he showed up at Angie's house, it might not sit well with Angie even though Mel knew it was just Tate being protective. Sort of like Joe having Manny babysit her. She didn't like it, was surprised by his choice, but knew that it meant he would do anything to keep her safe.

When Manny returned, Mel couldn't help but ask, "You don't think he had anything to do with Kristin's murder, do you?"

"No," he said. "Even if we ran with the theory that he mistook Kristin for Angie and in some crazy crime of passion decided that if he couldn't have her no one else could, Roach's alibi checks out. Plus, by all accounts, he doesn't even know which end of a gun to point, never mind how to shoot someone from a distance in a crowd."

"So Kristin was shot from a distance?" Mel asked.

Manny blew out a breath. "I didn't mean to tell you that. I'm not talking to you anymore."

He sat back down at the small table and studied his laptop. He punched keys with his big fingers, and Mel got the feeling he wasn't working so much as avoiding her. Maybe now that the Roach buffer and Stan buffer were gone, and since they'd had their little heart-to-heart, things were officially weird between them. Well, Mel wasn't going to let that stop her.

"At their wedding I remember someone telling me that Kristin was an accountant in a local firm," Mel said. "Could she have enemies of her own? Could it be that the shooting has nothing to do with Tucci or Angie or any of us?"

"What part of 'I am not talking to you about this' do you not understand?" he asked.

Twenty

Mel frowned at him and sank onto her futon. There was so much she didn't understand about this whole situation. She couldn't help feeling that if she just had more information, she could figure out if Angie had really been the target.

The pictures of Frank Tucci's known associates had done nothing for her. She didn't recognize any of them as regulars in the bakery or from the zombie walk. Still, now she had names. She could look in the bakery records and see if she'd ever done a custom order for any of these guys. If she had, it would make more sense that there might be a tie to the bakery other than the one time she had delivered cupcakes to Frank and Mickey's.

Of course, there was no way that she was going to tell Manny what she was thinking. Joe, Stan, and Manny were being overprotective as it was, Tate and the brothers were the same with Angie, and now Roach was neurotic as well. As far as she and Angie went, they were hip deep in men with no answers. This really didn't work for Mel. And Manny tapping away on his laptop while she slept wasn't going to work for her, either.

How could Joe not know how weird this was? Did he think now that she'd agreed to give him another chance she was immune to the detective? Or did it just signify that he trusted her completely? That was so Joe, it made her smile.

Then she thought about spending a night alone with Manny in her apartment, and she was sure Joe was out of his mind. Did he think she was made of stone?

"I can't sleep," she said. "I'm going down to the bakery to restock the many cupcakes that the brothers ate today."

"You're going down to bake *now*?" Manny asked.

"No time like the present," she said.

"Is this because I'm here?" he asked.

Mel thought about lying, but really what was the point? He knew her too well.

"Yes," she said. "How am I supposed to sleep with you in the room? It's just . . . weird."

Manny gave her a lopsided smile. "That's what a guy wants to hear."

"You know what I mean," she said.

"I do," he said. "Look, you won't even know I'm here. I'm reviewing all of the camera footage we collected from the zombie walk via security cameras and cell phones in an effort to find something, anything that gives us a clue as to who shot our victim. It'll take hours and I promise I won't make a sound."

"Good thing you can do that down in the bakery," Mel said. "You can sit out front with Captain Jack while I work in the kitchen."

Manny rubbed his jaw and stared at her. Then he smiled. It was a slow smile that started at one corner of his mouth and slid across his lips with the same brilliance and promise of a sunrise.

Mel swallowed. "What?"

"You're afraid to be alone with me," he said.

"Pah!" Mel scoffed but she could feel the heat in her face and knew she was blushing. She grabbed a sweatshirt off of the hook by the back door and yanked it over her head. "I am not."

Her sweatshirt got stuck and she knew her words were lost as she tried to wrestle the stupid thing on. She felt a pair of hands tug on the hem of her sweatshirt, and when her head popped through the neck hole it was to find Manny standing very close, smiling down at her.

"What was that?" he asked. "I couldn't hear you."

"I am not afraid to be alone with you," she said. She didn't meet his eyes. "I simply have a lot of work to do and, thanks to Roach's visit, a raging case of adrenaline-induced insomnia."

"Uh-huh," he said.

"Come on, Jack." She made kissy noises and Jack scampered to the door. He loved it when Mel went down to the bakery at night. He shot out the door and down the stairs right to the kitchen entrance of the bakery. Mel followed with Manny right behind her, his laptop under his arm.

Mel switched on the kitchen light and locked the back door behind them.

"I don't let Jack run around the kitchen while I'm baking," she said. She offered Manny a cupcake to take into the front of the bakery with him. "Can you keep him entertained out front?"

"Sure, come on little fella," he said. "You sure you don't want us in here with you?"

"Yes," Mel said. Mostly, she needed to put some space between herself and Manny for her own peace of mind, but also she didn't let Jack hang out in the kitchen when she was cooking. "Cat hair."

Manny nodded. He double-checked the back door and the inside shutters, which Mel closed every night to keep the bakery secure.

"No one can see in through these," he said. "If you hear anything, or even if you just get a funky feeling, call me."

"Will do," she said.

He stood in the kitchen and assessed the room one more time. Finally, with a nod, he and Jack disappeared through the swinging doors into the front of the bakery.

Mel had to admit that having him here made her feel much more at ease than she would have felt alone. She quickly gathered her ingredients for a batch of Cookies and Cream cupcakes. She preheated her convection oven and got out her industrial-sized cupcake pan that baked thirty-six.

She wondered how Angie was doing. Then she thought about the brothers. Good grief. Would tomorrow bring more of the same? She didn't know if she could handle that. Then she wondered what Joe had to say about his brothers' job as bodyguards. She could only imagine how he must have felt if he sent Manny here for the graveyard shift.

She wondered how Joe was feeling about his case. Then

she wondered how Scott Streubel was doing. She whisked her dry ingredients while her wet ingredients were beating in her large mixer. Slowly she added her dry ingredients to the bigger bowl. She watched as the beaters churned the cupcake batter until it was smooth.

Once it was finished, she grabbed a clean ice cream scoop and used it to plop the batter into the paper liners in the cupcake pan. Using the scoop kept the amounts uniform so that all of the cupcakes were the same size.

She slid the pan into the oven and set the timer. While those baked, she whipped up a batch of buttercream frosting with crushed Oreo cookies in it. She thought about poking her head through the door and checking on Manny, but she knew he had to work. She wondered how looking at endless footage of the zombie walk was going for a guy who didn't like zombies.

She was curious but not enough to engage him in conversation. She knew playing with fire often led to third-degree burns, and she had no desire to be scorched.

None of this would matter if she and Joe were together. Heck, if she and Joe were together, Manny wouldn't even be here. That sort of made her feel bad, which made her confused, so she shook it off and focused on the task in front of her. She put aside the frosting and prepped another batch of cupcakes, using another industrial cupcake pan.

The goopy texture of the batter reminded Mel of her personal life, which was a mess and as far as she could tell there was absolutely nothing she could do about it; not even shoving it in a three-hundred-and-fifty-degree oven to bake would help. Darn it. Why couldn't relationships be as simple as cooking?

Baking was simple science. Flour and eggs were the foundation of the cake, which was moistened by the fat and sugar. For a perfect cupcake, all Mel needed to do was mind the ratio of foundation to moistness. Why couldn't relationships be this simple? Too much flour and eggs, and the cake was tough and dry. Too much fat and sugar, and the cake was soupy and wouldn't set.

She felt like maybe her relationship with Joe had too much fat and sugar since they couldn't seem to get it set. Hmm. Joe did have a legendary sweet tooth; maybe there was more to her theory than she realized.

Ugh. She shook her head. She wasn't going to think about it anymore. Instead, she thought about all she'd learned about the case Joe was working on. He'd refused to talk to her about any of it, determined to keep her as far away from it as possible.

Fine. Whatever. She had more information now than she had since the whole nightmare began. She walked by the swinging kitchen doors to see Manny sitting in a booth, looking at his laptop, while Captain Jack played hockey with the crinkled-up cupcake wrapper from Manny's lemon cupcake.

Since they both seemed occupied, she thought this might be a good time to see if any of Tucci's thugs were in her customer file.

She stepped into her tiny office, which was formerly the supply closet. She switched on her desktop computer and waited. The sound the computer made once it was fully functional made her cringe. She hoped Manny hadn't heard it. But so what if he had? She would just say she was looking up a cupcake recipe.

Wait, why did she have to explain herself at all? So what if she wanted to look through her customer files. Surely, that wasn't a crime, right? Okay, even Mel could see she was already too defensive. She blamed it on the exhaustion hovering around her brain, making her grumpy.

She opened her customer file on her desktop. Since she had first opened Fairy Tale Cupcakes, she had meticulously collected the mailing addresses of all of her special order customers. They were alphabetic by name, so checking to see if any of Tucci's thugs had placed an order with the bakery should be pretty snappy.

She scrolled through the list, jumping through the alphabet by clicking on the letter of the alphabet that corresponded with the thug's last name. Of course, for Tommy the Knuckle, she was out of luck, as she seriously doubted that he had done business with the bakery using his nickname, and Manny hadn't told her his real name.

She was almost done with her list when the oven timer went off. She went out to grab her first batch of cupcakes before they were burnt. She slid the next batch into the oven and paused by the kitchen door to check on Manny and Jack.

Manny had shifted so that he was leaning back in the booth. He had Captain Jack in his arms, and the two of them looked to be half-asleep. Mel figured she'd better get them a pillow and blanket. Manny could say he was going to stay up all night, but that didn't mean he wasn't going to need a power nap.

Since Mel was prone to pulling all-nighters, using her office to take quick catnaps, she kept a couple of pillows and fluffy blankets in the cupboard in her office. She retrieved her favorite Strawberry Shortcake pillow and fleece blankie and brought them out to Manny.

He glanced from his computer screen to her and back. He tapped a button on the keypad and looked at her.

"Tell me that is not for me," he said.

"Okay, it's not for you, it's for Captain Jack," she said. "It gets chilly in here at night; you might want to keep warm, er, that is, keep Captain Jack warm."

Manny took the pillow and tucked it behind his head while pulling the big blanket over his lap.

"Okay, but just for Jack," he said. "You seriously don't have anything more manly than this?"

"Sorry, no," she said.

Manny rubbed Jack's ears. "Don't worry about it, buddy, it'll be our secret, and next time I see you, I'll hook you up with a cool Avengers blanket. I promise."

Mel turned away before he caught her smiling. Honestly, she could have given him the Spider-Man blanket that Tate kept in the office for his power naps, but what would be the fun in that?

"How much longer will you be baking?" Manny asked.

"One more batch," Mel said over her shoulder. "I promise."

Manny nodded and she noted that he looked exhausted. She could only imagine the kind of pressure he and Stan were facing from above to try to solve this murder. Not to mention the extra incentive of tying it to Frank Tucci.

She saw Jack begin to knead the fuzzy blanket where it draped across Manny's chest. It looked like the boys were settled in. She hurried back to the kitchen to check on her cupcakes and finish looking at her customer list.

She took the second batch out of the oven to cool. She'd wait to frost them. She put her mixing bowls into her industrial dishwasher and then slipped into her office to finish her search.

She finished her customer list and came up with only two possibilities. She'd dig further tomorrow and see if there was a match. On a whim, the last name she checked was Tucci. She knew her old order for the party would be listed there but wondered if they'd ever ordered anything else.

Mel clicked on the letter *T* and then scrolled to the bottom. Sure enough, the name Tucci was listed. When she opened the order, she saw that the order had been made by Vincent Tucci, so nothing for Frank then. She reread the order, wondering if at the time she'd had any inkling of what was to come.

Twenty-one

Mel read the order. It was for three dozen of her Tiramisu cupcakes. She remembered now. She had delivered the cupcakes to Frank and Mickey's for an anniversary party. She checked the date. It had been two years ago, but if she remembered right, the cupcakes had been a huge hit and there had been some polite talk about Mel baking for Frank and Mickey's on a weekly basis.

Shortly thereafter Frank had been arrested, so Mel was quite sure the family's priorities had shifted; still she wondered if it would give her reason enough to stop by the restaurant just to network as it were.

No, she couldn't do that. She could already hear the yelling from Joe, Uncle Stan, and Manny, not to mention the rest of the DeLaura brothers, Tate, Oz, and Marty. Angie might be on board, but since she could be a target, Mel couldn't ask her to join her in her information gathering.

Mel blew out a breath. She shut down her computer and resigned herself to storing her cooled cupcakes and frosting and going to bed. She glanced through the kitchen window and saw Manny with his head lolled back on the pillow in the wide corner booth. His computer looked as if it had gone dark, and Jack was curled up into a little ball on his chest.

She didn't have the heart to wake him up so she could sleep in her bed while he crashed on, what, the tiny armchair in her living room? No, the booths here in the bakery were wide and pretty comfy. Goodness knew she had slept in them often enough.

She grabbed Tate's Spider-Man pillow and blanket and climbed into the booth next to Manny's and stretched out. Her feet dangled off the edge so she moved one of her free-standing chairs to the end of the bench seat so that her feet were secure. Wrapping the fuzzy blanket around her body like a snuggly cocoon, Mel thought about how she could plausibly just pop in at Frank and Mickey's. An idea came to her in a flash but before it was fully formed, she slipped into a deep sleep.

"How big of a beating do you think Manny will put on me when he finds out I took a picture of him in that blanket?"

"I'm thinking you're going to need a body cast."

Mel pulled her blanket up around her ears trying to block the noise. Why were people talking in the middle of the night? Didn't they know this was sleepy time?

"I think it was worth the risk. In fact, I'm going to take two."

A bright light flashed and Mel felt it poke her eyelids.

"What the hell?" a deep voice barked.

"Easy, big fella."

Mel sighed and eased the blanket off of her head. It took her a moment to remember that she was sacked out in one of the bakery booths. Then she moved her head and her neck got locked in a crooked position.

"Ow, ow, ow," she said as she sat up. Captain Jack was sprawled along the top of the booth with his feet hanging over on each side. Mel gingerly turned her head and saw Manny blinking at her over the feline's back.

"Mornin'," he said.

"Hi," Mel said. She felt unaccountably shy, which was ridiculous since they really hadn't done anything but sleep. She tried to toss her bangs out of her eyes, and her neck gave a sharp spasm. "Ow."

Manny put his hand on the back of his neck and winced. "Ugh, we must have slept in some weird positions. I feel like a broken pretzel."

Mel smiled. She glanced up to see Marty and Oz staring down at her and Manny. Oz was holding his phone so they could both see it. Judging by the snorting noises they were making, they were trying very hard not to laugh.

"If you are standing there without coffee already brewing, you had better rethink your priorities," Mel growled.

Marty and Oz exchanged an alarmed look. They began to back away from the booths until they were halfway across the room, at which point they turned around and jogged into the kitchen.

"I didn't think I was that scary," Mel said.

"I think it's just your bed head," Manny said. He appeared to be biting the inside of his cheek, and Mel got the feeling it was to keep from laughing.

She picked up a silver napkin holder and glanced at her reflection. She barely managed to stifle her scream. Her blond bangs were doing some sort of vertical lift, making her look like she'd recently done the mambo with two hundred amperes of electricity.

She carefully pulled the Spider-Man blanket over her head, letting just her face peer out from beneath the colorful fleece.

"Much better," Manny said. "Spider-Man, huh?"

"I found it after you were asleep," she said.

"Uh-huh," he said.

They were both quiet. The only sound in the bakery was Jack, who was purr-snoring from his spot on the booth back between them.

"I should get him home," Mel said.

"Yeah, I need to check in with Stan and get into the station," Manny said.

Still, neither of them moved.

"Thanks for staying last night," Mel said. "I don't really think I need protection, but it was good of you to be here."

"Just because you haven't seen the threat doesn't mean it doesn't exist," Manny said. "Tucci's thugs are not stupid, There is a reason they haven't been convicted for all of the heinous things they've done."

"Good lawyers?" Mel guessed.

"Partly," he said. "But mostly, it's because they leave no witnesses behind."

Manny's dark eyes were as serious as a heart attack, and Mel nodded. She understood. A man didn't get a nickname like "Tommy the Knuckle" because he ate too many pork joints.

The kitchen door swung open and Marty arrived bearing a tray loaded with two steaming mugs of coffee, creamers, and sugar. Mel could have kissed his bald head.

"Here's a little go juice for you," Marty said as he plopped down the tray.

Mel and Manny began to fix their coffee while Marty stood watching. Mel fumbled when she and Manny reached for the sugar at the same time. It had not escaped her that while she woke up looking like something Jack had coughed up, Manny was disarmingly rumpled. His close-cropped dark hair wasn't even mussed, and he still gave off his usual manly citrus smell. Annoying.

"Well?" Marty asked.

"Well what?" Manny said.

"What happened last night?" Marty asked.

"Nothing!" Mel protested, her face getting hot.

Manny blew on his coffee before taking a sip. He glanced at her over the rim, and she could see his dark eyes were amused.

"I think he means why did he find us down here asleep in the booths," Manny said.

"Oh," Mel said. She took a sip of the scalding brew and refused to meet anyone's eyes.

"Yeah, what did you think I meant?" Marty asked. Then he paused. "Oh, well that didn't happen, did it?"

"Whatever happened to minding your own business?" Mel asked.

"Hey, don't bring it up, if you don't want to talk about it," Marty said.

"Mel wanted to replace what the DeLaura brothers ate

yesterday," Manny said. "We must have zonked out in the middle of the night."

Mel looked at Manny and noted that he didn't mention Roach's late-night visit, so she assumed it was a need-to-know-only sort of thing.

Marty looked at Manny as if he was disappointed in him.

"You have the woman to yourself for a whole night and the best you can do is fall asleep while she bakes," he grunted. "No wonder DeLaura has you beat."

"Marty!" Mel chided him.

"I'm just stating the obvious," he said.

"How about noticing that we're going to be opening soon and we need to get cleaned up and restocked, and Oz should get cracking on another big batch of cupcakes?" Mel said. She knew she sounded downright ornery, but mortification will do that to a girl.

"I need to jog upstairs and get my overnight bag," Manny said. "Want me to take Jack up, too?"

Mel scooped up the sleeping feline, who had all the consistency of a sack of pudding, and draped him over her shoulder.

"I'll come with you," she said. "I need to wash up and feed the boy."

Manny nodded and folded up his blanket, leaving it in the booth where he'd slept. Mel was still using hers to cover her bed head and refused to give it up. They both refilled their coffee in the kitchen before heading upstairs, and Mel caught Oz giving them a speculative look.

She refused to engage. She noted Tony's camera in the kitchen blinking its red light at them. She wondered what he'd made of their night sacked out in the bakery. She had no doubt he'd burned the cell towers down to call Joe and report in. She felt a twitch of annoyance and suddenly, Angie's well-known temper made perfect sense to her.

Mel loved her brother, Charlie, dearly, but if there had been six more of him hovering around her while they grew up, watching her every move, reporting to their parents, and basically shadowing her very existence, she suspected she'd have developed a wee bit of an anger management issue herself.

She put more sugar in her coffee and led the way to the back door. They took the steps quickly, and Mel wondered if Manny was nervous to have her out in the open. It seemed ridiculous, but she'd spent enough time around Uncle Stan to see how a cop's brain worked, pretty much in a state of constant vigilance.

She closed the door behind them, and Manny crossed over to where he'd left his bag. He unzipped it and fished around until he found his toothbrush.

"Do you mind?" he asked.

"No, not at all," Mel said as she put Jack down. She waved Manny in the direction of the bathroom. "Have at it."

As soon as the door closed behind him, she crossed to her wardrobe and popped open the door with the mirror. She threw off her blanket and finger combed her hair, trying to get it to calm down just a little. The static from the blanket was not helping the dire situation.

Giving up, she crossed over to the kitchenette and got her fingers wet by running them under the tap. She shoved them into her hair and tried to pat down the mess. It helped a little.

She was just opening a can of food for Jack when Manny came out of the tiny bathroom. He looked as if he'd stuck his head under the faucet, too, and Mel imagined they were both going to need long, hot showers to restore them to their original selves. Separately, of course.

"Well, I'd better go," Manny said. "I'm sure Stan will have a lot to share about his meeting with the chief last night."

"Yeah, tell him I said hey," Mel said.

"Will do," Manny said. He hesitated and then said, "About last night."

Mel looked at him. He wanted to talk about last night? What about last night? Nothing happened. She realized she was sort of disappointed by that observation, and then shook her head. Obviously, sleep deprivation was kicking in, and she was losing it.

She scooped up her coffee mug and took a fortifying sip. Was this where Manny would tell her that he wished it had played out differently? That he would have put a move on her if he could? She would shut him down gently. It would be okay. Her heart thumped hard in her chest, making it hard to focus on his words.

Twenty-two

"You remember those pics I showed you of Tucci's associates," Manny said.

Mel felt her insides deflate like a cake after a loud bang. So, he was not talking about them, rather he was back on the case.

"Hard to forget," she said.

"If any of them come into the bakery, you leave," he said.

He strolled across the room so that he was standing right in front of her. Mel glanced up from her coffee and met his stare. His black eyes crackled with an intensity that made her all too aware of every facial flaw she had ever noted about herself, beginning with her eyes that were too close together and ending with the scar on her chin received from a playground swing-to-face incident that lived on in Pueblo Elementary School lore to this day.

"If they come in, I leave," Mel said. "Got it."

Manny narrowed his gaze at her as if he suspected her of something. Surely, he could not know that she had checked to see if any of the goons were customers. Could he? Mel gave him her best toothless smile of innocence.

"No, I'm not buying it," he said. He leaned closer. "You have a knack for getting into trouble."

"Me?" Mel put her hand on her chest as if she couldn't be more shocked. "I beg to differ. Trouble seems to find me even when I'm looking the other way."

A slow smile spread across Manny's face. It took Mel a second to realize that he thought she was calling him trouble. In that, while she was looking at Joe, Manny had found her.

"What I meant was—" she began but he interrupted her.

"I know what you meant."

They stood quietly staring at each other. There were a thousand words that could have been or should have been spoken between them, but Mel felt like words would diminish their connection somehow. Manny gave her a small nod and she knew he felt the same.

Was it wrong to feel a bond with this man? They had almost died together once. Maybe it was just the natural outcome of surviving a near-death experience together . . . or maybe it was more. Mel swallowed and it was audible. Manny's smile deepened.

"You may be in love with DeLaura," he said as he stepped back. "But at least I know you're not immune to me."

"No, I'm not," Mel said. Her voice sounded strained, and Manny looked pleased.

"I can live with that," he said. He shifted his bag onto his shoulder and turned towards the door. Over his shoulder, he said, "Lock up behind me and remember what I said. If any of Tucci's thugs show up, you leave."

"I promise," she said.

✓´`\¨

And she meant it. Right up until Angie showed up for work, looking as stressed out and miserable as Mel had ever seen her. Gone was Angie's usual sparkle; instead, she looked more like the zombie she'd been dressed as just a few days before.

"What's going on with her?" Mel asked Tate.

He sighed. "This murder is killing her."

Mel cringed at the poor word choice.

"Sorry," he said. "I can't get through to her that it's not her fault. She can't sleep. She won't eat. Having everyone watching her as if she's about to be gunned down is making her a nervous wreck. This morning I found her sobbing in the bathroom because a chunk of her hair fell out. And yet, I can't get her to leave town, not even for a day. It's like she's determined to stay to prove that she wasn't the intended victim. Honestly, I'd love to prove that just to give her peace of mind."

"Maybe I can help," Mel said.

"Sorry, kid," Tate said. "But I don't think there's a cupcake in the world that can solve this."

Mel watched him trail after Angie. It hurt her heart to see her friend so beaten up by life. If only she could do something, use her connections to figure out if Tucci's thugs were behind the shooting. But what connection did she have? Vincent Tucci. He was it. The only tie she had to the whole stinking mess. She needed to talk to him, but how?

Help came in the guise of her mother, Joyce. Mel loved her mom and they were very close, but even so, she had never been so happy to have her mom pop into the shop and demand a mother-daughter lunch.

Mel knew it was probably her mother's sly way of making sure she was okay after the whole zombie walk body in a casket nightmare, but Mel and the others had downplayed the event and its connection to Angie and Joe's case, specifically to keep Joyce from worrying. Still, Joyce was a good mom, and worry was her middle name.

"I just need to know that my baby is okay," Joyce said. She was standing in the bakery kitchen, watching while Mel frosted the cupcakes she had baked the night before.

"I'm fine, Mom," Mel said. "Really."

"And the others?" Joyce asked. "I couldn't help but notice that Angie doesn't seem herself. She looks like she's been crying, and she keeps checking her hair. Is there something wrong with it?"

Mel wondered how much to say. If she mentioned that Angie might have been the actual target, her mom was going to freak out. Mercifully, she was saved from having to answer.

"What are you still doing here?" Angie asked as she plowed through the swinging door into the kitchen. "Go have lunch with your mom. We got this."

Tate was hot on her heels, and Mel could tell he was still not letting her out of his sight.

"You sure?" she asked as she handed Angie her pastry bag full of frosting.

"Yes, go before I take your place," Angie said.

"Okay," Mel said. She untied her apron and hung it on the hook by her office.

She grabbed her purse out of her desk, pausing to check that there were no batter or frosting smears on her denim capri pants or pink T-shirt, which sported the atomic Fairy Tale Cupcake logo.

Joyce tilted her head as she took in Mel's appearance. "Lipstick, honey; you are on the market after all."

Mel rolled her eyes and went back into her office. She fished her pale pink lipstick out of her purse and dabbed it on her lips. She quickly checked that she had managed to color within the lines in the reflection of her cell phone before she hurried back out.

"Better?" she asked.

"Much," Joyce said. She led the way to the back door. "You just never know when you're going to meet Mr. Right. You have to be prepared."

Mel glanced over her shoulder at Angie and Tate, who were grinning at her; she made an exasperated face and they laughed. Mel closed the door behind her, locking it just to be on the safe side.

She glanced at her mother as they made their way to Mel's Mini Cooper, which was parked in a lot across the alley from the bakery. With the same fair coloring as Mel, Joyce looked adorable in a turquoise-and-white-striped blouse over a knee-length beige skirt. Joyce had matched her sandals and purse to the turquoise in her shirt, and Mel felt exhausted just looking at how put together her mother was.

Honestly, there were days when if Mel managed to shower, she considered it a big achievement.

"Any idea on where you'd like to grab lunch?" Joyce asked. "It's my treat."

Mel glanced over the top of her car at her mother while pushing the fob to unlock the doors. "How do you feel about Italian?"

"Oh, I could use a nice antipasto," Joyce said.

"I hear Frank and Mickey's over on Hayden Road makes a nice one, lots of good cheese," Mel said.

"Your father used to love that place. And they have outside seating," Joyce said. "Perfect, let's go."

Mel felt the tiniest pinch of guilt for not telling her mother everything, yeah, and for walking into the lion's den, which she knew Joe and Manny would not approve of, but then she shook it off. She was just having lunch with her mother. What was wrong with that?

When Mel walked into the restaurant, she couldn't help but notice how the place resembled a mobster's hangout. Dim lighting, check. Dark, paneled walls, check. Buxom blond hostess, check. The place was a cliché; then again, that meant the food would be excellent.

"Hi, I'm Heather," the hostess greeted them. "Would you like to sit inside or outside?"

"Outside, please," Joyce answered for them.

"Certainly, follow me," Heather said.

Heather was six foot four in her platform heels. Her low-cut, skintight, micromini black dress hugged her assets with the adhesive property of cling wrap, and her blond ponytail swung back and forth when she walked. She was mesmerizing and Mel noted that every male in the room stopped chewing to stare at her as she walked by.

Mel glanced down at her work clothes and felt as dowdy as a head of lettuce. Then she acknowledged that if she ever attempted to walk in shoes like those, she would do a face-plant and probably break her nose, so yeah, she was just fine the way she was.

Heather guided them to a table on the patio and told them their server would be with them shortly. They took their seats and Mel's mother took her reading glasses out of her purse.

"I have to say that was disappointing," Joyce said.

"What do you mean?" Mel asked. They hadn't even eaten yet; how could Joyce be disappointed?

"If they insist on hiring strippers for hostesses, I should think she would at least give us a pole dance while walking us to our table," Joyce said with a sniff. Mel laughed and her mother met her gaze with a teasing twinkle in her eyes.

Joyce reached across the table and patted Mel's hand. "Have I ever told you how proud I am that you're a woman of substance?"

"Aw, thanks, Mom," Mel said. "I learned from the best."

Joyce grinned and went back to her menu. A busboy brought them water, and soon after the waiter appeared to take their order.

"Good afternoon, ladies," he said. He was tall and broad and looked like he'd be more at home wrestling bears than serving food, but Mel liked the way he met her gaze with a straightforwardness that she found refreshing. "My name is Brian, but everyone calls me Meatball."

"Meatball?" Joyce asked. "Good heavens! Why?"

Meatball opened his mouth very wide and then closed it. "I won the contest for who could hold the most meatballs in his mouth at once."

Joyce wagged a finger at him. "You could have choked."

He grinned. "You sound like my mom."

"So, how many for the win?" Mel asked.

"Eleven," Meatball answered. Mel noted his chest puffed out a little when he said it.

"Impressive," she said.

"Don't encourage him, Mel," Joyce said behind her menu.

Mel and Meatball exchanged a smile before he said, "Let me tell you about our specials."

Joyce listened attentively while Mel scoped out the patio. She didn't see any of Tucci's thugs out here, but she was hoping not to run into any of them anyway, so she didn't consider that a bad thing.

When Meatball was done, Joyce ordered her antipasto and a Chicken Scarpariello, while Mel ordered Crab Louie. They both passed on wine and ordered iced tea instead. Mel figured she could use the caffeine.

After each order, Meatball would give them a pleased look and say, "Excellent choice."

It made Mel smile and she thought it might be something to incorporate at the bakery. She could hear Marty saying "Excellent choice" to their customers, and it almost made her laugh out loud.

As Meatball departed, Joyce leaned back in her chair and said, "Do you know who owns this restaurant?"

Mel put on her best blank look. "No, but I'm assuming they're named Frank and Mickey."

Joyce leaned over the table and whispered, "Yes, Frank and Mickey *Tucci*."

Twenty-three

"No!" Mel said. "You mean the same Frank Tucci that is on trial right now?"

Joyce narrowed her eyes at Mel. "Really, honey, how stupid do you think I am?"

Mel opened her mouth in what she hoped was a look of stunned disbelief. Luckily, Meatball took that moment to reappear with their iced tea.

"Here you go, ladies, and your order will be up shortly," he said.

"Wonderful, thank you," Joyce said. Then she turned her gaze back to Mel. "You were saying."

Mel shook her head. "Nope, I'm pretty sure I wasn't saying anything."

"Uh-huh," Joyce said. "On the grounds that you'd incriminate yourself, no doubt."

Mel picked up the lemon wedge on the edge of her glass and squeezed it over the tea. She dropped it into the glass and pushed it down with her straw. She hoped if she kept busy, her mother would get distracted. No such luck.

Joyce pulled her purse onto her lap and popped open the clasp. She pulled her phone out and glanced at the screen. "Let's see. I know I had Joe in my contacts when you were dating. It's such a beautiful day, I bet he'd love to join us for lunch."

"Mom!" Mel yelped. "You can't tell Joe we're here."

Joyce looked at her over the top edge of her reading glasses. "Why not?"

"Because he's at work right now," Mel said.

"He still gets to eat lunch," Joyce said.

"Mom, don't. Just don't."

Joyce leaned back and studied her.

"All right, fine," Mel said. "What do you want to know?"

"Why are we here?" Joyce asked. "Why does Angie seem so on edge? Why does it seem like one of the brothers is always around? And why did Manny spend the night at the bakery last night?"

Mel goggled at her mother. "How do you know all of these things?"

"Uncle Stan," Joyce said.

"He told you?" Mel asked.

"He talks in his sleep," Joyce said.

"What?!" Mel asked. "How do you know what he does in his sleep? Oh, my god, are you sleeping with Uncle Stan?"

"Melanie Cooper, lower your voice," Joyce hissed. "You are making a scene."

"*I'm* making a scene?" Mel roared. "You tell me you're

sleeping with my uncle over antipasto, and I'm making a scene."

"I never said I was sleeping with Stan," Joyce said. "But even if I was, how is that your business?"

"Because you're my mom and he's my uncle, totally my business," Mel said.

"No, it isn't," Joyce argued. "Now for the record, Stan came over to watch *Sherlock* with me last night after his meeting with the chief, and he fell asleep on the couch."

"Where he apparently spilled his guts," Mel said.

Joyce heaved a put-upon sigh. "Good thing he did, because it's not like you're telling me anything."

There was a note of hurt in her mother's voice that cracked Mel's chest open like a rib spreader.

"Fine," Mel said. "I didn't want you to worry but since it's too late for that, here it is. We're afraid that Kristin, the woman killed at the zombie walk, was a professional hit that was supposed to be Angie. That's why the brothers are always around and why Angie is upset. Manny was at the bakery to keep an eye on me because I refused to go to your house on the very, very, very off chance that I might be a target, too, because of my previous relationship with Joe."

"Is that everything?" Joyce asked.

"Yes," Mel said.

"Then why are we here?"

Mel thought about claiming it was all a coincidence, but one look at her mom and she knew it wouldn't fly.

"Angie is struggling with the idea that Kristin's death is somehow her fault, and by struggling, I mean it's really tearing her up, as in she's losing chunks of her hair," Mel said.

"Oh, that poor girl," Joyce said and put a hand over her chest. "Her hair really is her crowning glory."

"And with the brothers hovering and Tate trying to hustle her out of town, it's just getting worse and worse," Mel said. "Honestly, I'd do anything to help her."

"And you think you can help how?" Joyce asked.

"I don't know," Mel said. "Manny mentioned the Tucci family owned this place and I just thought—"

"What?" Joyce asked. "That you'd come and have lunch here and figure out who shot Kristin? Did it not occur to you that you might be putting yourself in danger?"

"I'm not—" Mel began but she paused when Meatball arrived at their table with their food. He put their plates down with a flourish.

"Can I get you anything else?" he asked.

"No, thank you," Joyce said. She wasn't rude exactly but it was clearly dismissive, and Mel smiled at Meatball to let him know it wasn't him.

Meatball nodded and headed off to his next table.

"I'm not in danger, Mom," Mel said. "Joe and I have been apart long enough that I am not associated with him anymore. There has been no indication that anyone is out to harm me."

Joyce closed her eyes and Mel couldn't tell if she was praying or trying to dig deep to find her patience.

"Well, I suppose that's something at any rate," Joyce said as she opened her eyes. "I still don't see why you thought coming to lunch here was a good idea, but I understand that you're trying to help Angie."

"I didn't think I'd discover who shot Kristin so much as I might find out who didn't," Mel said.

Joyce tipped her head, clearly not understanding Mel's line of thinking.

"I thought if I saw Vincent Tucci and he remembered me for my Tiramisu Cupcakes and we talked shop a bit, then it would clearly indicate that it's not the Tuccis who were after Angie but that it was someone after Kristin instead," Mel explained.

"I'm going to give on this one," Joyce said. "Not by choice, however."

Mel couldn't hide her surprise. "Really, Mom? Wow, and here I thought—"

"Save it," Joyce interrupted her. "If I'm right and I think I am, Vincent Tucci is headed our way. No, don't turn around. Then he'll know we're talking about him."

It took everything Mel had to pick up her fork and take a bite of her Crab Louie instead of turning around to see if Vincent was actually coming towards them. How did her mother even know who he was?

"I've lived here a lot longer than you," Joyce said as if answering her unspoken question. "And I read the papers."

"Melanie Cooper, is that you?"

Mel swallowed her mouthful and turned in her seat, hoping she looked surprised by the greeting.

"Mr. Tucci," she said. "How are you?"

"Please call me Vincent," he said. He took her hand in both of his and gave it a reassuring squeeze. "Mr. Tucci is my father, and I'd rather not be confused with him at the moment."

His smile was wide and welcoming, and Mel felt her nerves settle. Dressed in gray slacks with creases sharp enough to slice bread, Vincent was long and lean, but with broad shoulders that were accentuated by his form-fitting white dress shirt. His thick black hair was tousled, his chin clean shaven, and his dark brown eyes seemed to take in everything at once, making Mel feel reassured at the same time it made her edgy.

"Understood," she said. "Vincent, this is my mother, Joyce Cooper."

"Mother?" Vincent asked. "I would have sworn she was your sister."

He clasped Joyce's hand in his the same way he had with Mel, and Joyce tittered at the compliment. It was all Mel could do not to shake her head.

Their waiter was cruising by and Vincent signaled for him to stop. "Meatball, these lovely ladies are having lunch on me today."

"Oh, no, we couldn't," Mel protested.

"Yes, you can and you will," Vincent said. His tone was good-natured but brooked no argument.

"Understood, sir," Meatball said with a nod.

Mel exchanged a helpless glance with her mother. Her first thought was that Joe, Manny, and Stan could never find out about this. With a mobster's son buying them lunch, they'd fit her for cement shoes themselves if they ever found out. Judging by the concerned look in Joyce's eyes, she was thinking the same thing.

Vincent pulled out the empty chair next to Mel's and sat down.

"I have to apologize, Melanie," he said. "I have not forgotten how we talked about carrying your Tiramisu cupcakes in the restaurant, but as you can imagine, things have been rather hectic since, well, my father . . ."

Mel nodded. She could tell it was painful for him to talk

about. She remembered Manny telling her that by all accounts Vincent was legit. She couldn't imagine how hard it must be for him to be so with a mob boss for a dad.

"Don't worry about it," Mel said. "When life is less complicated, we can certainly work out the details."

"Sounds terrific," Vincent said. He glanced at the door to the restaurant and Mel followed his gaze to see the bodacious hostess Heather waving at Vincent. "Excuse me. It appears that I'm needed."

He rose from his seat and smoothed the front of his shirt then glanced back down at Mel.

His handsome face looked serious and not a little intimidating. "You'll stop by my office before you leave."

"Of course," Mel said.

Mel and Joyce watched him go; as soon as he cleared the door, Joyce starting having palpitations.

"Oh, my god, oh, my god, oh, my god," Joyce wailed. "He's going to kill us. He knows Joe was at your place the other night. He knows you're still Joe's weakness. He's going to kill you as a warning to Joe. We have to get out of here."

"Mom, breathe," Mel said. She leaned over the table and whispered. "We're in a public place. Nothing is going to happen to us. I'm sure it's just about business."

"He could talk business out here," Joyce said.

"Everything all right here, ladies?" Meatball appeared at their table.

Glancing up, Mel noted that Meatball didn't just appear to be a big man, rather he seemed ripped with muscles. A veritable behemoth who could tie a person into cute little balloon animals if he felt like it. *Gulp!*

"Everything is great," Mel said. She forced the corners

of her lips up even though everything inside of her wanted to open her mouth wide and wail.

Meatball nodded and backed away.

"Maybe we should ask him for help," Joyce said.

"Mom, he works for Tucci, does that really seem like the best idea?" Mel asked.

"No, but what are we going to do?" she asked.

"I'm going to meet him in his office while you wait in the ladies' room," Mel said. "We'll stay connected through our cell phones and if anything goes wrong, you can call the police and they'll get you out of here."

"What about you?" Joyce asked.

"I'll be okay," Mel said. "I'll stall him as long as I can and if that doesn't work, I'll let him know he's being monitored and if he hurts me, he'll give us all the evidence we need against him and his father."

Joyce reached across the table and patted Mel's hand. "I don't know whether to be proud of how brave you are or horrified."

"Proud works," Mel said with a shaky smile.

"You're sure we can't just hop the rail and run?" Joyce asked.

Mel tipped her head in the direction of the door. Meatball was standing beside the open door with his arms over his chest, watching them.

"Oh," Joyce said.

"Eat up," Mel ordered. "This might be our last meal."

"Not funny," Joyce said. "But at least it's a good one. Maybe if you praise the food, he won't kill you."

"I'll cling to that," Mel said. She tried to savor her Crab Louie, but even with avocados and black olives, it tasted like dirt.

When they had lingered as long as they could and kicked around four other ways to get out of there without having to meet with Vincent, Mel finally pulled her napkin from her lap and tossed it onto her cleared plate. She couldn't ever remember a time where she had felt as if she was literally throwing in the towel.

"Okay, Mom, call me," Mel said.

Joyce took out her phone with shaking fingers. She dialed Mel's number and Mel felt her phone vibrate in her hand. She answered it and checked the display to see that the call was connected. She carefully put her phone in her purse and kept the top of her bag open for the best reception.

"Okay, I'll go pop in on Vincent and you hit the restroom," Mel said. Joyce kept her phone to her ear as if she was taking a call. She nodded, letting Mel know she had heard her through the phone as well.

Mel threw a fifty down on the table as a tip for Meatball. If things turned ugly, this might be the tip that saved her life. A guy couldn't kill a woman who gave him a fifty-dollar tip on lunch, right?

Twenty-four

Once in the restaurant, Mel stopped by Heather's hostess station while Joyce went on to the bathroom.

"Hi," Mel said. She noticed her voice was breathy, probably because she felt like hyperventilating, and her palms were sweaty. "Um, Vincent asked me to stop by his office on my way out."

Heather glanced up. She looked Mel over as if trying to decide if Mel was competition or not. She gave Mel a scornful look, making it very apparent that, no, Mel was not considered a threat.

Mel knew it was ridiculous to feel insulted, but she did. She stood straighter and pushed her bosom out a bit as she followed the sashaying Heather passed the entrance to the kitchen and down a dark hallway at the back of the restaurant.

Heather rapped lightly on the office door. She looked

back at Mel and then said, "Vincent, that baker is here to see you."

She made it sound as if Mel was pursuing Vincent instead of Vincent being the one who had asked to see her.

"Great, send her in," Vincent called from inside.

Heather pushed open the door, and Mel brushed by her. She had a feeling Heather was trying to intimidate her by not moving out of the doorway enough for Mel to go through. Mel was forced to rub up against Heather's hip, and that's when she noticed the bulge at Heather's upper thigh. She'd seen Uncle Stan's Glock enough to know exactly what the bulge was. The woman was packing!

Mel scuttled quickly by the woman, feeling her heart pound in her chest. As the door swung shut and Heather click-clacked away on her stilettos, Mel let out a pent-up breath.

The interior of the office was surprisingly bright and airy, painted in a soft eggshell color. The red maple furniture was upholstered in bold shades of green, giving the room a surprisingly upbeat feel.

Framed awards for Best of Phoenix and Best in Arizona lined the wall as well as pictures of Frank Tucci and Vincent Tucci with celebrity diners.

"Mel, thanks for stopping in," Vincent said. He stood up behind his desk. "But where is your mother?"

"She went to freshen up," Mel said. "I'm sorry, I have to . . . do you know your hostess carries a gun?"

Vincent lowered his head and gave her a small smile of understanding. "You saw that, huh?"

"More like felt it when I walked by her. I don't think I've ever eaten in a place where the hostess is armed," Mel said. "I know it's Arizona and all, but . . . yikes."

"Heather is more than a hostess," Vincent said. "She's my personal bodyguard."

"Bodyguard?" Mel asked. Her voice sounded faint.

"Since my father's incarceration, he's made some threats," Vincent said. "I have to be very careful."

"Oh," Mel said. She felt herself relax. That, at least, made sense.

"Don't worry," he said. "No one has tried to kill me, lately. You're perfectly safe here. Go ahead and have a seat."

He gestured to one of the green chairs on the other side of his desk. Despite his reassurances, she wondered if he could see how her knees were knocking together.

"I have to confess, I have a personal motive for inviting you back to my office," he said.

Mel swallowed and she was pretty sure she heard a *yip* come from her phone. She ignored it. Tossing her blond bangs out of her eyes, she hoped she looked casual when she asked, "Oh, and what's that?"

"I desperately want to talk shop with someone who understands," he said.

"Shop?" Mel asked. "But I don't know anything about the restaurant business."

"I'm not talking about restaurants," he said with a small smile. "I'm talking culinary arts."

"You mean baking?" Mel repeated

"Yes," he said. "I don't think I told you before that I went to culinary school."

Mel couldn't have been more surprised if he'd poked her with a cake tester. "Really? Savory or sweet?"

"Sweet, definitely sweet," he said. "I was one of three males in my class."

"What was your specialty?" she asked.

"Pâte brisée," he said.

"Hmm, my favorite piecrust," Mel said. "To be perfect it has to be rich and buttery with a crisp and crumbly texture, which is so tricky to master. In France, I learned to make pâte brisée with aged cheddar and then fill it with apples, cinnamon, and raisins. It was melt-in-your-mouth amazing."

Vincent leaned forward. "You have to share the recipe. My best was a frangipane pear tart."

"Almond custard and pears," Mel said with a sigh. Her nerves vanished with the talk of food. "Perfection."

Vincent grinned. "I thought so. I do miss it. Sadly, when you have to sit on this side of the desk there is no time for playing in the kitchen."

"I know what you mean," Mel said. Quite unexpectedly, she found herself confiding in Vincent about her fears of franchising. "My partners want to take the bakery to the next level."

"You sound reluctant," he said.

"I'm not," Mel said. "No, that's a lie. I'm terrified that the quality will suffer."

Vincent gave her a sympathetic smile. "That's because you're an artist."

Mel felt her face grow warm under his praise. "I wouldn't say that."

"I would," he said. He looked very earnest. "I've seen your work. You have a true culinary gift, Melanie. Don't let anyone diminish that."

"Thank you," she said. "I'll do my best. You've never considered franchising the restaurant?"

"No," Vincent said. He looked away and then he looked back and Mel got the feeling something was bothering him. "Listen, I lied to you."

"Oh," Mel said. "So, you didn't go to cooking school?"

"No, that's true," Vincent said.

"Oh, good because I really want that frangipane pear tart recipe," she said.

"It's yours," he promised. "What I lied about was my father."

"The Frank in Frank and Mickey's?" she asked.

"Yes," he said. "Thank goodness my mother didn't live to see this disgrace, god rest her soul."

He crossed himself and Mel wondered if she was supposed to do the same. She was pretty sure she wasn't so she stayed still, hoping her lack of motion wouldn't be too obvious if she was supposed to cross herself.

"What I lied about was saying my father had made some threats," he said. "It's more than that. My father has tried to kill me."

"Oh," Mel said. She knew her mouth was hanging open a bit, but she didn't know what to say. *I'm sorry* seemed woefully inadequate.

"Listen, Melanie, my father is an evil man, and I don't doubt he's guilty of everything he's been accused of," Vincent said. Mel's eyes went wide. "I know it's shockingly disloyal of me to admit that."

"Do you have proof?" Mel asked. She was thinking Joe's case could be made if Frank's son testified against him.

"No, unfortunately," Vincent said. "My father kept all of his business dealings from me. On her deathbed, my mother made him swear that he would never let me become a part of the life. As far as I know, it's the only promise my father has ever kept."

"Why are you telling me this?" Mel asked.

"Because I've been watching the news," Vincent said. "That woman who was killed at the zombie walk, she wasn't just a random victim."

"What do you know?" Mel asked.

Vincent cursed. "Nothing for sure, but I know my father is behind it. That woman's body was put in a coffin in front of your cupcake van. Do you think that was a coincidence?"

"I don't know," Mel said.

"It wasn't," Vincent said. "That woman is married to that man who works in the prosecutor's office, right?"

It was public information, so Mel nodded.

"Melanie, it could have been you," he said. She glanced up at him in surprise, and he added, "Everyone knows you used to date Joe DeLaura. And doesn't his sister work for you, too?"

Mel's throat felt suddenly dry and when she swallowed, it hurt. Vincent was confirming her worst fears.

"Joe and I are no longer together," she said.

"That won't matter to my father if he suspects that DeLaura still cares about you," Vincent said.

"He doesn't," Mel said. She wasn't sure why she felt the need to lie when Vincent seemed to loathe his father as much as she did, but her instincts were guiding her.

"Why would your father go after Joe's sister?" Mel asked.

"To destroy him," Vincent said. "It would work, wouldn't it?"

Mel didn't answer. She couldn't.

"Do you think the woman who was murdered was supposed to be one of us?" she asked. She was pleased that her voice didn't shake when she asked the question.

"As I told the police, I don't know," Vincent said. "My father has kept me out of that part of his life. But would I put it past him? No. Melanie, until my father is locked away for good, I must warn you to be very, very careful."

Mel nodded. Her heart felt like a stone sinking in her chest. She did not want to report this conversation to Angie or anyone else for that matter.

A knock sounded on the office door right before it was shoved open, and Heather stepped into the room.

"The beer distributor wants to talk to you," she said. She crossed her arms over her chest, looking between them with an unhappy expression on her face.

Mel didn't need to be told twice. She rose from her seat and Vincent did the same, coming around the desk to join her. He put his hand on her lower back as they walked to the door.

"We'll have to get together again and compare cooking tips," he said. "You know, when things are . . . calmer."

"Absolutely," Mel said.

"And I really do want to get Fairy Tale Cupcakes in here and on our menu," he said.

"That would be great," Mel said. She felt as if her enthusiasm was forced since all she could think about was Vincent's revelation that Angie may very well have been the one marked for death.

She shivered and felt Vincent's hand move up and down her back in a soothing gesture. He leaned close and whispered, "Remember what I said. Please, be careful."

"I will," Mel whispered back. "Thank you."

Once outside the office, she turned and bolted down the hallway. She could feel Heather's narrowed gaze on her back, which did nothing to calm her nerves. Holding her purse up to her face she saw that her phone connection was still open. She picked it up and put it to her ear.

"Mom, meet me by my car," she said.

"Sorry, cupcake, there's been a change of plan." It was Joe who answered. "Now do exactly as I say."

Twenty-five

Mel gasped.

"Don't say my name," Joe ordered. "Just act casual and get your butt outside. Your mom is already out here."

Mel was halfway through the restaurant and saw Meatball standing by the bar, watching her leave. She gave him a little wave just as she would have had this been a normal lunch. To her relief, he waved back. Yes, the tip had definitely been worth it.

Mel stepped out into the daylight. She blinked against the sun's brightness and scanned the area, looking for her mother.

She heard Joe expel a relieved breath on the phone. Then he ruined it by sounding bossy. "Walk right to your car, do not turn around, do not pause, do not even think about avoiding me by trying to catch the city bus."

"Fine," Mel said. She trudged across the parking lot, where

she had left her Mini Cooper. When she got there she glanced in to see Joe back in his redneck disguise, sitting in the driver's seat of her car, holding her mother's phone to his ear.

She opened the passenger door and climbed in. Joe barely waited until she'd shut the door before he hit the gas and zipped out of the parking lot.

"Where's—" Mel began but Joe interrupted her.

"Joyce is with Stan, who is taking her home," he said. His jaw was clamped so tight Mel was surprised he could get the words out. "It's probably best if you do not speak right now."

Mel was about to argue, but self-preservation made her close her yap. Joe was the most even-tempered person she'd ever met, but he did not look like that now. In fact, his resemblance to Angie when she blew a fuse was alarming to say the least.

He drove to the lot behind the bakery, where he parked in her usual spot. Mel went to climb out but Joe halted her by putting his hand on her arm.

"We need to talk. Your apartment. Now."

Mel did not like his tone, but wisely realized that this might not be the best time to point it out to him. Instead, she got out of her car and strode across the alley to the stairs that led up to her apartment. She could hear Joe behind her, mostly because he was stomping his feet as if trying to exercise his foul mood on the steps.

Mel unlocked her door and pushed her way in. Captain Jack was snuggled in his favorite blanket and only blinked at the interruption before burying his nose in his tail and falling back to sleep.

"How did you know—" Mel began but Joe interrupted her again.

"No," he said. He ripped off his beard and hat and pillow gut and stood in just a loose gray T-shirt and jeans. He shoved his hands through his hair. "I get to ask the questions."

"Shouldn't you be in court?" Mel asked. She was hoping he'd forgotten and would now have to hurry back.

"We're recessed for the day," he said. He crossed his arms over his chest and glared at her. "Explain yourself."

"There's nothing to explain," Mel said. "Mom wanted to go out for lunch, so we went to Frank and Mickey's."

"How dumb do you think I am?" he yelled.

Mel blinked. Joe sounded crazy mad. He never sounded crazy or mad. In fact, she couldn't recall a single time when they'd been dating where Joe had yelled at her like this. And since they weren't dating, she really didn't know where he got off thinking he could yell at her like this right now.

"Hey, hey, hey," she said. She planted her hands on her hips and assumed her fighter's stance. "Don't you raise your voice to me."

"Are you kidding me?" Joe asked. "This is nothing. You're lucky I didn't storm into that restaurant and carry you out over my shoulder caveman style."

"You wouldn't!"

"Wouldn't I?"

Mel shook her head. There was no way she should find this domineering male thing he had going on attractive. And yet a tiny little feminine part of her swooned, which made the liberated woman inside of her vomit. She put her hand to her forehead. This was all too much to process.

She turned on her heel and headed to the giant ceramic cupcake on the counter where she kept her candy stash. She lifted off the lid and peered inside.

It was a sad state of affairs in there. She had a few stale chocolate hearts left over from Valentine's Day and half of a candy cane from Christmas. St. Patrick's Day wasn't known so much for candy as it was for beer, so that wasn't helpful. Thankfully, Easter was only a few weeks away. After that there really wasn't a good candy holiday until Halloween. Someone really needed to get on that. The Fourth of July needed its own candy with foil-wrapped chocolate stars or chocolate flags or something.

"Candy?" Joe asked. "You're foraging for candy *now*?" He leaned over her shoulder to check out the stash.

"Can you think of a better time?" she asked.

"That's pitiful," he said, eyeing the contents.

"Don't I know it," Mel said. She reached in and grabbed the two hearts. She held one out to Joe. He was the only person alive who had a sweet tooth to rival her own.

He took the heart and gave her a severe look. "Do not think that by taking this candy I am in any way saying that what you did today is okay."

"Noted," Mel said. She unwrapped her candy heart and shoved it in her mouth. "But I don't like shouting, so if you could dial it back that would be great."

Joe shoved his chocolate into his mouth, too. Mel wondered if it was to keep himself from yelling at her again. She glanced back into the cupcake. *Barren* was the word that leapt to mind. She sighed. If she had been planning to bribe him, she was out of luck.

"I'm sorry I yelled," Joe said. "No, actually, I'm not. In fact, I feel like yelling a whole lot more."

His volume started to go up, and Mel could feel her own temper kicking in.

"Stop!" she said. "We are not together anymore. You have no right to tell me what I can or can't do."

"I have every right," Joe argued. Mel opened her mouth to argue, but he held up his hand in a "stop" gesture. "Maybe not as your boyfriend but as the prosecutor in a very delicate case, you bet I do."

"My eating at a restaurant that is open to the public has nothing to do with your case," she said.

"Really?" he asked. He glowered at her but Mel refused to knuckle under to his glower. "Then explain to me why you were alone in a room with the son of a man who is likely responsible for a woman's death and why even Vincent the son was warning you to be careful, that his father is evil, and that you could very well be a target."

"Ah," Mel gasped. "How do you know all that?" She patted her clothes. "Do you have me bugged?"

For the first time a tiny smile lifted the corner of Joe's lips. He scowled, forcing it back.

"No, we have the restaurant under surveillance," he said. "We have for ages. How do you think Stan and I knew you were there?"

"Oh," Mel said.

Joe crossed his arms over his chest and frowned. "I must say you and Vincent certainly seemed to hit it off over pâte brisée."

"I had no idea he had been to culinary school," Mel said "Small world, huh?"

"Mel, just because he can roll out a piecrust doesn't mean he isn't dangerous," Joe said.

"But you heard what he said, his father made his mother a promise on her deathbed to keep him out of the family business," Mel said.

"Yeah, and because Frank Tucci is known for being a man of his word, I totally believe he did just that. Not. Just because we can't find any criminal activity in Vincent Tucci's past doesn't mean there isn't any. What the hell were you thinking going there for lunch?"

"I wanted to help Angie," Mel shouted. She couldn't help it; her nerves were shot.

"How?" Joe shouted in return. "By getting yourself killed?"

"No, by using my connection to the restaurant to see if it was likely that Angie was the target," Mel yelled. "The woman is losing her hair, Joe, I had to do something."

"Hair grows back," Joe argued. "But once you're dead, you're dead. You took a horrible risk. You have no idea what Tucci's goons could do to you."

Mel thought about Tommy the Knuckle and shivered. "I do know. Manny told me about his associates."

Joe was quiet for a while. "So, how did it go last night with Manny here?"

His voice sounded overly casual as if he was trying very hard to sound ambivalent.

"It was great," Mel said. She wasn't sure what made her do it, but the devil flew into her and she added, "You know, minus the lack of sleep."

Joe's brows lowered over his eyes. "Lack of sleep?"

"Yeah, we were up most of the night, if you know what I mean." Mel turned away from him so he couldn't see her smirk.

"No, I don't," he said. "Define 'up.' "

Mel glanced over her shoulder at him. She let her gaze lower to the portion of his anatomy that had the ability to rise up, so to speak. But instead of answering him, she strode into the kitchen to attend the dishes she had neglected over the past few days.

As she opened her small dishwasher, she began to whistle. She could see Joe begin to mutter and pace in her peripheral vision. A part of her felt bad for teasing him, but the part of her that was still sore at him for being so insufferably bossy did not.

Finally, he stopped muttering and leaned over the counter and demanded, "You're enjoying this, aren't you?"

Mel put the last glass in the dishwasher and closed it. She turned to face him. He looked punchy, tired, and utterly drained. She was pretty sure he'd lost at least ten pounds, and the bags under his eyes looked like they were packed and ready to head to the nearest deserted island they could find. She was enjoying nothing about this.

She leaned over the counter, meeting him halfway and putting them just inches away from each other.

"No, I'm not," she said. "It hurts me to see you like this, and I'm mad at you for pushing me away when I could help you."

He looked at her as if to say, *Oh but no.*

"I could," she insisted. "At the very least, I'd make sure you were eating and sleeping."

Joe's warm brown eyes grew soft. "So, I don't have to worry about you and Manny?"

"You know you don't," she said. She shook her head. "The cameras in the bakery would have made it perfectly clear that we slept in separate booths last night."

Joe had the grace and good sense to look down and away. "Yeah, I knew that."

"I figured you did," she said. "Otherwise, I wouldn't have teased you. Manny's a good man."

"He is," he said.

"But I'm otherwise engaged," she said.

"Engaged?" he asked. "Interesting word choice."

Mel felt her face get hot. "I just meant that I'm not available right now."

Joe smiled. "I like it the other way better."

"Really?" she asked. "So, if I asked you to marry me right now, would you?"

"Oh, no," he said. "It's too dangerous."

It was Mel's turn to glower. She hadn't really expected him to hustle her out the door to the nearest JP, but she had thought he'd be okay with the general idea of marriage. Then again, maybe when he'd said no a few weeks back, it hadn't been just about this case. Maybe Joe really didn't want a happy ever after with her.

"Really? Too dangerous?" she asked. "Tell me this, Joe, when is it not going to be too dangerous?"

"Mel, you know I never wanted to end things between us. I'm just trying to keep you safe."

"Not from a broken heart, apparently."

"I'm sorry," he said. "You caught me off guard there. Of course I want to—"

"Save it," she snapped. "You know what I think? I think you don't want me but you don't want anyone else to have me, either."

"Not true," he protested. "My only thought has been to keep you safe by any means possible. I never wanted to hurt you.

Hell, I never wanted to break up with you. I wanted to marry you. Remember? It was a go right before you dumped me."

"Oh, let's go there again," she said. "You know I was working through some stuff. I'm over it now."

"Are you?" he asked. "Then why do you take stupid risks and scare the beejezus out of me?"

"Lunch today had nothing to do with you," she shouted. She had hit her boiling point in frustration. "I was trying to help Angie."

"So you said, but how does putting yourself in the line of fire help Angie?" he asked. "Unless you think that being the one who gets killed will spare her, in which case isn't that a hell of a way to get out of being with me?"

Now they were both yelling—again. Captain Jack leapt onto the back of the couch and began to lick his foreleg. He looked disgusted with the both of them.

"That's the stupidest thing I've ever heard," she said. "Here's some reality. You don't really want to be with anyone, and you're always going to play the 'my life is too dangerous' card just to keep me, or anyone, away. Fine, then. I think we're done here. In fact, I want my key back and this time I mean it."

She held out her hand, knowing full well that Joe kept her key on his key ring.

He looked staggered by this, and Mel thought she might have gone too far. But that was crazy, right? Because they were broken up and fighting and despite any feelings they had for each other, the nature of his work meant he would never feel safe being married to her or anyone, or so she suspected.

Probably she should have insisted he give her key back weeks ago, but there had been this crazy little flame of hope inside of her that he would change his mind and come back to her. Now she knew. A relationship was never going to work between them, because every time Joe took on a scary case, and as a prosecutor when wouldn't he, he was going to dump her. Mel couldn't live like that. If they were going to be together, he had to be all in.

"Fine," he said. "If that's how you want it."

"It is."

Joe pulled his key ring out of his pocket and unfastened her key from it. When he handed it to her, their fingers brushed, and Mel felt the same pop of awareness she always felt when she came into contact with Joe. It made her want to cry, but she refused. She'd shed enough tears over Joe DeLaura.

He didn't seem inclined to move, so Mel took a deep breath and stepped around the counter. She marched to the door and unlocked it. Joe followed her, slapping his disguise back on as he went. Mel was relieved. It was a lot easier to say good-bye to redneck Joe than her Joe.

He paused in front of her. She noted that even behind his beard, his jaw jutted out, looking stubborn behind the synthetic hair.

"For the record, I don't give two hoots what you think you know about me, I'm still not calling it quits between us," he said.

Mel felt her heart flutter around in her chest until she smacked it with a mental flyswatter. No. She was not doing this again.

"Good-bye, Joe," she said.

He stepped through the door and she closed it after him. Immediately, she wanted to yank it open and throw herself at him, but she didn't. She supposed her strength of character should make her feel better, but it didn't.

Twenty-six

After she had calmed down, Mel headed back down to the bakery. She figured some good old-fashioned baking therapy was in order.

Did she feel bad about what was happening between her and Joe? Yes. Did it feel worse than what had already been happening? No, not really.

She stomped into the kitchen to find Angie there alone. The cupcakes she had left with Angie were all done, and she appeared to be beating the heck out of a lump of fondant, working a bright pink color into it.

"Everything okay in here?" she asked.

"It is now," Angie said. She motioned to the swinging door that led to the front of the bakery, and Mel noticed that a long board was wedged across it, barring anyone from entering or leaving.

"Okay, then; want some help?" Mel asked.

"You're not going to tell me to take it down?" Angie asked in surprise.

"Nope, I think I know exactly how you're feeling," Mel said.

"Crowded," Angie replied. "Shadowed, pinched, squeezed, suffocated."

"Harassed, nagged, scolded, and squelched," Mel added.

Angie paused in kneading the fondant and looked at Mel with her eyebrows raised in surprise.

"Do tell," she said.

"Mom and I had lunch at Frank and Mickey's over on Hayden Road," Mel said.

"Mel!" Angie squealed. "That's—"

"Frank Tucci's place," they said together.

"Yeah, I know," Mel said.

"What were you thinking?" Angie asked.

"Now, don't you start," Mel said. "I've had all the lecturing I'm going to take from your brother."

"Oh," Angie said. Her eyes and mouth making perfect O's in her heart-shaped face.

"I made him give me the key back to my apartment," Mel said.

Angie dropped the fondant and came around the worktable and hugged Mel.

"Oh, sweetie," Angie said as she squeezed her tight. "I'm so sorry."

"No, it's okay," Mel said. "It was overdue."

When Angie stepped back to study Mel's face, her own eyes were red and watery, and Mel found herself comforting her friend.

"It'll be okay," Mel said. "Someday."

Angie reached across the table, picked up the fondant, and said, "Have at it. I've found it very therapeutic to slap it around a bit. It's even better if I mold it into one of the brothers' or Tate's face and then put my fist in it."

Mel laughed. "You might be onto something there. I'll just go scrub up."

She washed up at the sink and then met Angie by the table, where she took a sizable ball of fondant out of a tub. Angie handed her the green food coloring, and Mel went to town working the color into the fondant until it was a solid bright apple green.

They worked in silence with Angie rolling out her fondant and then forming the shapes she needed for their order of specialty cupcakes. These were to have green fondant draped over a high mound of buttercream frosting with pretty pink roses on top.

Since some people were fondant resistant, Mel always put it over a good amount of buttercream. Although Mel ordered the fondant from a specialty company that created a marshmallow-flavored fondant with a firm consistency, some customers still balked at the taste. She couldn't argue because they were the customer, but also she knew fondant was an acquired taste.

The door banged and then there was a curse. Given the tone, Mel guessed that it was Marty.

"Angie, open up!" he bellowed. "I need to talk to Mel."

"What makes you think she's back here?" Angie yelled back.

"I saw that her car was back in its spot in the parking lot," he said. "Plus, a certain incognito DeLaura stopped by and bought a dozen cupcakes. It looked like a bout of pathetic comfort eating to me."

Mel sighed. Joe had bought cupcakes. Why did this endear him to her? She needed to stay mad at him. She gave the green ball of fondant a nose and two eyes, and then she punched it right in the kisser.

"Better now?" Angie asked.

"Maybe," Mel said.

"Can I let Marty, just Marty, in?"

"Yeah, he's okay," Mel said. "But if he starts lecturing—"

"Give him the heave-ho," Angie finished for her. "Got it."

She crossed the room and lifted the wooden two-by-four from across the door. Once she had propped it against the wall, she called out, "Okay, Marty, you and you alone may enter."

The door was pushed cautiously open, and Marty appeared around the edge. He glanced between the two of them as if to make sure they weren't going to throw anything at him.

"It's okay, Marty," Mel said. "You have clearance."

"Did you hear that?" Marty called back over his shoulder into the bakery. "I have clearance."

Mel could hear some disgruntled grumbling from the other side of the door, which she was pretty sure came from Tate and one of the brothers.

Marty strode into the kitchen and then gave Mel a desperate look. "Mel, you have to do something!"

"About what?" she asked.

"That conspiracy lunatic from the zombie walk is in the bakery, and he's spouting more of his usual crazy talk," Marty said. "He says he has a reporter coming to meet him here and that he has proof that Kristin was a zombie before she was killed."

Mel bolted for the door. There was no way she was having a reporter come here to talk about *that*. If Joe was angry about her going to lunch at Frank and Mickey's, he would be bezonkers if the bakery was the setting for an article about Kristin's murder.

She spotted Chad the second she entered the bakery. His zombie attire was gone but he was ever the hipster in skinny jeans, blue Converse sneakers, and a brown tweed coat. His hair was styled so that it stuck up in a point on the front of his head, and his black-framed glasses were perched on his nose, giving him a studious appearance. Mel wondered if they were prescription or just a prop.

"Chad, what are you doing here?" she asked.

"Meeting a reporter from the *New Times*," he said. "I'm going to give her an exclusive about the murder."

Mel slid into the booth across from Chad. She sensed that she needed to handle this in the most tactful way possible.

"How about a cupcake, Chad?" she asked.

"No, I'm good," he said. He peered past her at the door, and Mel forced herself not to turn around and look.

"Really?" she asked. "Because we're sort of in the cupcake-selling business and not so much the meeting-a-reporter-for-an-interview business."

Chad slid his gaze back to hers. He must have sensed she meant it, because he nodded.

"I guess a chocolate chip mint cupcake would be all right," he said.

"Great," Mel said. She'd actually been hoping he'd refuse

so she could show him the door, in the nicest possible way, of course. She glanced over at the counter and caught Marty's eye. "One mint chocolate chip."

"Roger that," Marty said. He made a face that led Mel to believe he, too, was disappointed in Chad's choice to stay.

"Chad, were you thinking of having another zombie walk next year?" Mel asked.

He shrugged and pushed his glasses up on his nose. "Assuming the government hasn't infected us all with this zombie plague."

"Why would the government do that?" Mel asked. As soon as the words left her mouth she knew it was a bad move.

Chad's eyes lit up like a sports commentator given an open mic. He was practically salivating with the opportunity to have his own monologue of stupid.

Mel held up her hand in a "stop" gesture. Chad looked like he swallowed his tongue. Marty delivered his cupcake, and Mel pushed it towards him.

"Listen, for you to have another zombie walk, you need the story about the zombie bride to go away, far, far away," she said. "No one is going to go to a zombie walk where people get shot."

"But they killed her because she was an experiment gone wrong," Chad said. "Don't you see? Any one of us could be Kristin Streubel."

Mel thought about how true his statement was in a totally different way. She shivered.

"Chad, I appreciate your concerns, but we don't know anything about Kristin except that she was a nice woman who worked as an accountant and was married to an equally nice man who was a law clerk."

"Lies!" Chad shouted and raised his index finger to point up in the air.

"What?" Mel asked. She glanced at the clock. Time was passing and she needed him out of here.

"She wasn't an accountant and she wasn't married," he said. "I checked. There's no wedding license on file, and the company she said she worked for has never heard of her."

"Dude, seriously?" Mel asked. "I was at her wedding. I saw her get married."

"No, you didn't," Chad said. He had the crazy eyes thing going on behind his glasses, and yet Mel couldn't look away. "She works for the government and so does he."

"He who?" Mel asked.

"Her bogus husband," he said. "They're in on it. They're a part of the plan to kill us all."

Mel blew out a breath and rubbed her very weary eyes with the heels of her hands. She needed inspiration, and in his paranoia, there it was.

"Why do you think this reporter is willing to meet with you?" Mel asked. Chad gave her a blank look, and Mel leaned over the table and opened her eyes wide for dramatic effect. She whispered in what she hoped was an undercover agent sort of voice, "She's one of them."

Chad yelped and dropped his cupcake. "Are you sure?"

"Positive," Mel said.

Chad's eyes darted around the room. Mel felt a little bad about playing into his conspiracy theory malarkey, but she was aiming for the greater good here.

"I have to go." Chad bolted out of the booth, leaving his half-eaten cupcake behind. He shot across the bakery, towards the door. It opened with a jingle of bells, and a young woman stepped into the bakery. She had reporter written all over her, and Chad must have sensed it because when she went to greet him, he dodged away from her outstretched hand and ran around her and out the door.

"Hey wait!" the reporter said. "Aren't you—?"

Mel watched as she rushed out after Chad. Mel turned to the window and watched the young woman chase Chad through the streets of Old Town, no doubt only convincing Chad more and more that she was "one of them."

Marty came to stand beside her. "Okay, so how did you do it?"

"First, I appealed to the businessman in him," Mel said. "That didn't work, so I changed it up and preyed on his paranoia."

"Kind of mean," Marty said.

"But effective," Mel countered. She bussed Chad's plate back to the kitchen, where she found Angie had taken over the green fondant and was draping it over the buttercream and then adding her pretty pink rosebuds.

She glanced up when Mel came in. "Crisis averted?"

"Barely," Mel said. "So, you want to tell me why Tate is out there with his sad puppy face and why Ray is sitting at a table with his eyes trained on this door as if afraid he'll miss something?"

"Tate and I are fighting," she said. "Roach is having a big CD release party blowout and I feel like I owe it to him to go, since he got hauled in for questioning as a suspect and all. Well, that and our breakup was a tad messy, but Tate— are you ready for this?—Tate forbade me from going."

"Did you really want to go?" Mel asked. She wondered

if now would be the time to tell Angie about Roach's late-night appearance but hesitated.

"That is so not the point," Angie said.

Mel nodded. "It was the forbidding thing, wasn't it?"

"Uh, yeah," Angie said. "Just because we're engaged does not mean he can boss me around. It would set a horrible precedent for our marriage."

"Agreed," Mel said. She thought about the spat she and Joe had had. It had started with him being a bossy boots; small wonder it had deteriorated.

"How did you leave things?" Mel asked.

"Funny you should ask," Angie said. "I told him I was sleeping at your place tonight because I needed some space."

"*Gilmore Girls* marathon?" Mel asked.

"Or *Buffy the Vampire Slayer*," Angie said. "I'm in a bit of an ass kicking mood right now."

"I hear you," Mel said.

"So, it's okay that I stay over?" Angie asked.

"Always," Mel said.

"Yay!" Angie grinned, looking happy for the first time all day. "And maybe we can ditch our surveillance team and sneak out and attend Roach's party."

Twenty-seven

"Wha—what?" Mel cried. "No, no, no! You can't do that. Oh, my god, Tate would filet us both with a rusty blade."

"Just hear me out," Angie said. "I have a plan."

"What plan?" Mel asked. "To get yourself killed?"

"Stop!" Angie said. "No one has come after me. No one. I really think the target was Kristin."

"Does that make sense?" Mel asked.

The kitchen door opened and Tate poked his head in.

"Hi, girls," he said in his most chipper voice.

"Get out," Angie snapped.

"There's my blushing bride," Tate said. "Have I told you how beautiful you are today? Because you are truly breathtaking."

Angie held up her hand and pointed for Tate to go back the way he came.

"Okay, then; I'll just be out front if you need me," he said. The door swung shut behind him.

"How long do you plan to torture him?" Mel asked.

"Until the lesson sticks," Angie said. "He's a bright boy. He should get it by this time tomorrow."

"It would be very difficult for any of Tucci's associates to make a move on you since you've had your own personal security detail, so your argument that nothing has happened is shaky at best."

"No, it's not," Angie said. "Listen, there's stuff you don't know about Kristin Streubel."

"Such as?" Mel asked.

"First, there is no record of a marriage between her and Scott Streubel," Angie said.

"How do you know that?" Mel asked.

"Marty told me what Chad Bowman said when he was here before," Angie said. "So I double-checked and he's right. There is no record of a marriage."

"So what? You know how long it takes to file these things," Mel said. "Maybe the paperwork got held up."

Angie just stared at her. "Then why does the accounting firm she was supposed to have worked for have no record or even a recollection of her?"

Mel felt her heart pound hard in her chest. Could it be possible that Kristin wasn't who Mel had thought she was?

"If you tell me next that the government caused her to be a real zombie and then executed her so that people wouldn't find out, I'm calling the hallucination hotel and booking you a room," Mel said.

"No, I'm not all the way around the bend yet," Angie said. "But you have to admit, it's fishy."

"Still not worth putting yourself out there to be shot," Mel said.

She took a slab of the rolled-out green fondant and began to shape delicate green leaves to put around the rosebuds.

"Maybe, but if they really wanted to whack me, they would have by now," Angie argued. "That's why I'm sure the target must have been Kristin, and if I go to Roach's party unencumbered and nothing happens to me that will prove it."

"That's a big risk to take to prove you're right," Mel said.

"No bigger than taking your mother to lunch at Frank and Mickey's restaurant," Angie argued. "Wouldn't you do it?"

"Maybe," Mel lied, knowing full well she would. "Let's review the situation one more time."

"I have gone over and over this in my head," Angie said. "It's taken the place of counting sheep for me."

Mel looked at the dark circles under Angie's eyes. She knew her friend well enough to know that Angie was taking Kristin's death very much to heart. She couldn't blame her. She could only imagine the mix of emotions she'd have if she thought someone had been killed because they'd been mistaken for her.

"The suspect list on a homicide usually starts with the person closest to the victim," Mel said. "That would be her husband Scott."

"He looked truly messed up over it to me," Angie said.

"Maybe," Mel said.

Angie paused in placing another rose and squinted at Mel.

"What do you know?"

"Nothing," Mel said. "It's just that . . ."

Angie waited and Mel knew she had gone too far to stop now.

"The brothers," Mel began but Angie interrupted.

"My brothers?"

"No, the two boys who have been targeting Marty as a ghoul," Mel said. "They said that they saw Scott at the festival kissing another woman, a zombie with blue hair."

Angie's eyes went wide.

"I know," Mel said. "I thought they must be wrong because I just couldn't believe it, but now . . ."

"Oh, my god, this whole thing could be about a man trying to get rid of his wife," Angie said and clapped a hand over her mouth. "And wouldn't it be the perfect cover to have everyone think it was a mob hit?"

Mel held up her hands. "Whoa, whoa, whoa, slow down the crazy talk."

"It's not crazy!" Angie said. "It makes perfect sense."

"It makes no sense!" Mel argued.

"Think about it," Angie said. "Scott Streubel is married to Kristin but in love with someone else. How does he get out of it?"

"No!" Mel said. "I was at their wedding. Joe gave a speech. It was very touching."

"Because you were with Joe or because there was heartfelt emotion going on there?" Angie asked.

Mel tried to think back to the day of the wedding. She could only remember bits and pieces as most of her attention was caught up in being with Joe. She sighed.

"What if Leo and Atom were wrong?" she asked. "What if they were mistaken and the blue-haired zombie woman was kissing someone else? I don't think I can risk putting Scott through an accusation like that."

"Then we know what we have to do," Angie said. "We need to find the blue-haired zombie woman."

Mel blinked at her. "You have lost your mind."

"Hear me out," Angie said. "Samurai Comics had a free photo booth at the zombie walk and they posted the pictures online. Maybe they took a picture of her."

"How do you know this?" Mel asked.

Angie glanced away. "I pay attention to stuff."

Mel knew she wasn't getting the whole story but she decided to let it go, for now. "Even if they did, how are we going to figure out who she is?"

"First things first," Angie said. She wiped her hands on her apron and hurried into the office. She came back holding the laptop Tate kept in the office.

Mel glanced at the door to the bakery. All was quiet. She supposed it didn't hurt to just look for the blue-haired zombie. After all, it was incredibly unlikely that they'd find her.

"All right, go ahead," Mel said. She knew she sounded reluctant as she pressed her little green leaves onto the base of a rosebud.

"You know I have to do this, right?" Angie asked. "Please don't judge me. I've been a wreck."

"I know," Mel said. "I can't imagine . . ." Realizing she was about to say something really stupid, she let her words trail off, but the damage was done.

"What it feels like to think it's your fault a woman was killed. I can't sleep, I can't eat," Angie paused to sob and then reached up and pushed her hair aside and pointed to what was clearly a bald spot, "and I'm losing my hair."

Mel circled the table and hugged her friend close. Angie sobbed on her shoulder and Mel patted her back and rocked her as if she were one of Mel's nephews with a boo-boo. When Angie quieted down, Mel pulled back and studied her friend.

"Angie, you have to know this isn't your fault," Mel said. "The person who killed Kristin is at fault. Not you."

"Maybe," Angie choked the word out. "I keep thinking what if Tate and I hadn't gone as a bride and groom. What if we'd gone as a zombified Fred Astaire and Ginger Rogers?"

"That was an option?" Mel asked.

"Not really. Tate can't dance and we figured even as zombies they'd have been able to bust a move," Angie said. "But there were so many other things we could have gone as. But if it wasn't Frank Tucci behind the shooting, if it was someone else . . ."

"Then she would have been killed either way," Mel said.

"Yeah," Angie said. "How sick am I to hope that's the case?"

"Not sick," Mel said. "A little warped perhaps . . ."

Angie gave her a weak smile in return for her attempt at humor. Mel returned to her cupcakes while Angie dug into the pictures posted from the zombie walk.

Mel pressed a circular cookie cutter into the green fondant and then carefully lifted the circle of fondant off of the parchment paper. She placed it over the buttercream on a cupcake and smoothed the sides down with her fingers. She then brushed a little bit of water onto the top of the fondant-covered cupcake before placing a leaf cutout and one of her rosebuds on top. She gently pressed them onto the base and then leaned back to admire the results.

She finished off a dozen while Angie hunched over the laptop, saying nothing. Mel was about to suggest she give it a rest, when Angie gasped.

Mel glanced at her and then hurried back around the table to look at the screen. "Did you find her?"

"I think so. Look." Angie tapped the screen, and Mel saw a blue-haired zombie woman posing for the camera. She was about to point out that there could be many blue-haired zombie women at the festival, but then she remembered the boys had said the one they saw was wearing a lab coat.

"That has to be her," Mel said. "She's dressed just as the boys said."

"Yes, but it gets even better," Angie said. "Look at this." She scrolled through the photos until she came to another page that had several pictures including the blue-haired woman. "This is an open invite from the Sewers to these selected zombies to attend the Sewers CD release party tonight."

"What? Why?" Mel asked.

"When I talked to Roach, he said—"

"You talked to him?" Mel asked.

"Briefly, after Tate refused to let him drop off the VIP passes, I 'bumped' into him when I stopped at Echo Coffee."

"'Bumped' meaning it was a setup?" Mel asked.

Angie shrugged and then continued. "Because of the . . . situation . . . the band doesn't want to use the promotional pictures they took at the zombie walk and are calling back their favorite zombies for photo ops at the party tonight. You realize what this means, right?"

"That we should call Roach and ask if he knows who she is?"

"No, it means I'm going to Roach's party tonight," Angie said. "I need to make peace with him anyway."

"You're fighting?" Mel asked.

"Not fighting so much as there's a lot left unsaid between us," Angie said. "When I ran into him at the coffee joint, we started to talk, but then Tate and two of the brothers arrived. We agreed to talk later, but later never happened, as I didn't want another dustup between him and Tate. Hey, those look really beautiful."

Angie pointed to the cupcakes. They were lovely with the pink rosebuds perched on tiny green leaves on the lighter green fondant base.

"They remind me of the simple beauty of a petit four," Mel said.

"We could add some bright pink swirls if they want to jazz it up a bit," Angie said.

Mel nodded but she wasn't thinking about the cupcakes. It was time. She took a deep breath.

"Roach came to see me last night," she said. "Before you 'bumped' into him at Echo."

"What?" Angie asked. "And you're just telling me now?"

"It's been kind of crazy," Mel said. "Plus, I wasn't sure how it would go over with you and Tate and, gah, why is it all so complicated?"

"Agreed." Angie blew out a breath. She studied Mel's face. "What did he say?"

"He still cares about you very much," Mel said. "He seemed worried."

"I know," Angie said. "I need to go see him, especially if it helps us track down the blue-haired woman."

Mel was silent for a moment. She needed to contact

Manny and tell him what they'd found out about Scott. Maybe in the footage he'd been reviewing, he'd pick up Scott and this woman. The thought made her stomach hurt.

"What time do you want to leave tonight?" she asked.

Angie's big brown eyes met hers. "You're in? You'll go with me?"

"Well, I'm not letting you go alone," Mel said. "Assuming you'll let me."

Angie got a mischievous twinkle in her eye, and she looked at Mel and said, " 'An old friend is never an extra guest.' "

Mel frowned. Angie was quoting a classic movie, black-and-white, with a swoon-worthy Cary Grant and the incomparable Ingrid Bergman. What was it?

"Give up?" Angie asked.

"No . . . *Notorious*!" Mel said.

"Nailed it." Angie raised her hand and they exchanged a high five.

"All right, let's get these finished," Mel said. "I am sure my wardrobe does not have anything even remotely resembling what to wear to a CD release party."

"Actually, that's a good thing," Angie said. "Because I think I know how we're going to ditch our bodyguards."

Mel glanced up at the camera blinking at them from its perch atop the shelves in the corner.

"Tony didn't wire the place for sound, did he?" she asked.

"No," Angie said. "More accurately, he said he didn't." She glanced at the bakery door. "They'd be in here by now if they heard us planning, don't you think?"

"Probably," Mel said. She glanced inside her industrial mixer. The bowl below the beaters was empty, but she switched it on anyway. She gestured for Angie to join her. "Let's talk by the mixer just in case."

Mel leaned close as Angie outlined her plan. She supposed it was mental, but when she saw the dark circles under Angie's eyes, and the bald spot on her head, she knew her friend was driving herself slowly crazy. How could she not help her gain peace of mind?

Twenty-eight

"Don't you think it's highly suspicious that Tate just let me go like that?" Angie asked for the third time as they strode through the mall with Marty and Oz dragging their feet behind them like two prisoners of war.

Although Tate had been okay with the girls' night thing, when it came out that Mel and Angie were headed to the mall, suddenly Marty and Oz demanded to shadow them. Mel supposed they should be grateful that they didn't have all of the brothers trailing after them.

"You made it clear you were mad at him," Mel said. "He's probably relieved that you're doing a girls' night so he can recover from getting his butt chewed all day."

"It's his fault," Angie said. "Telling me what I can and can't do. You see where I had to nip this before we got to the 'until death us do part' portion of our relationship, right?"

"Absolutely," Mel said. "And I'm sure once Tate has enough time to think about it, he'll see the error of his ways, assuming he forgives you for this."

"I wasn't planning on telling him until our fifth or perhaps our tenth wedding anniversary," Angie said. "Besides we'll be in disguise; it'll be okay."

"Oh, here's a store for party girls," Mel said. She turned and looked at Marty and Oz. "We're going to buy underwear, you coming?"

It was hard to say what turned a brighter shade of red: Marty's bald head or the part of Oz's face that was visible beneath the fringe of hair he wore over his eyes.

"We'll wait out here," Marty said and Oz nodded in agreement.

Mel hooked Angie by the elbow and dragged her into the shop, which sported tiny dresses and very high heels in the window.

The salesgirl who approached them looked like she was twelve and had raided her mother's makeup case and jewelry box. Her hair was bright pink, her lipstick purple, and she was wearing a neon green minidress and white stiletto-heeled go-go boots.

She studied Mel and Angie through suspicious eyes as if she felt they might be too old or too fashion backwards to appreciate the store's merchandise. Mel had no worries that Angie would set the girl straight in a matter of moments.

Angie fished through her purse and pulled out her VIP pass to Roach's party.

"We're Mel and Angie, we own the Fairy Tale Cupcakes bakery, and yeah, I'm the Angie that Roach wrote the hit single about," Angie said. "Now we've been working all day and need to get dolled up for his CD release party which starts in about half an hour."

"Oh, my god, you're her?" The girl grabbed the VIP passes and looked from them to Angie and back.

"I have two extras for you, if you can work some magic on us," Angie said. "As in we need to be unrecognizable."

The girl squealed and informed them her name was Tracy and the other salesgirl was Paula and they would be happy to relieve Angie of her extra passes. Tracy looked like she might swoon, but she shook it off and the next thing Mel knew, she and Angie were being shoved into the fitting room with an armful of skimpy dresses.

"Try them all on," Tracy instructed. "I'm going for shoes. I'm looking at sizes seven and ten, correct?"

"Nine and a half," Mel said.

Tracy gave her a dubious look but Mel refused to look away. She was a nine and a half, most of the time. Mel tried on the dresses. She chose the only one that covered her butt—barely.

"I can't breathe," Mel said. She pulled back the curtain and stepped out of the room. She was wearing a pewter gray lace sheath dress that was so snug she was afraid to inhale too deeply.

"You?" Angie said. "Check this out."

She stepped out of the cubby next to Mel's. She was wearing a bold red embroidered organza dress with a fitted top and a flirty skirt that was sure to bring Tate to his knees, if he ever actually saw her in it.

"Okay, I brought nine and a half and tens for you," Tracy said as she joined them. She thrust two pair of strappy platform sandals in Mel's direction and two more at Angie. "And six and a half and sevens for you."

Mel looked at the shoes. She really had no idea how the gladiator-inspired footwear was supposed to go on.

"Here, let me help," Tracy said.

She knelt in front of Mel and opened up the straps for her. Mel put her right foot in and realized she couldn't even touch the ground with her other foot. The shoes made her well over six feet tall, but she figured it would make it easier to see over the crowd, which might come in handy so long as she didn't actually have to walk anywhere.

Tracy helped her with the other one and then stood back up to examine Mel's look.

"We need a dark lipstick and some eye makeup and you're good. Maybe we can add a pop of color to the hair, too."

She then turned to assess Angie, who had managed her stiletto red suede pumps all by herself.

"Paula, I need an assist back here!" Tracy yelled to the front.

The other salesgirl came trotting to the back. She wore black thigh-high boots and a hot pink minidress. Her black hair was styled in a thick braid that she wore wrapped around her head. She looked Mel and Angie over and came to the same assessment that Tracy did.

"I got this," she said. "Let me get my makeup bag."

She came back with what looked like a small carry-on to Mel. Immediately, she began unloading flat irons, curling wands, lotions, powders, lipsticks, and some stuff Mel couldn't identify.

"Fake eyelashes?" she asked Mel.

"No, no thank you," Mel said.

"No, really, those pale little brush things you've got going will not work," Paula said.

"Gee, thanks," Mel said.

"Lip liner," Tracy said to Paula while she worked on Angie. "This one has a very thin upper lip."

Mel met Angie's gaze over the girls' heads. She gave her a "what the hell?" look that made Angie's lips twitch, which was unfortunate because it caused Tracy to veer off course with the lip liner.

"Sit and close your eyes," Paula ordered. Duly intimidated, Mel did.

Finally, the two girls finished working their magic and stepped back from Mel and Angie.

"Serious wow," Paula said.

"Thanks," Mel said. She had a feeling this was one of the more sincere compliments she'd ever received.

Mel and Angie staggered over to the mirror. Mel felt her jaw drop. She had to pat her face to make sure it was actually her reflection staring back at her. They both looked like their legs were seven miles long and their curves fit and flared in all the right places. Mel had more makeup on than she'd ever had in her life, and her blond hair had vivid pink streaks in it.

She reached up to touch it, but Paula smacked her hand away. "Don't worry, it washes out."

Angie didn't have color in her hair. She didn't need it. Tracy had sculpted Angie's long, dark brown hair into a wavy mane of loose curls that neatly covered her bald spot. If she didn't know any better, Mel would have thought she and Angie were some freakish runway models in an haute couture fashion show. Crazy.

"Nice work, girls. We owe you," Angie said as she handed over two of the passes to the Sewers party.

Mel paid Tracy for their dresses and shoes, cringing only a little at the cost. A glance in the mirror and she convinced herself that really it was all worth it. Even her own mother wouldn't recognize them.

"Okay, if all goes well," Angie said, "we'll walk right by Marty and Oz and they won't even recognize us."

"We're ditching them?" Mel asked.

"You know they'd tattle on us," Angie said.

"Without even hesitating," Mel said.

"Okay, so here's what we do," Angie said. "We'll have the girls hold our clothes for us and then we'll sashay our way out the door. I bet we're long gone before the boys even realize it's us."

"Sashay? Hobble might be the more accurate description of me in these heels," Mel said.

"Come on, you just need practice," Angie said.

Mel glanced in the mirror one more time before sending up a quick prayer that she didn't get arrested for indecent exposure.

"Okay, let's do this," Angie said. She hooked her arm through Mel's and half dragged, half carried her out the front door.

To Mel's relief, Oz and Marty were not right out front, which certainly made things much simpler. In fact, when Mel looked around, she saw them halfway down the mall, lounging in the massage chairs a vendor had set up. As Mel and Angie walked by them, Oz looked half-asleep and Marty had saliva glistening in the corner of his open mouth, which Mel noted was emitting snores.

Neither of them noticed Mel or Angie as they let the chairs work their magic on them. Mel took this as a good sign. The salesperson working the area did notice Mel and Angie, and Mel was flattered that he looked too dumbstruck by the sight of them to trot out his sales pitch. Then again, he may have been scared of them, hard to say.

"Okay, let's catch a cab in front of the mall," Angie said. "The party is at the Black Dog Pub over on Mill Avenue in Tempe, so it's only about ten minutes away."

"Sounds like a plan," Mel said. As they rode the escalator to the lower level, she couldn't help asking, "How mad do you think they're going to be?"

"Eh," Angie grunted. "Marty's always mad."

"Let's send them a text telling them we went home," Mel said. "So they don't panic and run all over the mall looking for us."

"Once we're in the cab," Angie agreed.

A cab was waiting right outside, and in minutes they were driving south on Scottsdale Road. While in the car, Mel used the time to text Marty and Oz that they'd gone home, as well as send a text to Manny about the boys seeing Scott kiss the blue-haired zombie woman, while gently suggesting he look at the video footage from the zombie walk again.

Mel tugged the hem of her dress down when the cab took a sharp right onto Curry Road and a left onto Mill Avenue. The dress was really not made for sitting. She feared she was going to have a celebutante crotch shot moment when the cab pulled up to the curb, so she made Angie get out first and used her as a shield.

The line into the Black Dog Pub circled the block. Angie had no issues with sauntering past the people queued up for entrance. She fished her VIP passes out of her bag and flashed them at the beefy, bald bodybuilder guarding the door. He gave them a warm smile and lifted the rope to usher them through.

Mel had to admit there was something very cool about the VIP thing. She could see where people got hooked on special treatment. How did one go back to normal life when they were used to having all doors opened for them? She thought maybe it was just better not to get used to it.

The pub was dark and it took a moment for her eyes to adjust. Purple neon lights illuminated the dance floor, which was heaving with a crowd of bodies all gyrating to the music being spun by a DJ in the booth up in the balcony above the main floor. The stage was empty but the Sewers equipment was there just waiting for them to charge onto the stage.

Angie was searching the room, looking for the blue-haired zombie or Roach. Mel did the same but had no luck spotting the tall, long-haired, tattoo-encrusted musician. There were several bars, lots of tables, and three levels to the pub. Mel looked up and saw that the balcony gave a nice view of the whole place.

Mel nudged Angie and pointed up. Over the music, she yelled, "I think we need to be up there."

Angie nodded and together they worked their way to the stairs. Another large bodybuilder type was blocking the stairs. Angie showed their passes, and he studied the pass and then her face.

"Angie," he said as if he'd been expecting her. "Go on up, ladies."

They climbed the circular staircase to the level above. It was less crowded here, and Mel instantly saw two of the band members and the manager sitting on the plush couches that filled the long, narrow space. Their section was roped off from the rest of the loft that was packed tight with bodies.

Mel realized that a person could come up and shank her or Angie, and no amount of undercover security would be able to save them. The thought made her dizzy, and she grabbed Angie's arm and held her close. She would not let anything happen to her friend.

Angie had no such fear. She sauntered right into the thick of it, not hesitating and not breaking her stride until she stood right next to Jimbo, the band's manager.

He glanced up with a practiced smile until recognition kicked in. Then he scowled and snarled, "What are you doing here, Angie?"

"I came to see Roach," she said.

"Haven't you done enough damage?" shouted the singer whose name Mel couldn't remember as he jumped to his feet, looking like he was going to square off with Angie. Not a great plan.

"Roach gave me passes so I came to see him," Angie said. "If you have a problem with it, take it up with him."

Jimbo narrowed his gaze at Angie as if he was thinking through this turn of events. "You know he didn't have anything to do with that shooting, don't you?"

"Yes, of course," Angie said. "I've said that all along."

"Maybe it's good that you're here then," he said. "There's a lot of media. If you show support for Roach, maybe they'll get off his back."

"My thoughts exactly," Angie said.

"You know he's still in love with you, right?" the singer asked. His tone was hostile.

Angie nodded, looking uncomfortable.

"You still engaged to that other guy?" Jimbo asked.

Angie nodded again. "Listen, I'm marrying Tate Harper. That's not going to change, ever, but I will always care about Roach. Always."

"Well, if that's all I can have, I guess I'll have to learn to live with it."

Mel whirled around to find Roach standing behind them. The love in his eyes when he looked at Angie was painful to take in. Mel glanced away and she noted that the singer and Jimbo did, too.

"Oh, Roach," Angie sighed. She stepped forward with her arms wide and hugged him close. "Why are you musicians so damn sensitive?"

He gave her a sad smile. "It makes us better songwriters."

Angie nodded and pressed the top of her head into his chest. He wrapped his arms around her, and they stood for just a moment as if no one else was there.

When Angie stepped back, Mel watched as Roach let his hands slide down her arms as if memorizing the feel of her before he let her go one last time. Mel felt her throat get tight, but she forced herself to smile when Roach's eyes, which were a bit damp, turned to her. He blinked.

"Good golly, Miss Molly!" he cried. "Is there a fire alarm ringing? Because, Melanie Cooper, you are smoking hot!"

Twenty-nine

Mel laughed out loud. She knew she'd always liked Roach for a reason.

"You big flatterer," she said as she hugged him.

"Just speaking the truth," Roach said with a grin. He turned back to Angie. "I can't believe you actually came. Is Todd with you?"

Angie closed her eyes for a moment, obviously channeling her patience.

"His name is Tate, which you know," she said. "And no, he did not. Actually, I came to talk to you. Do you have a minute?"

Roach looked over her head at his manager. Jimbo glanced between them and gave a sharp nod.

"Ten minutes until showtime," he warned.

"Cool," Roach said. He took Angie's elbow to lead her to the far corner, and Mel fell in behind them.

She supposed they wanted to talk alone, but there was no way she was letting Angie out of her sight. She followed behind them, all the while scanning the place for the blue-haired zombie.

"Are you really coming with us?" Angie asked her.

"Yes," Mel said.

"We're safe. No one knows we're here," Angie said. "Relax."

Roach glanced between them. "What do you mean no one knows you're here?"

They were off in a corner of the loft now. On one side of them was a blue glass wall separating them from the DJ's lair. The thirty-foot drop from the loft was on either side of them, and a substantial crowd filled the space. Mel tried to stand between Angie and the rest of the room.

"Mel's being paranoid," Angie said.

"No, I'm not," Mel protested. "I'm being cautious."

"You can leave us alone to talk," Angie said. "No one is going to gun me down up here. Security is too tight."

"You two can say anything you have to right in front of me," Mel said. "I won't even listen. I'll just keep an eye on the crowd."

"Whoa, whoa, whoa. Gun you down?" Roach asked. "What are you talking about?"

"You know the police think that Kristin, the woman at the zombie walk, might have been murdered because she was mistaken for me," Angie said. "I am trying to prove that they're wrong."

"By coming here and putting yourself in harm's way?" Roach asked. "Look when I invited you, I figured you'd bring all of the brothers or that the murderer would have been caught. Are you crazy coming here on your own? That is so irresponsible!"

"No, it's not!" Angie retorted. "You sent me passes and I wanted to come and clear the air with you. Besides, we have a mission. We're looking for one of the zombies from the zombie walk who was invited back for pictures."

Roach stared at her for a moment then he pulled out his phone and began tapping a text message.

"What are you doing?" Angie demanded.

"I'm texting Tate to let him know what his crazy fiancée is up to," he snapped.

"What?" Angie cried. "How did you get his number?"

"Hey, you called him Tate," Mel said.

"I have his number from when you called him using my phone back when we were dating," he said. "I kept it. No idea why."

Roach tapped the screen one more time, which Mel assumed meant he sent the message. Then he glanced at Angie with a frown. He looked as if he was seeing her in a whole new light and not a flattering one.

"You know for the first time ever, I'm glad you're his headache," he said. "I can't handle you, but I'm betting he can, which is why you didn't tell him you were coming here, did you?"

Two red spots flared on Angie's cheeks. "It so happens that I'm not speaking to him right now."

Roach glanced at his phone. "Well, you'd better get over that because he'll be here in ten minutes."

Mel glanced between them, uncertain how Angie's temper was going to manifest itself and that's when she saw movement, a large shadow, against the blue glass wall. It occurred to her that the DJ's song sounded more like it was skipping than it was a repetitive beat. Her instincts went into overdrive and she lurched forward, catching Angie and Roach in an awkward tackle, which sent them all down to the ground.

Despite the VIP locale, the floor was sticky and dirty and smelled of stale alcohol and feet. Mel would have poked her head up but sharp popping sounds, not part of the skipping song, pierced the air over her head. She used her full body weight to keep both Angie and Roach down on the ground.

"What the—?" Angie cried.

"Someone's shooting at us," Mel cried. "Stay down!"

Roach swore and yanked Mel down beneath him, blocking both her and Angie with his body. Mel's face was inches from Angie's and she could see the terror in her friend's face, which slowly gave way to rage.

Screams sounded behind them, and Mel glanced under Roach's arm to see that the rest of the VIP section was down on the ground as well. The big bouncer who had been at the bottom of the stairs came charging into the area with more security behind him.

Mel glanced at the blue glass and noted that the shadow was gone, the music was still skipping, and there appeared to be several bullet holes in the glass. She felt dizzy and thought she might throw up, but she forced it back down. One of the security personnel planted himself in front of their group.

"Are you all right?" he asked.

As one, the three of them nodded. Mel wondered if Roach could feel her shaking, and then she realized it wasn't her but Angie who was trembling.

"Stay down until we clear the area," the officer ordered.

They waited on the hard floor while security accessed the DJ booth from another door in the wall. The men were gone just moments and the music abruptly stopped.

Another security guard, a female, came back and yelled, "The shooter is gone, but we need an ambulance. The DJ is alive but unconscious."

The man who had told them to stay down knelt beside them and helped them to their feet while speaking into a radio, asking for an ambulance to come to the scene.

"Angie!" a voice bellowed from below. "Mel!"

Angie and Mel exchanged a nervous glance. Roach gave them a disgusted look and walked over to the railing.

"They're fine," he called down. "They're right here."

In seconds, Tate came barreling at the two of them with the ferocity of a grizzly bear. He was pale, looking wild-eyed and terrified. Without pausing, he swept Mel and Angie into his arms in a hug that suffocated.

Mel felt tears burn her eyes. She hugged him back hard and then she began to blubber.

She could hear Angie beside her, also sobbing, saying "I'm sorry. I'm sorry. I'm so, so sorry."

Tate let them go. He stepped back and looked them over as if to be certain that they were all right. Then he looked at Roach.

The two men stared at each other and then Tate held out his hand. Roach clasped his hand in a solid shake, and then he gave him a solid thump on the shoulder.

"She's all yours, Tate," Roach said. "I never thought I'd say this, but she's just too much for me. I'll be at the bar drinking if you want to join me."

"Thanks," Tate said. "I might."

They watched as Roach joined his bandmates and manager at the bar. When Tate turned to face them, Mel expected his wrath to be unleashed. She was wrong. It wasn't anger that Tate let loose. It was worse. It was guilt.

He took one of their hands in each of his. "I think I aged five years when I got to the bar and heard there had been gunshots." He looked at Mel. "You're my best friend. I don't know what I'd do if I lost you."

Mel felt her throat close up. She would have apologized, but she couldn't seem to unclench her vocal cords. Instead, she squeezed his hand really tight and hoped he understood her unspoken apology.

"And you," he said as he turned to Angie. "You are my life. I can't believe you would put yourself in harm's way and not tell me, no matter how mad you are at me."

Tears were coursing down Angie's cheeks, ruining her makeup and making her look like she was just a kid playing dress up.

"I'm so sorry," she choked.

Tate let go of Mel's hand and took Angie's free one in his so that they were holding hands and facing each other.

" 'Love means never having to say you're sorry,' " Tate said as he pressed his forehead to hers.

"Awww," Angie bawled. Sobs wracked her frame, and she used their clasped hands to wipe the tears dripping off her chin. "*Love Story*. Really? I can't believe you just used the stupidest movie quote ever on me."

She cried harder and Tate waited patiently while she got it all out.

"I really didn't think anything was going to happen. I would never have put myself or Mel at risk. You know that, right? I love you too much, way too much, to ever leave you, Tate."

"I know," he said. Tate let go of her hands and cupped her face. He wiped her tears away with his thumbs and kissed her lips. "I love you, Angie DeLaura, but we're going to have a long chat about acceptable risks and the lines of communication in this relationship. Yes?"

"Yes," Angie agreed. She looked crestfallen. "I thought, no, I really believed that it wasn't me that they were after."

"It wasn't," Detective Manny Martinez said as he joined them.

"You're here!" Mel exclaimed. She moved over to let Manny join their little group. He crossed his arms over his chest and glowered at her.

"What?" she asked. She self-consciously tugged at the back of her dress to make sure her rear was covered. It was.

"It wasn't Angie they were after, it was you," he said.

Thirty

"Now don't scare her just to get even," Uncle Stan said as he joined them. He was huffing and puffing, probably from the climb up the stairs.

"I'm not," Manny began but Stan interrupted.

"Yeah, you are, because seeing her here scared the snot out of you. Me, too," he said. He swept Mel into a fierce hug. "I'm glad you're okay, kiddo, quick thinking on the tackle, but if you ever do anything this stupid again, I swear I'll arrest you and throw away the key."

"I won't. I promise," Mel said. She felt like a sponge absorbing her uncle's solid strength into her shaking hands and knocking knees.

When Stan released her, Manny stepped forward and hugged her close, too. He pressed his face against her hair as if to reacquaint himself with the scent and feel of her.

When he stepped back, he looked like he wanted, well, more, but he just shook his head and cleared his throat.

"What he said," he growled.

Mel saw the concern on his face and it was heartwarming, until she realized there was no way he could be here so quickly unless . . .

"How did you know to be here?" Mel asked. She looked at Manny. "I only texted you a little while ago, and I did not mention that we were doing this."

Neither Stan nor Manny spoke. She raised her eyebrows. "You followed us, didn't you?"

"There might have been an undercover detail on Angie that tracked you from the mall to the club," Uncle Stan said. He did not look the least bit repentant, and given how it had played out, Mel didn't figure she had any moral high ground.

"Did you catch the shooter?" Mel asked.

Stan and Manny exchanged a look. Mel knew that look. It was the sort of look people make when they are trying to figure out how to phrase bad news.

"You didn't, did you?" she asked.

"No," Stan growled. "We had uniforms at every exit. He just disappeared like a freaking ghost."

"Unless he's still here," Tate said. He clutched Angie close and said, "Sorry, guys, if you have questions for the girls, you're going to have to ask them at home. I am getting these two out of here."

"I'll help," Manny agreed.

Uncle Stan scanned the nightclub as if looking for the barrel of a gun to poke out at them. He gave them a somber nod. "Take them through the back. Go!"

Manny hustled them down a staircase that was crawling with uniformed police officers. Once outside, he signaled two officers to escort them to Tate's car. The two men in vests bookended them until they were inside the vehicle.

"Take them straight home," Manny said. He looked at Mel. "Text me as soon as you're safe."

"I promise," she said. She leaned forward and put a hand on his cheek just to let him know she cared. She hated to think of him out there with a shooter at large.

"You saved several lives tonight, including your own," he said. He looked chagrined. "That's not how this—" he gestured between them—"is supposed to work."

"Maybe not," she said. She thought about the shooter being trapped inside. "Promise you'll be careful."

"Always," he said. He glanced at Angie, looking grim. "I know you were hoping that you weren't the target, but clearly, the shooter is gunning for you. I'll be sending a team to your house to watch over you and they'll be staying until the shooter is caught."

Tate shook Manny's hand. "Thanks."

"Be careful," Manny said.

Mel only got a glance at his face before Tate drove away, but as always, things remained complicated between her and the detective.

"I think we should book a room at a hotel," Tate said. "You know, someplace with an armed guard at the gate and vicious dogs roaming the grounds."

"My house will be fine," Angie said. "I imagine the brothers are already there, armed with righteous brotherly rage and in full lecture mode."

Tate gave her a sidelong glance that Mel took to mean yes, the brothers were there, and he was not admitting to being the one who called them.

"Drop me off at the bakery, please," she said.

Angie whipped her head around, and Tate frowned at her in the rearview mirror. They both opened their mouths to argue, but Mel held up her hand.

"I need to go home. I need to check on Captain Jack and the bakery, and I am not up for company right now."

"But . . ." Tate clearly was not getting her need for quiet.

"Tony's cameras are still on at the bakery," she said. "I'm sure he'll be monitoring my every movement."

"But what if—" Angie began but Mel interrupted her.

"I'll be fine," she said. "The shooter isn't after me."

There. She said it. Angie pressed her lips together. There was no argument to be made. Their mission to find the blue-haired zombie woman was futile. It hadn't been Scott Streubel trying to whack his wife and blame it on the mob. The shooter had been aiming for Angie and had killed Kristin by mistake, and everyone knew it.

Angie looked like she would argue, but Mel wasn't up for that.

"If you don't drop me off now I'll just catch a cab from your place, which would be infinitely more dangerous, don't you think?"

Angie and Tate exchanged a look. They did not look happy with her choice. Too bad. She was feeling borderline hysterical and needed to hold her cat and sob into her pillow.

"Fine, but it's under protest," Angie said.

"Noted," Mel said.

Tate dropped her off at the lot behind her house and then

walked her up the stairs. Mel jogged up the steps as best as she could in her ridiculously high heels, because she didn't want Angie left alone in the car. The whole night had shaken her right down to her strappy shoes, and the need to wail and moan was becoming too hard to keep a lid on.

At the door, Tate grabbed her arm and hugged her close. When he stepped back, he wagged his finger at her.

"Any weird noise, a footstep, a cough, a sigh, and you call me right away. Got it?"

"Yes," she said. She hugged him quick and then shooed him away. "Take Angie home and text me when you get there."

Tate nodded. He turned and bolted down the stairs as soon as Mel shut the door behind her.

Captain Jack came skidding across the floor almost as if his feline senses had told him something traumatic had happened to his kitty mama. Mel scooped him close and then buried her nose in his fur while he purred like an idling V-8 engine.

Mel felt the shiver start at the top of her head and rocket through her body like a summer storm, short but powerful. She'd thought she'd be doubled up and sobbing, but instead the memory of the moment she realized there was someone behind the blue glass wall kept replaying in her head like a film loop. Something was bothering her about it, but she couldn't figure out what.

She crossed her apartment with Captain Jack in her arms. The only light she turned on was the living room light. She felt less exposed that way. She didn't really think anyone was after her, but she couldn't help but be wary.

She glanced at the window but since it was dark outside all she could see was her reflection, and her slinky dress sure gave her a heck of a reflection. That's when it hit her. The air pushed out of her lungs in a whoosh. The shadow she had seen behind the blue glass had been the silhouette of a woman.

It was a woman who was the shooter! This changed everything. None of Tucci's goons that Manny had told her about were women, so who was she and how did she fit in? Mel racked her brain trying to think of any women tied to the Tucci case. There were none, at least none that anyone knew about.

Then a horrible thought struck, and her hands started to shake. What if it was the woman Scott had been kissing? What if she was the shooter? And what if she was still gunning for Angie, trying to make it look like it was a professional hit to keep the suspicion off of Scott? She had to tell Joe.

She lifted Captain Jack up to her face. The black patch of fur over his eye gave him the air of being one who considers the rules more as guidelines. She knew he'd understand what she had to do.

"I have to tell him," she said. "He's the one who will know if Frank Tucci has a female thug on his payroll or whether this woman is in league with Scott."

Jack cocked his head to the side and shoved the top of his head into her hand. She took it as an affirmative.

"I'm not calling him," she said. "What if the phone is tapped or he's not in his office. Or worse, what if Scott answers? I don't think I could fake any sympathy or friendliness right now. No, I need to talk to Joe face-to-face. If anyone comes by, tell them I'm in the bathroom."

As she put him down on the counter, she was pretty sure he winked at her. She locked the door behind her and hurried down the stairs. She couldn't help but feel as if eyes were watching her, but then she remembered Tony's camera. This was not going to go over well with Tate and Angie. She really didn't care. The need to see Joe was overriding every lick of common sense she had.

Mel knew the first place to look was Joe's office. He had a couch in the front room that he used for power naps. If the trial was as dicey as the media had reported, she knew every non-courtroom moment he had would be spent in his office. When they had first begun dating he'd had an all-consuming case, so she knew the drill.

She hopped into her Mini and sped over to Joe's office. It was located in downtown Phoenix in a square-shaped building that she'd always assumed was built that way to intimidate criminals or wannabe criminals.

Although it was probably locked up for the night, she figured she could either charm the security guard into letting her in or call Joe when she was right outside and give him no choice but to let her in.

The streets were quiet at this time of night, and she managed to get to Joe's office in no time. She parked on the street, grateful that there was no major sporting event clogging up the available parking. She hurried to the entrance of the building and yanked on the doors. They were locked.

She pressed her hands up against the glass, feeling like a kid checking out a candy store after hours. The security desk was empty so she couldn't even flag someone over to open the door.

She fumbled for her cell phone. She still had Joe in her contacts list. She tried his cell phone first hoping he'd answer. On the fourth ring, he did.

"Mel, you shouldn't be calling me," he said. He sounded tired. "It's too dangerous. Cell phones can be compromised."

"Given that a bullet almost made Swiss cheese out of me an hour ago, the cell phone thing, yeah, not really that scary," she said. "But standing outside your office in the dark right now, yeah, kind of creepy."

"What?" Joe shouted. "Hang on!"

In less time than it took to order a pizza, Mel saw a security guard racing towards the door. Nice to see her man, former man, whatever, had some pull.

She recognized Jesus Gonzales from when she used to come downtown to have lunch with Joe. He had a tight military crew cut and was broad shouldered, making the seams on his security uniform strain. Mel hadn't thought she was nervous until he unlocked the door and hustled her inside. As he closed and locked the door behind her, she felt her shoulders drop from around her ears.

"Hi, Jesus," she said.

He gave her a flat look with no returning smile. "You shouldn't be here."

"I know but it's important," she said.

"Mel!"

She turned towards the bank of elevators and there was Joe. She didn't pause to think about what she was doing. Despite the ridiculous height of her heels and the very real probability that she might break her leg on the polished floor, she broke into a gimpy run. Joe surpassed her speed, sprinting towards her in an unbuttoned, necktie-askew, disheveled state that warmed her heart.

They met in the middle of the lobby. Joe crushed her to him in a hug that left her short of breath in the best possible way. Then he kissed her. It consumed her from the inside out like a fire burning away all of the oxygen in her bloodstream. She didn't care.

Mel clung to him. When bullets had zipped overhead, she had realized with the clarity that only comes from an unfortunate staring contest with death that the only regret she had in life was not being with Joe.

"Ahem."

Mel wasn't sure how many times Jesus had cleared his throat to get their attention, but she suspected it was more than once. She broke the kiss before Joe did, but when she would have stepped back, he kept her close.

Then he whispered in her ear, "Your phone call about stopped my heart, but the dress is going to kill me for sure."

Mel pressed her forehead against his. "Oh, Joe."

"Not to break it up, but you two might want to get out of sight of the windows," Jesus said.

"Yes, of course," Joe said. He moved away from her with great reluctance, but twined his fingers with hers as he led her to the elevator. "She's coming with me."

"Understood," Jesus said. "I have my radio if you need me."

Joe led Mel into the elevator. When the doors closed and it began to rise, his gaze moved over her in a way that made Mel blush.

"Sorry," he said. His grin belied his apology but Mel didn't mind. "It's just—wow!"

Mel grinned. "Thanks. I went to Roach's CD release party with Angie tonight so we had to dress the part."

The heat in his warm brown eyes went from sexy to seriously, crazy mad in a nanosecond. She could tell because when he spoke, his words came out with ice crystals forming on them.

"You went where?"

Mel blew out a breath. Moment of truth. Best to get it over with as quickly as possible. She took a big breath hoping to get it all out in one long, detail-loaded sentence.

"The Bonehead Investigators, Leo and Atom, brothers and very cute, told me that they saw Scott kissing a blue-haired zombie at the zombie walk. Angie and I thought this might bust the shooting case wide open, thinking that Scott used the zombie walk to whack his wife and blame it on the mob to cover his affair with this other woman. Angie is losing chunks of hair. It's bad. So when we saw the blue-haired zombie was invited for a photo op at Roach's CD release party, we decided to go."

Joe opened his mouth to speak but Mel didn't give him the chance.

"Anyway, at the party when we were about to ask Roach about the blue-haired zombie, I saw a shadow and instinctively knocked Angie and Roach to the ground. A couple of bullets whizzed overhead but missed everyone, thank god. Tate, Manny, and Stan showed up and they hustled us out of there. Angie is pretty upset that it looks like she was the target after all, but she's got Tate, the brothers, and an entourage looking after her, so I think she'll be all right. But now I think we were wrong since I realized the shooter was a woman."

The doors to the elevator opened, and Joe just stood there staring at her as if trying to comprehend what all she had said. As the doors began to close, Mel shoved her arm in the opening to stop them.

"Joe?" she asked.

He shook himself like a dog after a bath and gestured for her to go first. Then he followed her. Mel noted he did not take her hand for the short walk down the hall to his office.

The cubicles that surrounded the open floor space outside his office were deserted. There was an ominous feeling to the rows and rows of empty desks. She had only been here during the day before when the room buzzed and hummed with activity. She wondered if Joe felt it, too, or if after so many late nights he was used to it and probably preferred it.

Joe pushed open his office door. He gestured for her to go inside, and Mel went. When he followed he crossed his arms over his chest with such careful precision that she wondered if it was taking everything he had not to blow up and yell at her. But that was silly; Joe never yelled, well, except for that one time when he was dressed like a redneck, but she wasn't sure that counted. He was the chief negotiator and peacekeeper of the DeLaura family. In all the time they'd been dating, he'd never raised his voice.

"Sit," he said.

Mel's eyes went wide. She glanced at the hem of her dress. Yeah, no, sitting was out. How did women wear these micromini things? She liked to sit, she wished she could sit, but if she did, she had no doubt Joe would see more of her than perhaps he wanted to at this juncture.

"No thank you," she said as if it had been optional.

Joe strode towards her, stopped just in front of her, and loomed.

"I am really struggling here," he said. "I am torn between kissing you again and yelling at you until my vocal cords bleed and I. Am. Not. A. Yeller."

He looked frazzled and a little bit deranged, and Mel

couldn't help but feel her heart go *smoosh* as she took in his agitated state and knew it was her fault. Mostly.

"Do I get to weigh in on this?" she asked.

"No," he said. He shoved both of his hands into his hair. "Cupcake, if anything had happened to you or Angie . . ."

Mel stepped forward and grabbed his arms, forcing him to look at her. "But it didn't."

He blew out a breath and his face sagged.

"I've been watching Scott struggle with Kristin's death every single day, and all I can think about is . . ." He grabbed her and held her close. "I can't even say it."

"Then don't," Mel said. She wrapped her arms around him and pressed her cheek on his shoulder. It felt so good to be close to him again.

"Mel," Joe whispered her name. She was so tall in her shoes that his lips were close to her ear, and the brush of his breath against her skin distracted her from her purpose.

"Yeah?"

"Why are you here?" he asked.

"Hmm?" she asked.

"Why are you here?"

Mel shook her head, trying to clear it. At the moment, the only thing she could think was that the need to see him had been all consuming. But that wasn't it. There had been something else. Something important. She stepped back from him.

"Oh, yeah," she said. "The shooter. I have to know, does Tucci have any female goons?"

"Huh?" He frowned at her and she got the feeling he had been hoping she was here for a different reason. "What do you mean?"

"The shooter at the club," she said again. "It was a woman."

"Did you tell the police this?" he asked.

"I texted Uncle Stan on my way over—at a red light," she said. "But then I figured you know everything about Tucci, so you would know for sure, but I didn't want to ask on the phone because—"

"Let me get this straight," he interrupted. Mel noticed that he sounded very disgruntled. "You thought you'd race over here and put yourself in harm's way out in the open when you could have just called me."

"Yes, I could have called you," she said. "But I felt under the circumstances that it was imperative to talk to you directly."

Joe narrowed his eyes. "Why?"

Mel glanced around the empty office. "Because what if Angie and I were right? Given that the shooter was a woman, what if Scott was having an affair with the blue-haired woman, and this whole thing was just a ruse to get rid of his wife?"

"What?" a voice cried from the door.

Mel whipped around to see Scott standing there.

Thirty-one

"How can you say that?" Scott asked. He looked equal parts grief struck and outraged.

Mel felt a spasm of guilt but she shook it off. No, the boys had seen him with a woman, and the two of them could have plotted the whole thing. That blue-haired zombie could be the female shooter, killing Scott's wife so she could have him and then going after Angie again to make it look like a mob hit.

"I know you were with another woman at the zombie walk," Mel said.

Scott gave her a confused look. Then he looked at Joe, who shrugged. Mel gave Joe an irritated glance and then turned back to Scott.

"Someone saw you," she said. "You were cozied up with

a woman with blue hair, and you were seen fooling around together."

Mel thought it spoke very well of her that she didn't add, *So there!* to her accusation.

Scott frowned at her as if he was trying to figure out what language she was speaking. Then he raised his eyebrows and turned away from them, walking out of the room.

Mel nudged Joe with her elbow and gestured for him to follow Scott. What if he tried to get away? Joe rubbed the spot where she'd poked him, but he made no move to follow.

"What if he goes to get a weapon?" she asked.

"He won't," he said. "He didn't hurt his wife."

"But there was that other woman at the zombie festival, and he was seen with her," Mel said. "What if she killed Kristin so that she and Scott could be together?"

"She didn't," Scott said, returning to the room. "And I know this because that blue-haired woman is my wife."

"Ah," Mel gasped. "You're married to two women?"

"In a manner of speaking," Scott said. He gave Joe a questioning look and Joe, after a short hesitation, nodded.

"She'll keep digging until she figures it out; you may as well tell her," he said.

Scott flipped open a two-sided wallet and held it out facing her. One side had a gold shield, and the other bore the unmistakable letters *FBI*.

Mel glanced over the wallet at him. "What is that?"

"My badge," he said. "I'm Special Agent Streubel, and Kristin, who was posing as my wife, was Special Agent O'Rourke."

Mel looked at Joe. "You knew?"

He nodded. "Yeah, they've been undercover working the Tucci case from day one."

"Oh, my god, Kristin was your *partner* not your wife," Mel said. "And your wedding was just part of the cover."

"Yeah," Scott said. "And Lauren, the blue-haired zombie, really is my wife. We thought if we could just see each other for a few minutes after so many months apart . . . what could it hurt?" He gave a harsh laugh. "Quite a bit it seems, since it got my partner killed."

Mel felt lower than dirt. Joe put a hand on her shoulder and squeezed. It was a gesture of comfort that she knew she didn't deserve. She hung her head.

"I am so sorry." She glanced up through her blond bangs to look at Scott. What she saw shattered her more than any anger would have. He looked desolate.

"No," he said. "You've been around Joe and this office enough to know that it usually is the spouse or significant other who is guilty. It was a natural conclusion, especially since you heard about me with my real wife."

"I'm sorry," Mel said. "Ugh, I'm such an idiot. But if the blue-haired woman, I'm sorry, Lauren, wasn't the shooter, then . . ." She turned to Joe and asked, "Did Tucci have any female goons?"

"Not as far as I know," Joe said. "He was pretty old school."

Mel felt a cold spot start on the top of her head and slowly drift down to her neck and shoulders, until her whole body was icy cold and she shivered.

"Maybe Frank Tucci was old school, but his son Vincent is not," she said. "I think I know who Kristin's shooter was, and I think I know who shot at us tonight."

"What?" Scott asked. "Who?"

"Yes, Melanie, who?"

Joe, Mel, and Scott all spun to face the door. In strode Vincent Tucci with the buxom restaurant hostess Heather at his side.

"Her," Mel said and she pointed at Heather.

Joe tried to push her behind him. She was having none of it. She refused to budge and stared at Vincent and Heather. As Heather stepped through the doorway and was backlit by the light in the hallway, Mel gasped. That was definitely the silhouette she had seen.

Vincent let out a weary sigh. "I am so sorry we won't be carrying your cupcakes at the restaurant, Melanie, but I'm sure you understand. It's not personal just business."

Joe frowned at Mel.

"What is he talking about?" Joe asked. "What do you want, Tucci, and how did you get in here?"

Heather pulled a very lethal-looking Glock out of the pink designer bag on her shoulder.

"That's Heather, she's the hostess at Frank and Mickey's," Mel said. "And apparently she's Vincent's hit man, excuse me, hit woman as well. Heather is the one who fired shots at us at Roach's party, and I'm betting she killed Kristin, too."

"It was you!" Scott said. "You killed my partner."

Vincent gave him a flat stare. "Your wife, you mean? Yes, that was an unfortunate mix-up since she thought she was shooting Mr. DeLaura's sister."

Mel felt woozy, as if all of the blood had just drained out of her head. Vincent was behind the shooting. Vincent had been trying to kill Angie all along.

"Of course, Melanie would have been the target if we'd known there was still a relationship between you two," Vincent said. He looked at Joe. "Very smart to dump her before the trial started."

Mel could hear Joe's teeth grinding, but his voice when he spoke was perfectly even, as if he wasn't fazed at all by having a gun pointed at his head.

"Why are you here?" he asked. Then he held up his hand. "Wait, let me guess. You want to be sure that Daddy dearest goes to jail so you can take over the family business?"

Vincent winked at him. "Yes, and this is so much easier than killing him myself. After Heather shoots the three of you, we'll stage it to look like one of my father's goons did it. That should ensure lethal injection for the old man."

Mel slid her hand into Joe's. If they were about to meet their maker, she wanted to do it together.

"This time don't miss," Vincent said and he slapped Heather on the butt as he left the room.

"That was your fault," Heather said. She looked at Mel in disgust. "I had a perfect shot until you took her down. Truthfully, I would have felt bad shooting Roach. I just love the Sewers. But since I knew you had seen me, or at least the outline of me, I knew I was going to have to take you out. We followed you from the bakery. Vincent figured this was even better. An innocent cupcake baker and two county attorneys murdered, yeah, everyone will want Frank's blood for this."

She started to hum the tune "Angie" by the Sewers and punctuated it by racking the slide on the gun, preparing to shoot. Mel wondered how badly the bullet would hurt. She wondered if Heather would shoot her in the head or the chest. She wondered if Joe knew how much she loved him.

She squeezed his hand with hers three times, meaning, *I love you.* Her throat closed up when Joe immediately did it back. At least he knew.

Heather appeared to be having a hard time choosing. She swiveled the gun wildly between them, and Mel realized she was practicing how she was going to spray the bullets. She had the gun pointed at Mel when Scott shouted and leapt forward.

The gun fired, but he was already on top of Heather, taking her down like a lion charging an antelope. Joe yanked Mel down hard and shoved her behind his big metal desk before diving back into the fray between Heather and Scott. Mel peeked around the edge to see if she could help. It wasn't necessary.

Scott pressed Heather's gun hand to the ground, and Joe used his full body weight to pin it. Mel heard the crunch of bones, and Heather screamed. Joe grabbed the gun, and Scott pulled some plastic restraints out of his pocket. In moments Heather's wrists and ankles were bound, and she sat sobbing and cradling her injured arm. Scott took the gun and pointed it at Heather.

Mel crawled out from behind the desk and crouched close to Joe and Scott. She noted that Scott's shirt had a bullet hole but there was no blood. She looked at Joe.

"Kevlar," he said.

Scott leaned in close to Heather, and in a voice Mel barely recognized as belonging to the affable county attorney he'd portrayed, he said, "I should kill you."

Joe held out a hand to Mel and helped her to her feet. She felt him tugging on the back of her dress and when she looked at him, he said, "Your dress, uh, yeah, you're good now."

She didn't think she'd ever seen Joe blush before. She leaned against him and said, "Thanks."

Three men and a woman, all of who reeked of being federal agents, burst into the office. Scott handed off Heather, looking as if he'd still really like to shoot her or at least torture her a bit.

"Vincent Tucci is in the building somewhere," Scott said. "We have to locate him. Casey, stay with these two. Javier, take our shooter into custody. The rest of you, let's split up and comb the building floor by floor."

In a blink the room was empty except Casey, who was a stocky bald man, standing in the doorway, watching the hallway like he'd shoot anything that pissed him off.

Mel wanted desperately to take her shoes off, but she knew she'd never get them back on again and who knew if she was going to need to run again. Instead, she looked at Joe and said, "I think you have some explaining to do."

Thirty-two

Joe rubbed his eyes. He looked more tired than Mel had ever seen him, and she had seen him do this before, working consecutive late nights to the point of being stupid tired.

"You can just give me the synopsis for now," she said.

He gave her a closed-lip smile that was full of fondness and gratitude.

"A few months ago, the death threats started," Joe said. "They appeared to be coming from Frank Tucci's associates, but we couldn't nail them down. I knew I had to close off from the family and you to keep you from being targets. I figured my family was still in danger, so we've been hypervigilant."

"So I noticed," Mel said. "It might have been easier if you told us the whole story."

"I didn't want to risk it," Joe said. He ran his knuckles

down her cheek. "I couldn't bear the thought of you being alone and afraid."

Mel rolled her eyes but she had to admit that deep down, she was touched by his concern.

She opened her mouth to ask another question, when a ruckus sounded outside. Casey assumed a fighter stance with his gun aimed.

"Stop or I'll shoot!" he shouted.

"No don't; I'm security. I have my badge. I'll show you."

Mel looked at Joe. "That's not Jesus's voice."

Joe stepped forward to look, pushing her down as he went. Mel refused to go. She popped up and followed him to the door.

Casey kept his gun trained on the man, who had his head down while he fished through his pocket for his ID. Joe stepped around Casey, who began to argue, but it was over in two hits. Joe hitting Vincent and Vincent hitting the ground.

"Call Scott," Joe ordered as he shook out his knuckles. "We got him."

Casey called it in to his radio, and the feds came at a run. By the time they got there, Vincent was trussed up just as Heather had been, except he had the beginnings of a purple shiner forming on his cheekbone.

"I'll sue you!" Vincent yelled. "I'll get your ass for assault and harassment and I'll walk. You can't prove anything."

"Shut up," Scott said and he walked over and popped Vincent right in the mouth. Vincent sagged against Casey, who'd been holding him upright. He slid right through Casey's arm and smacked his head on the floor on the way down. "That was for Kristin."

Joe gave him a look and Scott shrugged.

"Heather already rolled over on him. Funny how the thought of not getting to the hospital in time to have her arm set and thus being deformed for life made her go on record so fast for the murder of Kristin O'Rourke on Vincent Tucci's orders."

"Wow, I think the gunshot made my hearing go, because I can't hear a word you're saying," Joe said.

"Did she . . ." Mel hesitated. She wasn't sure how to ask this question, but she needed to know. "Did she kill Kristin because she thought she was Angie?"

Scott met her gaze and he blew out a breath. Then he nodded. Mel felt a rush of hot tears press against her eyelids.

"I'm sorry," she said.

"Don't be." Scott's voice was gritty. "Kristin died in the line of duty, and she will be honored just as a fallen agent should be. It's who she was. It's what we do."

Guilt and anguish were having a fistfight in Mel's chest. Guilt because she realized how close they'd come to losing Angie and how relieved she was that they hadn't, and anguish because the FBI had lost one hell of a special agent.

"We'll be there," Joe said. "And I'll do everything I can to see Vincent Tucci pays for everything he's done."

Scott nodded. He cleared his throat and studied the floor for a moment, obviously trying to get himself together. Then he looked up at Mel and Joe. He held out a hand to Joe and they shook hands.

"My law degree is a little rusty," Scott said. "But it's been a real pleasure watching you work."

"If you ever want to retire the shield, I'd take you on my team in a heartbeat," Joe said. "I'm glad you got your man."

"Me, too," Scott said. "I'm going to have Agent Gallegos

take your statements, but then you're free to go. It's been a hell of a night."

By the time they got out of there another two hours had passed. The arches of Mel's feet hurt so badly it was all she could do not to hobble, but the thought of walking barefoot on the city streets really didn't work for her, so she limped her way to her car. Joe took her keys out of her hand, insisting on driving her home.

"But how will you get home from there?" she asked.

He didn't answer and Mel felt her face get hot. Was he thinking he was spending the night? She wasn't sure what to make of that. Well, she did. Her insides were doing cartwheels, but given how confused things were between them, she wasn't sure that was an appropriate response.

Still, she said nothing and let him navigate the dark streets back to Old Town Scottsdale. It was a school night, so while there were still people milling about, it wasn't with the determined party air the weekenders maintained. Joe parked in the lot behind the bakery and together they crossed the alley to the steps that led up to Mel's apartment.

"Do you have time for coffee or a cupcake?" Mel asked. She realized she didn't want him to go, if that was his plan, so yeah, she was more than willing to sugar and caffeine him up if it meant she got more time with him, time to talk, decompress, or just be.

Joe nodded. "Yeah, I think I have time."

Mel took her keys and unlocked the door to the back of the bakery. She pulled the door wide but before she could step inside, Joe stopped her by taking her arm and turning her to face him.

"I wanted to ask you—" He paused.

"Yes?" Mel prompted.

He looked uncertain for a second and then he said, "That question you asked me a few weeks ago. Is that offer still open?"

Mel's ears started ringing with a sound like an air horn blasting. She shook her head, trying to clear it. She did not want to make a fool of herself by assuming the wrong thing.

"Are we talking the 'daily preferred flavor of cupcake' question or the one-time-only 'will you marry me' question?"

"The second one," Joe said.

Mel had to read his lips because the ringing in her ears was getting louder. She was about to open her mouth to answer him when the pink cupcake van owned by the shop came careening around the corner of the alley and screeched to a halt beside them.

The ringing in Mel's ears stopped, and she realized it was Marty and Oz who were hanging out the back window, brandishing air horns that had been making the racket.

The passenger side window rolled down, and Angie stuck her head out.

"There you are!" she cried. A huge smile lit up her face and she gestured for Mel and Joe to get in the van. "Come on, you two, get in! Tate and I are eloping!"

Recipes

Strawberry Brains

A Lemon Cake with Strawberry Icing
Piped to Look like a Brain

1 cup (2 sticks) unsalted butter, softened
2 cups granulated sugar, divided
4 extra-large eggs, room temperature
⅓ cup grated lemon zest (6–8 large lemons)
3 cups flour
½ teaspoon baking powder
½ teaspoon baking soda
1 teaspoon salt
¼ cup freshly squeezed lemon juice
¾ cup buttermilk, room temperature
1 teaspoon pure vanilla extract

Preheat oven to 350°. Put liners in muffin tin and set aside. Cream butter and 2 cups granulated sugar until fluffy—about 5 minutes. With the mixer on medium speed, add eggs, one at a time, and lemon zest. In medium bowl, sift together flour, baking powder, baking soda, and salt. In another bowl, combine lemon juice, buttermilk, and vanilla. Add flour and buttermilk mixtures alternately to the batter, beginning and ending with the flour. Use an ice-cream scoop to fill paper-lined cupcake pan. Bake 20 minutes. Makes 24.

‿ ╱ ╲ ╲ ╲

Strawberry Buttercream

½ cup (1 stick) salted butter, softened
½ cup (1 stick) unsalted butter, softened
4 cups sifted confectioners' sugar
1 cup finely chopped fresh strawberries

In large bowl, cream butter. Gradually add sugar, one cup at a time, beating well on medium speed. Scrape sides of bowl often. Add strawberries, and beat at medium speed until smooth. Makes 3 cups of icing.

Pipe icing with a fine pastry tip in squiggly lines to resemble brains. Yum.

Dark Chocolate Demise

A Chocolate Cake with Chocolate Chips
and Chocolate Icing, with a
Chocolate Coffin Lid on Top

1 ⅓ cups all-purpose flour
¼ teaspoon baking soda
2 teaspoons baking powder
¾ cup unsweetened cocoa powder
⅛ teaspoon salt
3 tablespoons butter, softened
1 ½ cups white sugar
2 eggs
¾ teaspoon vanilla extract
1 cup milk
1 bag semisweet chocolate chips

Preheat oven to 350°. Put liners in muffin tin and set aside. Sift together flour, baking powder, baking soda, cocoa powder, and salt. Set aside. In a large bowl, cream together butter and sugar until well blended. Add eggs one at a time, beating well with each addition, then stir in vanilla. Add the flour mixture alternately with the milk; beat well. Toss chocolate chips with flour and then add to the mixture. Bake 15–17 minutes. Makes 12.

Chocolate Icing

½ cup (1 stick) salted butter, softened
½ cup (1 stick) unsalted butter, softened
1 teaspoon vanilla extract
4 cups sifted confectioners' sugar
6 tablespoons unsweetened cocoa powder
2 tablespoons milk

In large bowl, sift sugar and cocoa powder together and set aside. In medium bowl, cream butter and vanilla. Gradually add sugar, one cup at a time, beating well on medium speed. Scrape sides of bowl often. Add milk, and beat at medium speed until light and fluffy. Makes 3 cups of icing.

Decorate with chocolate coffin lids or other ghoulish cupcake toppers.

`' / ' \`

Vanilla Eyeballs

Vanilla Cake with Vanilla Icing,
with a Gummy Eyeball Stuck in the Top

¾ cup butter
1 ½ cups sugar
2 eggs
1 ½ teaspoons vanilla extract

2 ½ teaspoons baking powder
¼ teaspoon salt
2 ½ cups flour
1 ¼ cups milk

Preheat oven to 350°. Sift together flour, baking powder, and salt. Set aside. Cream butter and sugar at medium speed, add two eggs, and beat until smooth. Beat in extract. Add in dry ingredients; beat until smooth. Fill cupcake liners ⅔ full. Bake until golden brown, about 20 minutes. Makes 24.

Vanilla Buttercream Frosting

½ cup (1 stick) salted butter, softened
½ cup (1 stick) unsalted butter, softened
1 teaspoon clear vanilla extract
4 cups sifted confectioners' sugar
2 tablespoons milk

In large bowl, cream butter. Add vanilla. Gradually add sugar, one cup at a time, beating well on medium speed. Scrape sides of bowl often. Add milk, and beat at medium speed until light and fluffy. Keep bowl covered with a damp cloth until ready to use. Makes 3 cups of icing.

Frost cupcakes with vanilla buttercream and place a gummy eyeball on top.

Marshmallow Mummies

Chocolate Cake with a Marshmallow Filling,
with Vanilla Icing Piped to Look like Mummy
Bandages with Two Candy Eyes Peeking Out

Chocolate Cupcake

2 ¾ cups flour
1 teaspoon baking soda
1 teaspoon baking powder
½ teaspoon salt
2 cups sugar
1 cup unsalted butter, room temperature
6 ounces semisweet chocolate, melted and cooled to
    room temperature
4 extra-large eggs, room temperature
2 tablespoons vanilla extract
1 cup sour cream
1 cup water

Preheat oven to 325°. Line 24 muffin tins with cupcake liners
and set aside. In medium bowl, whisk together flour, baking
soda, baking powder, and salt, and set aside. In the bowl of an
electric mixer fitted with the paddle attachment, cream
together sugar and butter until light and fluffy. Add chocolate
and beat on medium speed until well combined. Add eggs,

one at a time, mixing well after each addition. Add sour cream and vanilla and mix until well combined. With mixer on low speed, add the flour mixture and water, alternating between the two. Beat until just combined. Fill prepared muffin cups ¾ full with batter. Transfer to oven and bake 20 minutes, or until a toothpick inserted into the center of a cupcake comes out clean. Rotate the cupcake pans halfway through for even baking. Let cool completely before filling. Makes 24.

Marshmallow Filling

2 teaspoons hot water
¼ teaspoon salt
1 jar (7 ounces) marshmallow cream
½ cup shortening
½ teaspoon vanilla extract
⅓ cup confectioners' sugar

In small bowl, combine hot water and salt; stir until dissolved. Set aside to cool. In large bowl, beat marshmallow cream, shortening, and vanilla until fluffy. Gradually add sugar and saltwater mixture. Beat again until fluffy. Using a melon baller, scoop out the center of the cooled cupcakes and put the scoops of cake aside. Fill a pastry bag with marshmallow filling and insert into the hole in the cupcake. Gently squeeze the bag to fill each cupcake and replace the scoop of cake in the hole to seal the marshmallow filling inside.

Vanilla Buttercream Frosting

½ cup (1 stick) salted butter, softened
½ cup (1 stick) unsalted butter, softened
1 teaspoon clear vanilla extract
4 cups sifted confectioners' sugar
2 tablespoons milk

In large bowl, cream butter. Add vanilla. Gradually add sugar, one cup at a time, beating well on medium speed. Scrape sides of bowl often. Add milk and beat at medium speed until light and fluffy. Makes 3 cups of icing.

Using a smooth basket-weave pastry tip, pipe the icing across the cupcake, making it look like mummy bandages. Use candy eyes or any small round candy to give it an especially ghoulish look.

Tiramisu Cupcakes

A Delicate Sponge Cake Flavored with
Coffee and Rum, Topped with a Creamy
Mascarpone and Whipped Topping

Ladyfinger Cupcakes

5 eggs, separated
⅔ cup sugar, plus 2 tablespoons
1 teaspoon vanilla extract
1 cup flour
½ teaspoon baking powder

Preheat oven to 400°. Line a muffin tin with cupcake papers
and set aside. Using a small bowl, beat egg whites on high
until stiff peaks form. Add sugar and continue beating until
glossy. In another bowl, mix the remaining ⅔ cup of sugar
and egg yolks. Fold half of the egg whites into the yolk
mixture, then add in the flour, baking powder, and remaining
egg whites. Evenly distribute the batter into the cupcake
liners to about ¼ full. They will not rise to the top to leave
room for the mascarpone topping. Bake 8 minutes. Makes 12.

Tiramisu Frosting

6 egg yolks
¾ cup sugar
⅔ cup milk
1 ½ cups heavy cream
½ teaspoon vanilla extract
1 pound mascarpone cheese
1 cup strong black coffee, room temperature
2 tablespoons rum
1 tablespoon unsweetened cocoa powder

Using a medium saucepan, whisk together egg yolks and sugar. Add in milk and whisk over medium heat until mixture boils. Boil for one minute and then remove from heat. Once the mixture has cooled, cover it and put it in the refrigerator. After one hour, mix the mascarpone cheese into the egg and milk mixture until smooth. In another bowl, whip together cream and vanilla until stiff peaks form. In small bowl, mix together the coffee and rum. Pour 1 ½ tablespoons of the coffee and rum mixture over the cooled cupcakes and allow it to absorb into the cake. Distribute the mascarpone mixture over the cupcakes, spreading it evenly. Place a large dollop of the whipped cream over the mascarpone mixture and sprinkle with cocoa powder. Refrigerate 3–5 hours until set.

Don't miss the next
Cupcake Bakery Mystery, coming 2016.
Turn the page for a preview of Jenn McKinlay's
next Library Lover's Mystery . . .

A Likely Story

Coming November 2015 in hardcover
from Berkley Prime Crime!

"I need a plunger and a mop stat!" Lindsey Norris cried from the family restroom in the children's area of the Briar Creek Public Library. There was an inch of water on the floor, and the water spilling over the toilet bowl showed no signs of slowing.

The harried mother and daughter who had just been in the restroom stood by the door, with the young girl giving Lindsey big worried looks while the mother gushed apologies almost as fast as the toilet spilled water.

"I'm so sorry, so sorry, so very, very sorry," Kimberly Curtis said.

"It's fine," Lindsey lied. "Happens all the time."

She glanced down at the young girl, Madison Curtis, who was pulling her winter hat over her face as if to hide. She peeked at Lindsey from under the edge and said, "I sorry. Duck wanted to swim."

Lindsey felt her lips turn up in spite of the situation. She glanced at Kimberly and said, "It does make sense on one level."

Kimberly hugged her daughter and gave Lindsey an appreciative glance. "You're very kind, but there is nothing logical about flushing a stuffed duck down the toilet."

"Here's the mop!"

Lindsey glanced past Kimberly and Madison at her second in command. Her longtime friend, Beth Stanley, was coming at her with a mop in one hand and a plunger in the other, or more accurately, a mop under one wing and a plunger under the other.

"Wild guess, here," Lindsey said as she took in Beth's bright yellow hooded sweatshirt with wings on the sleeves and an orange beak and two large eyes sewn onto the hood, *"Make Way for Ducklings?"*

"McCloskey is the man!" Beth said. "Yes, story time was all the faves: *Ping, Come Along, Daisy!,* and *The Ugly Duckling,* natch."

"Well, you inspired little Madison here to set one free," Lindsey said.

"Uh-oh," Beth said. She looked past Lindsey at the bathroom floor.

"It's fine, I changed into my boots," Lindsey said. She pointed to her L.L.Bean snow boots. "I'll just waddle on in there and shut the water off."

"I'll help. I'm in boots, too. They look like duck feet, don't you think?" Beth asked.

"They do," Lindsey agreed. She looked at Kimberly and

Madison. "We're going to start cleaning, and then I'm going to call our maintenance people from the town and see if they can get your duck out of the pipes."

Madison's face crumpled, and she looked like she was going to have a complete meltdown. Beth, ever in touch with her story timers, saw the brewing storm and started having a conversation with Madison's duck.

"You're going where? Oh, sorry," she called into the toilet. She glanced at them with a chagrined look. "I forgot to speak in duck." She turned back to the toilet and said, "Quack, quack quackety quackers."

Madison's face went from distraught to hopeful. Beth kept on the conversation, making Madison laugh while Kimberly leaned close to Lindsey and said, "We won't need Fluffy back. When Madison made it her go-to stuffie, Beth advised me to buy more of the same. I bought three of them and I rotate them in and out so they have the same amount of wear."

"Brilliant," Lindsey whispered back. Then she hurried into the bathroom to shut the water off.

"When will Fluffy come back?" Madison asked Beth. Her four-year-old voice was so pitiful that Lindsey wanted to hug her.

"Fluffy says she's going to visit her sister and she'll be back." Beth paused to look at Kimberly, who nodded. "After dinner."

Madison beamed and clapped her hands as Beth and Lindsey sloshed back towards them.

"What do you say, Madison?" Kimberly asked her daughter.

"Thank you." Madison hugged Beth around the knees and then did the same to Lindsey.

"You're welcome," they said together. They waved as the mother and daughter bundled up to go out into the February cold.

"Maintenance is never going to get that duck out of there, are they?" Lindsey asked.

"Not a chance," Beth said. "But it's okay. Kim is smart and has backups."

"So she said," Lindsey said. "Great advice you gave her there."

"Sometimes I pull a good one out of my beak," Beth joked. "Quack."

"Clark from Maintenance just called. They are fixing an electrical issue with the town garage and can't get back here until late this afternoon," Ms. Cole said as she joined them. She looked at the bathroom with disapproval and said, "When Mr. Tupper was director we never had plumbing issues."

"That's ridicu—" Beth protested but Lindsey interrupted her.

"Thank you for calling them, Ms. Cole," Lindsey said.

When she had taken the job as director of the small town public library a couple of years ago, she'd had no idea that her skill set would evolve to include basic plumbing, but then there were a lot of things she hadn't expected when she took this job. She supposed the unexpected was what kept it interesting.

She glanced at her watch; speaking of interesting, she had a meeting to attend. Her weekly crafternoon meeting was scheduled for one hour from now, and she knew what she had to do. Mop.

A Likely Story

\\'/\\'/\\'\\

"Hurry!" Beth said as she and Lindsey hustled down the hallway.

It had been a couple of years now, and Lindsey was surprised at how much of an important part of her life their weekly crafternoon meetings had become for her.

Briar Creek was a small town nestled on the coast of Connecticut. Its claim to fame was that Captain Kidd had once buried treasure out in the Thumb Islands, which numbered into the hundreds if you counted big rocks, out in the bay. As yet, no one had found the treasure although plenty had tried.

When Lindsey had become the director of the library, she knew that in order to survive, she had to make the library a place that people really enjoyed spending time. One of her very first ideas had been to form a crafternoon club, a group of women who met every Thursday for lunch, book talk, and crafting. Men were welcome, too, but so far they'd had no takers.

Instead of just a program for the library, what Lindsey had gotten was a close-knit group of friends who shared her love of food and books and tolerated her inability to craft. She adored each and every one of them.

She and Beth skidded into the room to find Nancy Peyton, Lindsey's landlord; Violet La Rue, a retired Broadway actress; Charlene La Rue, Violet's daughter who was also a local newscaster; and Mary Murphy, owner of the local café and sister to Lindsey's ex-boyfriend Mike Sullivan, known to everyone as Sully, already engaged in conversation.

"Inspector Grant," Nancy Peyton said. "What do we think of him, ladies?"

"I like him," Violet La Rue said. "He has spunk."

Lindsey smiled as she and Beth hit the buffet spread and loaded up their plates. Nancy and Violet were two of the spunkiest ladies she'd ever met, so it was no surprise to her that they approved of Inspector Grant, the hero of this week's book under discussion, *The Daughter of Time* by Josephine Tey.

Charlene had brought the food today and it was an assortment of mini quiches, arugula salad, sweet tea, and chocolate cream pie for dessert. The quiches were still hot, and Lindsey felt her mouth begin to water. She'd had no idea that swabbing a bathroom floor could cause such an appetite.

Nancy's blue eyes twinkled as she looked at Lindsey. "Can you imagine trying to solve the mystery of whether King Richard III murdered the princess in the tower just because you were hospitalized for a broken leg and were bored? Who does that sort of thing, solve mysteries just because?"

Lindsey shoved a mini quiche into her mouth and then pointed to her lips to indicate she couldn't talk right now because she was chewing.

Charlene La Rue laughed. She was Violet's daughter and they shared the same dark complexion, striking features, and fierce intelligence. Charlene moved over on the couch so that Lindsey could sit next to her. Then she looked at Lindsey and said, "I think she's teasing you."

Lindsey swallowed. "You think?"

Charlene laughed and Mary joined in, saying, "We could always talk about who you're dating if that would be more comfortable for you than your penchant for amateur sleuthing."

Lindsey gave her a horrified look. She swallowed and said, "But I'm not even dating anyone right now."

"Really?" Mary asked. She sounded so disappointed.

Mary had been lobbying hard for Lindsey to get back together with her brother Sully for a while now.

"Sorry, it's complicated," Lindsey said.

"So, you're not dating anyone at all?" Violet clarified.

"Nobody," Lindsey said. Violet had a horse in the race for Lindsey's affections, an actor friend of hers named Robbie Vine, who was ridiculously charming and also married. Lindsey went for a subject change. "So, what did you think of Inspector Grant's uncanny ability to read a person's character from their face? Do you think it's possible?"

"I wish," Beth said, taking a seat next to Violet. "Every time I think I've nailed it, the guy turns out to be a toad. I've dated more than my share of toads."

"I thought you had a nice time with that young banker you went out to dinner with," Nancy said.

"Ugh," Beth grunted. "He's all about conspicuous consumption, you know, the big house, expensive car, designer label life. So shallow."

"That's too bad," Violet said. She patted Beth's shoulder. "Don't you worry, the right one will come along."

"Speaking of the right *one*," Charlene said. She turned her reporter's gaze on Lindsey. "Have you had any luck in narrowing down your choices?"

"Do we have enough paper for the paper flowers we're making?" Lindsey asked. "Maybe I should go check on that."

She hopped out of her seat and crossed the room to their crafting table. Today they were making bouquets of paper roses out of recycled office paper. Lindsey planned to use the bouquets to decorate the library and help fight off the winter doldrums.

Using paper with words printed on it, they used a template to cut the petals out, then they colored just the edges of the paper to give the flowers some pop. Next they would use a glue gun to layer the petals from biggest to smallest. Once the flowers were done, they would attach green florist wire for the stem.

She heard the women resume talking about the novel, and she heaved a sigh of relief. She loved them all dearly but she didn't want to talk about her love life, since it was rather complicated. Actually, it wasn't complicated so much as it was none of their business, but that seemed rude to say.

"Lindsey, can I talk to you for a sec?"

Lindsey glanced up at the door to see their library clerk Ann Marie standing there. The ladies all greeted Ann Marie warmly, and Nancy promised to bring her a batch of cookies for her two precocious boys.

"Sure, what is it?" Lindsey asked.

"We finally got that book in for Stewart Rosen," Ann Marie said. She held up the book in question. It was a medical text that they'd special ordered from a university for him. "They're giving us a very short turnaround on borrowing it. Just two weeks."

Lindsey glanced at the title and nodded. "Stewart will want this right away then."

"That's what I was thinking," Ann Marie said. "Do you want me to put a call in to Sully to see if the water taxi is available?"

"That'd be great," Lindsey said. She felt her heart kick up a notch at the thought of spending the afternoon with Sully.

"I think Stewart and Pete have some other books put

aside for them on the hold shelf as well. Could you check this one out to them and put it with the others?"

"You got it, boss," Ann Marie said. "Make sure you dress warm. The wind out on the water today is brutal."

"Will do," Lindsey said.

In her previous occupation as an academic librarian, Lindsey had never mopped up after overflowing toilets, but she'd never gotten to go on boat rides, either. Even though it was a chilly day in February, she couldn't help but be pleased that she was going out to the islands to deliver books to two of their homebound patrons. It was one of the parts of her job that made her feel as if she really was making a difference in her patrons' lives.

When Lindsey had become the librarian, she had made it her mission to reach out to the residents of the Thumb Islands and provide them with borrowing privileges, and they had responded with great enthusiasm. Stewart and Pete Rosen were elderly brothers who had lived their entire life on Star Island. They were definitely on the odd end of the spectrum, but Lindsey had become rather fond of them and their quirks.

Now if it just so happened that she had to use the local water taxi, operated by her ex-boyfriend Sully, well, what was a girl to do? Borrowers needed books, and Lindsey was all about giving excellent customer service.

Luckily, Star Island wasn't too far out in the bay. She could be out there and back within an hour. Easy peasy, or so she thought.

31901056937446

M1212AS1013